Fairy Tales, Fruitcake, and Murder

A Cozy Magic Midlife Mystery

Silver Circle Cat Rescue Mysteries
Book 4

Leanne Leeds

Fairy Tales, Fruitcake, and Murder
Silver Circle Cat Rescue Mysteries #4
ISBN: 978-1-950505-94-4

Published by Badchen Publishing
14125 W State Highway 29
Suite B-203 119
Liberty Hill, TX 78642 USA

In a cat's eye, all things belong to cats.
  -English Proverb

Contents

Chapter 1	1
Chapter 2	14
Chapter 3	30
Chapter 4	44
Chapter 5	59
Chapter 6	73
Chapter 7	88
Chapter 8	103
Chapter 9	117
Chapter 10	133
Chapter 11	147
Chapter 12	164
Chapter 13	177
Chapter 14	193
Chapter 15	209
Chapter 16	224
Chapter 17	238
Chapter 18	256
Chapter 19	270
Chapter 20	284
Chapter 21	299
KEEP UP WITH LEANNE LEEDS	317
Find a typo? Let us know!	319
Artificial Intelligence Statement	321

Chapter One

THE JANGLING SILVER BELLS ABOVE THE SILVER Circle Cat Rescue front door announced Alice Grey's arrival with their merry tune. I glanced up from wiping down the counter to see her breeze inside with her usual kind smile. "Morning ladies! Brrrr, it's brisk as the North Pole out there today!" Alice unwound her scarf, cheeks flushed rosy from the cold.

"It's actually going to warm up this afternoon, but enjoy it while it lasts," Darla said to the town librarian with her usual cheer, tossing a wave Alice's way. "The usual?"

"You know me so well," Alice laughed, making her way to the counter and placing her coffee tumbler on the counter.

"Well, you are in here every morning." I grabbed the tumbler, moved toward the origin of dark roast aroma permeating the cozy café, and called over my shoulder as

I filled, "Nothing better than a vanilla latte right now, Alice. This weather did sneak up on us. You think we might get a white Christmas in Texas this year?"

The lively chatter filling the coffee nook cut short as everyone erupted in laughter, the sound bouncing off the shelter's walls.

Everyone except Old Carl, that is, who sat frowning into his coffee. "Y'all laugh, but it could happen," he grumbled in his gravelly drawl. Heads around the café swiveled toward the weathered farmer as he stabbed a crooked finger at the air. "We had near a foot of snow on Christmas mornin' when I was a kid, I tell ya!"

Old Carl could've sworn there was a white Christmas in Austin when he was a kid, even if the weather records say differently. They go all the way back to the 1890s (while Old Carl only goes back to 1942) and don't show snow on the holiday—well, except for a tiny bit in 1939.

"I'm sure it was lovely, Carl." Alice leaned her elbows on the counter, sighing wistfully. "That would be magical. Everything would look so picturesque, with a fresh coat of snow on Christmas Eve."

"Well, at least we have that fake snow in the square," Darla said. "You must be excited about the tree lighting ceremony tonight." She did a little happy dance, blond ponytail bouncing. "I made little Santa hats for the shelter cats to wear."

Darla was so jazzed about making little Santa hats

for the cats that I didn't have the heart to tell her the cats would probably see them as playthings, not fashion.

"Aw, how cute!" Alice told Darla.

"Here you go," I slid the tumbler of frothy vanilla latte across the counter to Alice. "I can't believe it's already Christmas again. Last year, the shelter was in that small house on the edge of town, and this year, thanks to Fiona, we have ten times the cats we used to have. So much has changed."

"Good things," Alice told me, and then sipped her latte. "Oh, that's good."

"Well, now, you ladies won't catch me sippin' on one of them uppity coffees," Old Carl declared, bushy eyebrows raised. "Or peckin' away on a keyboard like those contraptions you got at the library. Ain't no computer better than the good Lord's printed words in a book, I tell you what."

Alice laughed. "Yes, Carl, I know how you feel about my lattes."

"I've made my thoughts on them dag-blamed computers perfectly clear, too," Old Carl said. "Don't you go forgetting my opinion on them dang blasted computers at the library."

"Well, Carl, you can ask Santa to take computers from children instead. It'll make for a refreshing change." I lowered my voice conspiratorially. "Santa will be there tonight. Our new mayor managed to convince my boyfriend to don the red suit."

"No way!" Darla's brown eyes went wide. She

swatted my arm. "Ellie, how could you keep such a big secret?"

Laughing, I raised my hands in mock surrender. "Hey, I just found out myself a couple of days ago. But can you imagine? This will definitely be a Christmas to remember." I smiled, picturing the festive scene.

"I love Tablerock's Christmas stuff." Alice nodded, wisps of steam rising from her latte. "It really brings the entire community together. All these little traditions make the season feel special." She glanced at her watch, sighing. "Well, time for me to open up the library. Enjoy the ceremony tonight, ladies! I'm sure I'll see you there!"

Scooping up her drink, Alice slid off the vinyl café stool. Her boots landed with a thud on the tiled floor as she tucked her chin into her wool scarf. The bells on the café door jingled merrily as Alice pushed her way out into the frosty December air.

After Alice left, I untied my apron. "I'm going to duck into the office and make sure we have enough supplies before half the places we order from start shutting down for the holidays."

"Sounds good!" Darla said. "I've got things up here."

I made my way to the office in back where I found my daughter, Evie, buried in adoption paperwork.

My daughter glanced up, brushing a strand of chestnut hair from her eyes. "Morning, Mom. Just doing the paperwork from the two cats adopted yesterday." Her face lit up. "And get this—one family drove from Dallas just to adopt from us!"

"Wow," I said, leaning in the doorway. "Looks like our little rescue's reputation is spreading."

"What's this about reputation?" With a dramatic swish of colorful silk and jangling bangles, Josephine Reynolds—the feline sanctuary's legal eagle and one of my closest confidants—burst into the tiny office. "My ears are burning, ladies. What mischief are you hatching without your trusty adviser present?" she teased.

I laughed. "Nothing. It's the holidays—I think we could use a vacation from mischief. Evie was just saying we had an adoption all the way from Dallas yesterday."

"Dallas!" Josephine trilled, placing her palm to her decolletage in feigned astonishment. "It's high time the pedestrian palates of greater Texas finally recognized the singular sophistication of our cosmopolitan oasis wrapped in a provincial little bow."

"Sometimes it truly shocks me you're a lawyer," I said with faux sincerity.

"That's by design. It's just another quiver in my arsenal."

Just then Laurie poked her head through the door. "Hey, all. What time should we meet tonight before the lighting ceremony?"

"How about five o'clock at the café?" I suggested. "We can walk over to the square together and get a view of the tree."

"Perfect!" Josephine clapped her rings together merrily. "We can sip cocoa with peppermint schnapps and get into the Christmas spirit." She winked at Evie.

I shot Laurie a look. "Don't be late."

"I'm never late."

"You're always late."

Evie grinned up at us. "If she's late, she can meet us there. I'm just excited to spend time with everyone. You know, the shelter has felt so full of holiday magic lately. This season feels extra special."

"It really does." I gave my daughter's shoulder a loving squeeze, smiling around at my quirky makeshift family. "This is going to be a wonderful Christmas."

Standing in front of my closet, I sifted through the clothes, contemplating what to wear to the tree lighting ceremony. My gaze landed on a festive red sweater dotted with white snowflakes that seemed perfect for the occasion.

As I changed, my thoughts turned to the election results from last month, and a satisfied smile crossed my face. The town had elected Waldo Monroe as our new mayor, finally ousting the flashy Jessa Winthrop.

If the dearly departed keep tabs on earthly happenings, Fiona must've toasted her rival's defeat on election night. Her post-living legal plans worked like a charm to dethrone her nemesis, Jessa Winthrop.

I wondered if Jessa would even show her face at the ceremony tonight after her defeat. Somehow I doubted she'd miss it—that woman hated to relinquish the spotlight. But if she did appear, I knew Waldo would handle it with his usual stoic grace. He was exactly the steady, community-driven leader our little town needed.

Zipping up my jeans, I glanced down as Belladonna wound between my legs, purring loudly. "Well, hello, there," I chuckled, reaching down to scratch under her chin. The black cat nuzzled against my hand affectionately. "I was just thinking about Fiona. You must miss her."

Belladonna let out a no-nonsense meow.

"I know. I kind of miss her, too."

It amazed me how far Belladonna and I had come since she first arrived at the shelter months ago. As the cat of the deceased eccentric Fiona Blackwell, she had clearly been through trauma losing her owner so abruptly. At first Belladonna had been wary and aloof with everyone, myself included. But over time, she had slowly opened up and begun to trust again.

She remained somewhat wary, with a mind of her own and an attitude to match, and at times she still behaved like the place belonged to her. But the once-distant queen cat often sought my company now, sprawling out in the café or my office or bedroom instead of staying in isolation.

I smiled as she leaned into my hand. "I wish you could tell me more about Fiona and that magic tray of hers," I mused, thinking back to the ornate platter downstairs that allowed cats to temporarily speak when standing on it.

Belladonna just blinked her intelligent golden eyes knowingly.

"Well, maybe you'll feel like sharing soon. If you know anything, anyway," I said. "For now, let's just enjoy Christmas, shall we?"

Evie appeared in the doorway. "Hey, Mom, can I borrow that red sweater with the snowflakes? Matt's picking me up any minute, but I can't find something adequately Christmas-y enough."

Well, there goes that idea.

"Sure, I was just about to put it on, but I can find something else." I tossed the sweater to her. "Perfect timing. Saves me an outfit change."

Evie quickly swapped her shirt for the festive sweater. "Thanks! Are you eager for tonight?"

"Definitely." I leaned against the dresser. "It's so nice having the whole town come together to celebrate. And wait until you see the town square—Landon sent me a picture, and it looks incredible with all the lights and decorations."

"I know. Matt was helping them finish setting up today. He says it's like a winter wonderland." Evie checked her reflection in the mirror and smoothed down a flyaway strand of chestnut hair. "He can't wait to see Landon dressed up as Santa Claus."

"I still can't believe he volunteered for that." I grinned, picturing our burly carpenter friend squeezed into a Santa suit. "Josephine will get a real kick out of it, that's for sure."

The front doorbell buzzed its familiar tune on the first story. "That's Matt." Evie gave me a quick hug. "See you there!"

I watched her hurry off in my red sweater.

I stood staring into the full-length mirror on the back of my closet door with a furrowed brow. Tugging at the hem of my plain white button-down shirt, I sighed. It wasn't quite the festive look I was going for. I guess I could dig out that green sweater instead...

I debated for a moment before plunging my hands into the messy depths of my closet. After some rummaging, I unearthed a lumpy emerald green sweater buried at the back of a shelf behind other clothes. Holding it up, a few stray cat hairs clung to the wool fibers.

With a shrug, I tugged it over my head.

The sweater was aggressively Christmas, I thought as I stared at myself in the mirror, with its bold green hue and patterns of reindeer dancing across the front.

I frowned.

I looked like a slightly clumsy elf.

Shaking my head, I grabbed my purse, gave Belladonna one last chin scratch and headed out into the crisply cold evening, ready to celebrate the spirit of Christmas with my daughter, friends, and our little Texas Hill County town.

A blanket of twinkling lights draped over the quaint shops surrounding the town square, reflecting off the storefront windows and making the ground sparkle. Crimson bows adorned each street lamp, adding festive pops of color. The air was alive with the mingling scents of cedar, cinnamon, and barbecue smoke.

"Wow," I murmured. "This is really something."

At the center of the square stood the towering pine, the town's Christmas tree. It stretched toward the night sky, its emerald boughs laden with shimmering ornaments. A five-pointed star glowed at its peak, waiting to blaze brightly during the evening's tree lighting ceremony.

Families bustled around the square, children darting about in light jackets, their laughter filling the slightly crisp air. The scene looked like something off a postcard, capturing the holiday spirit of this cozy Hill Country town.

I stood with Evie, Matt, and the rest of our friends, admiring the festive scene.

Just as Darla had promised, the rescue cats looked absolutely adorable lounging in their Santa hats within the large Christmas-decorated catio displays Landon had built. The enclosures were prominently displayed around the towering town tree, giving the cats cozy holiday abodes in the square.

The creative catios showed off Landon's handiwork while giving a few rescued kitties a festive atmosphere in the heart of the town's holiday cheer to show themselves off.

"Isn't the decor impressive this year?" Josephine said. "And sweet baby angels, that Christmas tree! It's got to be thirty feet of twinkling timber if it's a foot."

Landon chuckled. "Yeah, they go all out. I'm just hoping I don't trip over this costume getting up the ladder later." He held up the bag containing his Santa costume. "Speaking of, I probably need to go get changed."

"You're going to make the perfect Santa," I said.

As we chatted, Sarah Black strode over. "Evening, everyone. Sure is exciting, isn't it?" She gestured at the elaborately adorned square.

"It really is stunning," Josephine agreed politely. "You and Alice did such a marvelous job decorating the reading nook over there. If that doesn't get more kids to the library, I don't know what will."

Sarah's bright smile dimmed at the mention of Alice's name. She shifted from foot to foot, her gaze dropping to the floor. "I didn't have anything to do with it," she mumbled, a crease forming between her brows. "I don't work at the library anymore." She paused, hesitating before adding, "But yes, Alice always did excel at all those special projects for the children."

Was that a tinge of bitterness in her voice?

Before I could ponder Sarah's clipped tone any further, Henry Davis ambled over to join our small gathering. The elderly gentleman's steps were slow but steady, his back hunched slightly from age but his bright blue eyes as lively as ever. He grasped Josephine's hand warmly with both of his own wrinkled mitts, giving it a firm shake accompanied by a congenial smile that creased his weathered face.

"Wonderful to see you all here on this fine night," Henry said in his refined tones. He glanced around. "Is the charming Miss Grey here this evening? She and I have a little business we need to discuss, and I haven't seen her."

"Miss Grey, the librarian, or Ms. Gray, the veterinarian?" Josephine asked.

I looked at my watch. "Laurie's late as usual."

"The librarian," Henry said.

As he spoke, Sarah wrapped her arms across her chest, her fingernails picking at the wool of her sweater. She cleared her throat awkwardly and glanced up from beneath her lashes. "I see someone I know. Talk later?"

Before I could answer, she was gone.

"You know, I haven't seen Alice yet." Evie's forehead creased with worry as she scanned the bustling town square. "That's not like her to be late, especially for something like this."

I glanced around too, taking in the glowing lights, festive wreaths, and locals mingling with hot chocolates in hand. Alice was nowhere to be seen, even though the tree lighting would start any minute.

Alice was never late—her punctuality was legendary in our small town. She planned every minute of her day with meticulous precision. "I'm sure there's a reasonable explanation," I said.

But my gut felt off, like something was definitely amiss.

I checked my watch again, the minute hand seeming to tick by in slow motion. "You know, the library is just a couple blocks away," I said, trying to keep my voice steady. "Maybe we should go check on Alice, make sure everything is okay."

Evie and Landon exchanged a worried glance as I met their eyes.

"I bet she just needs help carrying something over for the ceremony," Landon added. The others quickly murmured agreement.

"If you see her, let her know I'm looking for her," Henry said, and then he moved on to say hello to another group of people milling about.

Before we got half a block, the still night air shattered with the sudden wail of police sirens. We all froze, dread creeping across our faces as the sirens drew closer. Silently, we took off once more down Main Street, the festive lights of the town square vanishing as we left them behind.

Even after the sirens cut off abruptly, I could still hear their shrill echo ringing in my ears, the residual sound cutting through the festive holiday atmosphere as the swirling lights flashed patterns across the library's brick walls.

Chapter Two

As we approached the library, the flashing lights of a police cruiser cut through the darkness, casting an eerie glow across the building's stately brick facade. My footsteps faltered, my heart pounding.

This couldn't be good.

A figure stepped out from behind the cruiser, and I recognized Mario Lopez, one of the town's police officers. He held up a hand, his usually cheerful face grim.

"Sorry, folks, the library's closed," Mario said. "I'm going to have to ask you to turn around."

"Mario, it's us," I called out. Mario's face remained unreadable, his dark eyes focusing in between the flashing of the bright lights until recognition spread across his face. "What's going on? Is everything okay?"

"Nope, definitely not okay. I really shouldn't..." Mario hesitated, his eyes flickering in the direction of the library entrance. He stepped closer, lowering his voice. "I suppose you'll find out in a few minutes anyway, with the way gossip spreads around here. There's been an incident. We just found Alice Grey deceased inside."

My breath caught in my throat as his words sunk in, Evie's hand flying to her mouth beside me. Just this morning, she had been her usual cheerful self at the café. And now...gone? A knot formed in my stomach as I pictured her lifeless body behind those doors.

What on earth had happened?

"What happened?" Landon asked, his question echoing my thoughts.

Mario shook his head. "Can't discuss the specific details of an ongoing investigation. But..." He trailed off, exhaling heavily. "This definitely looks to be a homicide. Alice was murdered. We called in the county immediately."

"No!" Darla cried, distraught. Tears filled her eyes. "Who would do that to Alice? She was so kind, so loving..."

"You were all at the tree lighting?"

I nodded. "Just for a bit. It hadn't even started yet."

"Did you folks see or hear anything out of the ordinary tonight?" Mario asked. "Anything at all could help."

We exchanged looks, shaking our heads—what the heck? I did a quick head count. Landon, Darla, Evie, Matt, me...one person was missing. Josephine was no longer standing with us. I strained my eyes toward the library, half-expecting to glimpse Josephine peeking through the doors.

I brought my attention back to Mario's question and racked my brain trying to piece together some sketchy action or suspicious words, but all I could recall were memories of the cheery chatter and festive bustle of families gathered around the Christmas tree. "I'm sorry. I didn't see anything suspicious."

"No, wait—Sarah Black." Evie gripped my arm. "Remember how weird she acted when Henry asked where Alice was?"

"Well, that's something, isn't it?" Mario's eyes sharpened with interest as he withdrew a small notebook and pen from his pocket. "Go on."

I nodded. "You must know Sarah, Mario. She used to work here at the library."

"She did, until she got fired," Evie told him.

"How do you know that?"

She shrugged at me. "Rumors. SocialBook. You know, the usual."

As he scribbled notes, I recounted the encounter with Sarah earlier that evening. Her bitter tone, the tension in her frame at the mention of Alice's name.

"But Evie's right," I said. "She definitely seemed uncomfortable talking about Alice. Resentful of Alice, even."

Mario tapped his pen on the pad of paper, contemplating. "I'll speak with her, see if we can confirm her whereabouts this evening." He glanced back toward the library doors. "The medical examiner is on the way. Once they've finished, forensics will sweep for evidence. But I appreciate you guys offering a lead."

"Of course, anything we can do to help," Landon told his friend.

Mario gave a tired smile. "I can't imagine the murder of a librarian would be all that complicated, right?" he said optimistically. "She was such a simple woman. I'm sure we'll have whatever happened wrapped up in no time."

Famous last words, I thought, suppressing an eye roll. No woman is simple. No murder, either, I suspected. He was in for a rude awakening, I suspected, if he thought this would be an open-and-shut investigation. No point in saying something and bursting his bubble just yet—he'd learn soon enough that librarians have more layers than cardigans.

He turned to head back inside, but Josephine—now back with the group as if she'd never left—caught his arm. "Mario, does the mayor know about this yet? The tree lighting ceremony is about to begin."

Mario winced. "Chief Yarbin or Sheriff Dixon will inform Mayor Monroe shortly, I imagine. If they haven't already." He gave his head a shake from side to side. "Terrible timing, with the whole town gathered. This will cast a real pall on the Christmas festivities."

With that solemn thought hanging in the air, he slipped back inside the library's heavy oak doors.

We stood in mournful silence next to the police cruiser's swirling lights, the red and blue staining our faces at intervals. Darla's body trembled as she wept quietly into my shoulder. I blinked back my own tears and rubbed her back, unable to find any words of comfort. "I've known her since I was in middle school," she whispered into my shoulder. "I can't imagine why anyone would kill her."

After a moment, Matt gently broke the silence. "We should get back. Mayor Winthrop might have carried on with a party after a murder, but I suspect Mayor Monroe will tell everyone what happened. I'd like to be there if and when he does." He squeezed Evie's hand. "Mario's right about this putting a damper on the Christmas spirit."

Evie just mutely nodded, leaning into him.

"Are you going to change first?" I asked Landon, gesturing at the baggy Santa costume hanging awkwardly on his lanky frame.

He grimaced down at the costume. "Yeah, give me a sec," he said, already fumbling to unzip the back. He shuffled behind a tree and emerged a moment later free of the bulky suit, now dressed in his usual faded jeans and button-down shirt.

With heavy hearts, we slowly made our way back to the square. The familiar holiday tunes and cheerful babble of the townsfolk celebrating Christmas Eve seemed almost vulgar now, considering Mario's news.

I felt like a pool of sadness had gathered within my chest, swallowing all merriment.

Back at the square, the crowds were still blissfully unaware of the somber events that had unfolded just blocks away. Parents cradled steaming mugs of hot cider, laughing and chatting amiably. Their jacket-clad children practically vibrated with excitement beside the towering tree, their faces upturned in wonder at the glittering lights and shimmering ornament.

For now, the Christmas spirit prevailed, as parents and children alike basked in the magical glow of the season, oblivious to the creeping darkness on the horizon. But we knew the carefree cheer wouldn't last once news spread.

At the front of the square, Mayor Monroe stood on a small dais next to Sheriff Dixon, looking dignified in a festive red bow tie. As we arrived, the mayor leaned over to murmur something to the sheriff, his expression somber.

Sheriff Dixon nodded, his craggy features creasing into a frown. He stepped up to the microphone.

"Evening, folks." His gravelly voice boomed out over the square. "So grateful to y'all for being here to celebrate this Christmas Eve together as a community." The sheriff shifted on his feet, clearing his throat. "I'm afraid I have some very troubling news. There's been a death tonight of someone dear to many of you."

Confused murmuring rippled through the crowd. Parents drew their children closer, their merry expressions shifting to worry and fear.

"The victim was Alice Grey, the town librarian."

Cries of dismay went up around the square. My friends and I stared at the sheriff, fresh tears pricking my eyes. Hearing it stated so bluntly somehow made it crushingly real. While the sheriff didn't state she was murdered—the one deference to the children in the square, I suspected—the use of the word "victim" made it subtly clear to the adults what had transpired.

Sheriff Dixon raised a hand, waiting for quiet. "Alice was a light in this community, and her loss pains me greatly. I wish I had better tidings on this Christmas holiday kickoff, but Mayor Monroe and I thought we should let everyone know as quick as we can since we'll need to cancel tonight's events and clear the square."

Gasps and angry shouts rose like steam from a boiling kettle. A small portion of the crowd bubbled with indignation at having their merrymaking cut short.

Josephine clicked her tongue in disapproval as she watched her fellow townsfolk work themselves into a tizzy. "I hope all that huffing and puffing is for poor Alice and not just for your evening plans being interrupted," she said loud enough that her voice carried.

A few people had the decency to look ashamed under her stern gaze. Most of those that shouted, however, continued grumbling about their disrupted holiday fun.

Josephine sighed and shook her head.

"I know emotions are running high, but let's not speculate," Sheriff Dixon continued. "My department, in conjunction with the Forkbridge Police Department, will conduct a swift, thorough investigation into what transpired. Right now, I ask that you look out for each other, and keep Alice's loved ones in your thoughts and prayers."

He stepped back, and Mayor Monroe moved to the microphone, his expression grim.

"My friends, this is a terrible blow, made even more heartbreaking with it falling on the beginning of our Christmas celebrations," he began, his resonant voice carrying solemnly across the crowd. "Alice was a treasured member of our community, and she will be sorely missed. While we grieve, let us also remember life is fleeting and find meaning in each other. Reach out to your neighbors, hold your loved ones close, and keep the spirit of goodness and humanity alive in Alice's honor."

He paused, looking out over the crowd. "In this time of darkness, we must be lights. While evil exists, there is still infinitely more good, hope, and love. That is what we must focus on as we move forward."

The mayor stepped back, nodding for the sheriff to proceed. Sheriff Dixon cleared his throat gruffly into the microphone. "Thank you all for your cooperation tonight. We will let you know more when we can. For now, please head home and be with your families."

As the grave announcement echoed across the hushed square, the carefree Christmas spirit evaporated in an instant. Parents gathered their children close, joyful smiles replaced by worried frowns.

"I guess we should go grab the cats in the catio display," Evie said.

As the town moved to clear out, Sheriff Dixon approached our huddled group, his face etched with grim lines. "Ellie, I'm glad I caught you all."

I turned. "Sheriff. What can I do for you?"

He removed his hat, his craggy face troubled. "I have a favor to ask. Deputy Markham is over at Alice's apartment with CSU, but there's an angry, hissing cat making things difficult and Markham's not that great at dealing with animals. We need someone to take the poor thing until Alice's family can be contacted."

"Of course, Sheriff," I said, my heart aching for the distressed feline and the poor thing having to put up with Don Markham's dislike of cats. "We'll get over there right away."

"I can go with you," Darla offered, wiping her eyes. "We have an extra cat carrier by the catios, too. I always bring an extra in case one breaks."

"That's great, Darla."

Landon nodded. "I can drive you both over."

"Thank you kindly." Sheriff Dixon sighed heavily as

he replaced his hat. "This entire business is just heart-breaking. Alice really was one of the good ones."

I gave his arm a gentle squeeze. "We'll take good care of Alice's cat until her family can make arrangements."

Matt and Evie headed back to the shelter to update Laurie on the tragic events as well as get the isolation room ready for a new occupant, while we grabbed the extra cat carrier and trudged over to Landon's beat-up work truck. I leaned my head against the window, watching the glowing decorations of Main Street fade behind us in the rear-view mirror.

Streetlights flashed by in a blur as we drove the short distance to Alice's apartment complex and parked beneath one of the tall lamp posts. We could see the swirling lights from multiple police cruisers illuminating the building ahead.

Landon drummed his fingers on the steering wheel, exhaling heavily. "I just can't wrap my head around it. Who would want to hurt someone as kind as Alice?"

"I know," Darla said from the back seat. "She didn't have any enemies. I mean, she couldn't have. Do you think it was a random burglar, someone who didn't know her? That would be even worse if it was just senseless violence. But who would rob a public library?"

"Hopefully, the police find evidence that will explain what happened," I said, though the thought provided little comfort. Either scenario was horrible—that she was murdered by a stranger, or someone she knew. "For now, let's just help her cat. That's the best way we can honor Alice right now."

We climbed from the truck and made our way inside, showing our IDs to the deputy stationed by the stairwell, and explained what we'd been sent to do. The sheriff must have let these guys know, because the deputy confirmed the apartment number and waved us up the stairs.

"I'll wait down here," Landon said. "Looks like a lot of people up there."

I nodded.

As we approached Alice's apartment, we found the front door swung open. Lively voices and police radio chatter echoed from within the home out onto the front porch.

Stepping inside, we entered a busy scene.

A police officer dressed in uniform stood in the living room, intently photographing the area. He glanced up from his camera to acknowledge us with a slight nod before focusing back on his work. Around him, forensic technicians brushed powders across surfaces and collected samples.

The space was disorderly, with cushions overturned and cabinets left open, and despite the decorative warmth it felt eerily still and sterile, like a museum exhibit rather than someone's home.

Photo frames crowded the shelves and side tables, each one holding a frozen moment of Alice's smiling face. Motivational posters promoting free speech and images of people protesting book banning covered the walls just above overflowing bookcases. Her plush, claw-foot sofa and reading chair by the window seemed to be waiting for Alice to come home, to sink into their soft embrace with a book in one hand and a steaming mug of cocoa in the other.

But Alice would not be coming home again.

Blinking back more tears, I turned my focus to locating Ginger. Poor thing was probably terrified with all these strangers traipsing through his territory and tearing up her house.

We found Deputy Markham in the kitchen, looking harried as he jotted notes, while another CSU tech swabbed down the counters for fingerprints. At our entrance, he glanced up, visibly relieved.

"Oh thank god, you're here for the cat." He thumb-hooked toward a closed door off the kitchen. "Little monster's been raising hell ever since we got here. Won't let any of us near it." He pointed to a picture. "I think its name is Ginger."

"His name is Ginger," I corrected Markham.

As if on cue, an angry yowl erupted from beyond the door, followed by the sound of objects crashing.

"Oh, poor baby." Darla hurried over and cautiously eased open the door. More hissing ensued, along with a blur of orange fur streaking between her ankles into the kitchen. "Whoa, easy, sweetheart!" She crouched down and began making soft kissing noises. "It's okay, Ginger. We're here to help you."

I could see the cat freeze mid-dash across the floor, his bottlebrush tail puffed up to triple its size. He pivoted to face Darla with wide, frightened eyes, back arched warily.

"I know. I know this is all very scary. There's a good boy." Darla extended a hand toward him. "Why don't you come with me, sweetheart? We're taking you somewhere safe."

After a tense moment, Ginger took a hesitant step forward and gave Darla's fingers a cautious sniff. The sight of the sweet ginger cat, who I knew had been Alice's cherished companion from countless stories she'd shared over coffee, tore at my heart.

"That's right, we're friends," Darla soothed. Slowly, gently, she scooped the still-rigid cat into her arms and cuddled him close. "Shh, I've got you now."

Ginger let out a pitiful mewl, but gradually relaxed against Darla, his claws retracting from Darla's sweater. Darla stroked the cat's head tenderly as she carried him toward the door. "We'll take care of you, I promise."

"How the hell do you people do that?" Deputy Markham asked, incredulous. He shook his head, running a hand through his short brown hair as he tried to understand our uncanny ability to be nice to animals in a way that soothed them.

"Be kind to a frightened creature? It's easy, Don. You should try it."

Darla flashed me a sly smile as I gave a nonchalant shrug in response to the deputy's shocked question, and then subtly angled her head toward the side of the room. My eyes followed the gesture, landing on an open bag of cat food placed next to Ginger's bowl.

"I'll grab some of his things to help Ginger feel comfortable," I told Deputy Markham. "Unless you need them?"

"No, no, go ahead."

I gathered up Ginger's food and water bowls, scooping the leftover kibble into a Ziploc bag. From his toy basket, I picked out a few worn toys hoping they were favorites—a catnip mouse, a feather wand, and a ball with a bell inside. Last, I carefully lifted his plush pet bed, still imprinted with the shape of his curled up body. I hoped having these familiar items would provide Ginger some measure of consolation during this difficult transition.

The poor cat meowed mournfully from the carrier as he watched me load everything into a duffel bag through the door. "I know, sweetheart, I know," I whispered. "Life can be very unfair."

Deputy Markham gave me an appreciative nod as we prepared to depart with Ginger. "Really appreciate you folks getting here quick and taking him tonight."

"No problem," I told him. "It's the least we could do."

He escorted us downstairs, shaking hands with Landon like they were old buddies, and I felt a twinge of exclusion. Sure, handshakes were just empty niceties —but they signaled an unspoken camaraderie that women in this town still hadn't quite managed to bust through.

It annoyed me.

As we made our way to Landon's truck, Ginger had quieted down in the box. I hoped it was more comfort than fear, but I doubted it. Finding small comfort for the poor orphaned cat might take a while.

The four of us were silent as we drove back across town, each lost in our own solemn thoughts.

Back at the shelter, Matt and Evie met us in the front hall, their faces etched with worry. Evie hurried over to peek at Ginger, nestled securely in the cat carrier.

"Oh, the poor thing," she murmured sympathetically. Darla just nodded, lips pressed together, as she carried the carrier toward the isolation room.

Landon slumped down heavily into one of the waiting area chairs. He scrubbed a hand across his beard, looking drained. "What an awful night."

"I know." I squeezed his shoulder. "Why don't you and Matt head home and try to get some rest? All of this can wait until morning."

Landon sighed heavily, then nodded. I pulled him to his feet and hugged him as Matt shuffled over to Evie and gave her a kiss goodnight. They leaned on each other for support like comrades stumbling back from battle.

"You'll call us if there are any updates?" Matt asked over his shoulder as they slowly made their way to the exit.

"Of course," Evie said with a wave.

I watched their retreating forms, my own eyelids heavy. The adrenaline was rapidly fading, leaving a bone-deep weariness in its wake.

But I couldn't rest yet.

I knew for certain that sleep would not come easily until I talked to Ginger and let him know that his beloved Alice was gone.

Chapter Three

Standing outside the quarantine room, I paused to collect myself, taking a deep breath to calm my nerves. On the other side of the door, Ginger awaited—a cat who had just lost his most cherished companion. My heart broke for the orange cat, whose world had been upended through no fault of his own. I steeled myself before entering, resolved to provide whatever small comfort I could.

As I stepped inside, I saw Darla sitting cross-legged on the floor. Ginger was still in his carrier, peering out warily through the open door.

"How's our new friend doing?" I asked.

Darla shook her head sadly. "He's understandably very frightened and confused. I figured it would be best to let him come out when he feels ready."

I crouched down, offering my hand to him. He approached tentatively, then nudged his head against my palm, meowing softly. "There's a good boy," I told him. My gaze traveled around the small room. A few cat toys and Ginger's bed and bowls sat neatly arranged in one corner, familiar items awaiting their owner.

Up on the windowsill, Belladonna observed the scene curiously.

"Darla, let's move Ginger's carrier over by the cubby," I suggested.

Darla carefully grasped the plastic handles of Ginger's cat carrier, lifting it up and positioning it directly in front of the cubbyhole entrance. I swung the metal door open fully so that it aligned with the small tunnel.

For a moment, Ginger was still, eyeing the unfamiliar space distrustfully. His ears swiveled, listening for any sounds within. Tentatively, he stepped forward, peeking his head out to inspect the cubby, his orange legs following as he inched into the tunnel, tail swishing cautiously. Once all four paws were inside, he glanced back at us as if seeking reassurance.

I gave him an encouraging smile. "There you go," I cooed gently. "I know you must be very confused right now."

Ginger remained poised to flee, his pale gold eyes wide and frightened. We had to make him understand what happened, as impossible as that would be.

"It's okay, sweetie. Come, step on this." I gestured toward the crystal plate.

In response, Ginger looked up at Belladonna—who,

much to my surprise, remained still and rather uncharacteristically non-defensive. Most knew Fiona's black cat had a fierce temperament, yet for once she remained unusually calm and non-aggressive. The newcomer stretched his neck up toward her, and Belladonna dropped her head down slowly in return.

This seemed to reassure the orange cat.

Hesitantly, Ginger stepped onto the ornate platter. He glanced down in surprise as it glowed brighter, illuminating his ginger fur with an ethereal emerald light.

"Ginger?" I asked softly. "Can you understand me?"

The cat's gaze snapped to mine. "Y-yes," he stammered in a distinctly masculine voice. "How are you doing that?"

I chuckled. "The easiest way to explain it is magic. But that doesn't matter right now. Ginger, something terrible has happened..."

I hesitated, unsure how to continue. Darla placed a comforting hand on my shoulder.

"I'm so sorry to have to tell you this, sweetheart," Darla said gently. "Your owner, Alice...she passed away tonight."

Ginger stared at us in stunned silence. Then his back arched and he hissed angrily. "No! I don't believe you. This is some kind of trick."

My shoulders slumped. Of course he didn't want to believe it. "I'm afraid it's true," I said. "The police found her at the library. She's gone. I'm so very sorry. That's why all those people were in your apartment. The police want to find out who would do such a terrible thing."

Ginger's golden eyes clouded with grief and he sank down on the shimmering platter. "Not Alice," he whimpered. "She knew every trick and trap. My clever Alice was too smart to die! Tell me what happened."

I exchanged a surprised glance with Darla.

Too clever to die?

Alice always struck me as a kind and studious person, and, of course, she'd read so many books that her knowledge was impressive—but I wouldn't exactly call her clever or crafty. Those words didn't really fit the polite, reserved woman I knew.

"The police told us she was murdered," I explained. "We don't know all the details yet. But I want you to know I am so sorry for your loss, Ginger. Alice was a wonderful woman. She was so sweet and caring, always thinking of others."

Ginger narrowed his eyes. "Sweet and caring?" He flicked his tail in irritation. "You didn't know Alice at all! She was cunning and brilliant. A crime maestro! She knew things no one else did."

I stared at him.

Darla looked at Ginger as well, seemingly equally surprised by his words. "I'm sorry, but are you certain we're talking about the same Alice Grey?" she asked carefully. "The librarian?"

"That sweet librarian persona was just a front," Ginger declared. "At home, the real Alice emerged—

cunning, crafty, always cooking up new schemes. She hid her brilliant underworld mind behind a mask of politeness and simplicity. But I knew the truth."

Darla and I exchanged a baffled look.

What on earth was he talking about?

The Alice we knew was a simple small town librarian, friendly and kind to everyone.

I took a deep breath. "I'm sorry, Ginger, but I think there must be some misunderstanding," I said, and then thought better of arguing with a grief-stricken cat. "Tell you what—why don't you tell us more about the Alice you knew? We'd love to understand what you mean."

Ginger eyed me suspiciously for a moment, then began pacing the glowing plate. "I guess it doesn't matter now. Where to start?" he mused. "I suppose with her rare book theft ring..."

I blinked.

Her rare book what now?

As Ginger launched into his shocking descriptions of Alice's double life, Darla and I listened in dismayed disbelief. The gentle soul we thought we knew apparently was someone else entirely.

Ginger finished his shocking account of Alice's supposed criminal enterprises with a swish of his tail, and my mind reeled trying to reconcile his descriptions of thievery, blackmail and worse with the gentle, kind librarian Darla and I thought we knew.

Beside me, Darla seemed equally dumbfounded. "This has to be some kind of game she played at home that the cat is mixing up for reality, or maybe an audio-book Alice listened to a lot," she said, shaking her head. "There's no way Alice was a blackmailing book thief. She was one of the kindest souls in town. Everyone loved her."

"Brought people soup when they were sick? Delivered meals on wheels to the elderly—always managing to get assigned to the ones that had a lot of books?" Ginger lashed his tail in agitation. "I'm telling you, it was all an act. Just a cover to divert suspicion from her true self—or further her goals. My Alice was a felony architect of the first order."

"She loved books and fairy tales," I argued weakly. "How could someone who loved fairy tales and children the way she did be a criminal mastermind?"

"I think he said felony architect," Darla corrected.

"She was a villainous virtuoso!" The orange cat narrowed his eyes. "Obviously, that was all calculated to paint her as harmless. I told you. She was brilliant. Only I and her partners knew her real capacities for cunning and strategy."

Just then, the door creaked open a sliver and Evie peeked in. "Everything okay in here? What's going on?" she asked, glancing between us and Ginger illuminated on the glowing plate. "You two look like you've seen a ghost."

Darla quickly explained the troubling things Ginger had revealed about Alice's supposed hidden life.

"Oh, come on." Evie's eyes went wide. "That can't be true!" She wagged her head as if clearing water from her ears. "Alice was wonderful—kind, sweet, totally harmless. This cat must be confused."

Ginger bristled at that, arching his back. "How dare you!" he spat. "I knew Alice better than anyone. Everything I said is true!"

Belladonna gracefully jumped up onto the glowing plate next to where Ginger stood bristling at Evie's words. The elegant cat sat tall, her tail curled neatly around her paws. She looked at each of us gathered there, her eyes calm yet piercing. "Why are you all so quick to dismiss Ginger's claims?" she asked calmly.

Her golden eyes were curious but non-judgmental.

Which, I had to admit, was weird.

"Because the Alice we knew wasn't anything like he described," I said. "She was just a small town librarian to us. She seemed utterly unobjectionable."

Belladonna tipped her head thoughtfully. "And why does that make Ginger's claims about his mistress impossible?" she pressed. "Is it not natural for humans to conceal parts of themselves?"

I hesitated.

She had a point.

"True, sometimes people aren't always what they

seem on the surface," I conceded. "But the difference between what we saw and what Ginger saw? They're practically diametrically opposed."

"So?" Belladonna languidly swished her plumed tail. "You, of all people, should know that hidden truths can sometimes be shockingly opposite to what the world sees. Do you not hide this very room and the plate I stand upon from public knowledge?"

Another good point.

Evie looked sheepish. "I guess I shouldn't be so quick to judge," she said. "I'm sorry if I offended you, Ginger."

"I still don't understand. Why would she pretend to be someone she wasn't?" Darla asked, still confused. "I can't believe the person I knew wasn't real. That's just crazy."

"Perhaps she wasn't pretending. Perhaps she is both things at once. Why she did it is not, in my mind, for us to speculate," Belladonna replied calmly. "I just wish to remind you that we should not dismiss another's truth because it does not align with our own experience."

Properly admonished by the black cat (at least in her mind), we all fell silent under her steady gaze.

After a moment, Belladonna turned her attention back to Ginger. "My friend, while your claims seem unlikely to those who thought they knew Alice, I can see you speak sincerely," she said. "I shall not disregard your truth. And you should be prepared that your mistress may have had layers beyond what even you realized."

Ginger looked somewhat mollified by her assurances. With all the speed of an internet connection circa 1995, he nodded. "I suppose that's possible," he acknowledged begrudgingly. "Not likely, though."

Belladonna dipped her head. "Oh, there are always deeper truths beneath the surface," she said cryptically. Then she leaped delicately down from the plate and slipped out through the room's cracked door.

An awkward silence descended.

I cleared my throat.

"I'm sorry I didn't believe you, Ginger," I said sincerely. "Belladonna's right—I shouldn't have dismissed your claims so quickly. I guess I just..." I trailed off, struggling to find the right words.

"You had an image in your mind of who Alice was," Ginger finished. "And it didn't fit with what I told you." He lashed his tail, but his tone was less heated now.

"Exactly." I gave him an apologetic look. "But that wasn't fair of me. Clearly you knew a different side of Alice."

Ginger held my gaze for a long moment. Finally, he gave a slow nod. "Apology accepted," he declared, then turned his piercing eyes on Evie and Darla. "Do you two also concede your mistake?"

Were all arrogant cats determined to beat dead horses? I could have sworn the girls had already apologized. Once before, and this was now twice. I hoped our esteemed guest was not intent on hammering home their regret until the end of time.

With an inward groan, I realized I now had two arrogant cats with superiority complexes lurking around.
And that was aside from the normal feline one.

As if one entitled furball wasn't enough.

No wonder Belladonna came to his defense.

"Absolutely," Darla said earnestly. "We're so sorry."

"Me too," Evie quickly agreed. "That was wrong
of us."

Satisfied, Ginger sat back on his haunches. An air of
grief descended on him again now that the momentary
distraction had passed.

"She's really gone, then?" He sounded so lost and
alone.

"I'm afraid so."

Ginger closed his eyes, looking small and vulnerable.
"I still can't believe it. My Alice, murdered! Oh, when I
get my claws on whoever did this..."

He trailed off, overcome with emotion.

Carefully, I reached out and stroked his head. "I
know. But for now, just try to rest." I gestured to his bed
and toys arranged nearby. "We'll take good care of you, I
promise."

Ginger stepped off the plate, its glow fading. He
stared morosely at the toys from Alice's apartment as
Darla and Evie came over to fuss softly over him.

Our minds still spinning from the startling claims Ginger had made about Alice, the three of us left the isolation room and stood in the second floor hallway. I pulled the heavy door shut behind us with a soft click, and then we stood in bewildered silence, trying to process what had just transpired.

"I don't want to get the cat riled up again, but I can't believe it," Darla whispered, leaning back against the wall. "Alice Grey, a criminal mastermind?" She shook her head, clearly as dumbfounded as I felt. "Can cats be delusional? Because that one has to be delusional."

"I'm with Darla, Mom. You can't actually believe that nonsense...right?" Evie asked uncertainly. She wrapped her arms around herself. "I mean, a whole rare book theft ring and everything? In Tablerock?"

I hesitated. "I'm not sure what to believe," I told the girls. "But you have to admit, Ginger seemed completely convinced."

We stood motionless in the hallway, a heavy silence settling over us. We were all grappling to make sense of what we had heard, and Darla was right—no matter what assurances we all gave Ginger, the gentle, bookish Alice we knew seemed impossible to reconcile with the cunning criminal mastermind her cat had described.

If what Ginger said was true, what did that mean for Alice's murder?

Darla voiced the question I was likely just about to ponder. "Should we tell Mario about this?"

"I think we have to tell him," I said. "He knows

about the plate, so he'll take it seriously. And any information might help the investigation. It's possible Alice really was a mastermind, and the police don't even know about the double life Ginger claims she led."

Evie nodded reluctantly. "You're right. Mario needs to know."

"I wish we knew more. It's going to be really tough for him to use any of what we heard tonight," Darla said. "It's so out there."

"I know. I don't envy him coming up with a way to explain it." I exhaled heavily. "Okay. I'll call Mario first thing in the morning and have him come to the shelter. Maybe he already knows about it and can make sense of all this better than we can."

Having decided to share with Mario, I felt a slight sense of relief at having a plan to move forward—but as we walked along the second floor balcony toward the lobby stairs, I noticed Evie and Darla had the same uneasy looks that likely matched my own.

"Do you really think it could all be true?" Darla asked as we walked. "Could Alice truly have been some secret criminal mastermind?"

"I don't know," I admitted. "It doesn't seem possible. But clearly there are things about her we never realized."

We reached the front lobby. I glanced through the doors, watching our feline residents lounging and playing in the enclosed cat café, blissfully unaware of human troubles.

"Nothing is ever as simple as it appears, is it?" I mused with a tired sigh.

"I was really looking forward to this Christmas," Evie whispered. Her face was pale and drawn, the twinkling lights of the Christmas tree reflected in her downcast eyes.

"I know. We'll try not to let this ruin it," I said.

Darla turned her head to look at me, unshed tears glistening. "I thought everything was going to be perfect, you know? The tree lighting, the Christmas bake-off..." Her voice broke a little. "Ugh, I need to stop this. I won't be able to see the road home."

I squeezed her hand and then stifled a yawn, suddenly feeling the weight of the long emotional night pressing down on me. "Why don't you stay in the guest room, Darla, and we can all try to get some rest," I suggested. "It's been a rough night for everyone, and I don't want you driving home when you feel this out of sorts."

Darla looked reluctant but too exhausted to argue. We exchanged hugs and murmured goodnights before they shuffled back up the stairs toward the human living quarters.

Alone in the silent lobby, I sank down into one of the waiting room chairs, emotionally drained. My jumbled thoughts kept returning to Alice and the secrets she may have carried quietly in her heart alongside the sweet librarian persona we'd known.

People and animals alike hid parts of themselves

away. And sometimes people were gone before you ever had the chance to fully understand them.

With that disquieting thought swirling in my tired mind, I finally headed upstairs to find some desperately needed sleep.

Chapter Four

Mario stared at me, mouth agape.

"You're telling me sweet little librarian Alice Grey was some kind of criminal mastermind?" The Tablerock police officer scoffed in disbelief. "Did she mastermind heists between shelving books? Coordinate international smuggling rings using the library's interlibrary loan system? Hide microfilm in the biography section?"

"Mario, we're not joking," Evie told him.

But he wasn't done.

"Was her book cart actually a high-tech getaway vehicle? Did she threaten unruly patrons with a knife instead of a ruler? I appreciate what you're saying, Evie, but come on—this has gotta be a joke. I've never seen such an unlikely villain in all my years on the force." He paused, staring off into space for a moment as if a thought had just occurred to him. "Though I suppose it does explain why she was always shushing people.

Trying to keep them from uncovering her secret life of crime, no doubt."

"You didn't get much sleep last night, did you?" Landon asked his friend.

"How could you tell?"

I sighed, glancing around at the circle of faces in my small living room. Landon and Evie occupied the sofa, while Laurie, Matt, and Darla were sprawled across the armchairs and floor. Belladonna observed us all imperiously from her perch atop the bookcase.

"Look, I'm sure the cat's going through a rough time, but..." He held up his hands, clearly still not buying the idea of a librarian gone rogue. "Come on, Alice was a sweet lady who wouldn't hurt a fly! This has got to be some kind of prank."

"Believe me, I wish it was a joke," I told Mario. "But Ginger seemed completely convinced. He told us all about Alice's supposed rare book theft ring and black-mail schemes. Said she had this whole secret identity that none of us realized."

Mario looked at Matt. "You're awful quiet."

"Yes. Because I don't know what to believe, either," Matt admitted. "I just got assigned a case that might relate to all this, if you can believe it." Matt's Uncle Javier, the head of an Austin detective agency, had recently hired his nephew as a private investigator. This assignment was Matt's first real case on his own since joining the agency. "Some fancy old book was stolen from a collector's library. A first edition of some fairy tale book worth a fortune." He pulled out his notepad, flipping through pages. "Here it is—a first edition of Grimm Brothers, valued at over $10,000."

I raised my eyebrows. That seemed like an odd coincidence.

"The victim is a wealthy retired lawyer that lives in Tablerock named Henry Davis," Matt continued. "My abuela says he used to be around town quite a bit, but she hasn't seen him out and about much for the last few years. Notes say the book just vanished one night out of his library. No signs of forced entry or anything."

"Maybe he's not around town much, but Henry Davis was at the tree lighting asking about Alice last night," I said, then looked at Mario. "Did he call the police? I think his home is within the bounds of Tablerock. You should have a police report, right?"

"Interesting." Mario's eyes narrowed. "I would think so. I'll have to follow up with him. Could be connected." He shook his head. "Man, what a mess. If Alice really was mixed up in shady stuff, that probably gives us a whole new set of potential suspects."

"I find it hard to believe one of them will be Henry David," I said. "The man must be in his early eighties. It looked like he could barely walk without a cane and stay upright."

"He's got money, though," Landon pointed out. "People with money can hire people to do things for them. They don't have to do their own dirty work."

"We can't rule anything out yet." Mario scribbled

some notes. "We just don't have enough to narrow down a direction, but we'll investigate the claims thoroughly one way or another." He glanced at Matt. "Ginger's intel could really break this case open. I'll keep you all posted if we find anything to support what the cat said."

I nodded reluctantly. "Let us know if there's any way we can help or if you want to talk to Ginger yourself."

"Will do, though I'd like to wait on that in case I have to interrogate him."

My eyes went wide with astonishment. "Interrogate?"

"Hopefully, it won't come to that." Mario tucked away his notebook and stood. "I should get back to the station. We've all got a lot of digging to do."

"Mario, wait," Darla said as he turned. "How exactly was Alice...you know..." Her voice dropped. "How did she die?"

Mario hesitated, then sighed. "She was bludgeoned with one of those fruitcakes that were on sale to raise money for the library's reading program. The ones set up on a table by the entrance."

"A fruitcake?" Landon repeated in disbelief.

"Yep. Killer must have grabbed one right there in the lobby. Big sucker too, heavy as a brick on a metal platter. Did some real damage." Mario shook his head. "Wouldn't have thought it."

"Wow," I murmured. "Who kills someone with a charity fruitcake?"

"Well, it definitely wasn't premeditated. Crime of

passion, maybe? Grabbed whatever was handy nearby?" Matt speculated. "The library has better weapons than a fruitcake. Someone wasn't thinking."

"Could be. Or meant to send some kind of twisted Christmas message?" Mario shrugged. "We're looking into it. We're looking into everything. I don't think the fruitcake meant anything, but you never know."

Landon and I hurried out into the crisp morning air, the sun already climbing in the pale blue sky. His beat-up old pickup sat waiting, the chipped paint dull in the cool light. As he turned the key, the truck sputtered to life, the rumble shattering the quiet of the back lot at the shelter. I climbed inside, rubbing my hands together against the chill.

I stared out the dusty window as we drove, the passing houses a blur. I couldn't believe Christmas was in just a week or so, with all its cheer and light.

Right now, it felt far away.

Josephine had missed the group meeting at my place because of some high-stakes court case she was tangled up in, so Landon and I drove over to her law office to fill her in. While we were doing that, Darla volunteered to go next door to the vet clinic so she could get Laurie up to date about everything that had transpired.

Oh, to be a fly on the wall when Laurie found out about the fruitcake...

It certainly was shocking.

Bludgeoned with a fruitcake.

Who on earth would bludgeon someone with a fruitcake?

"A fruitcake. I still can't get over it," Landon said under his breath as he navigated the streets toward Josephine's office. "Of all the things to kill someone with."

"I know. It's just so strange," I agreed. "Nothing about this case makes any sense. First, we find out Alice may have had this whole secret criminal life. And then she's murdered in such a bizarre way."

"It's just a hunch, but I feel like one has to do with the other."

"Probably." I shook my head, gazing out the window at the passing shops decorated for the holidays, trying to reconcile this darkness with the surrounding cheer. "If the cat's telling the truth, anyway. Which we still don't know."

Landon's weathered pickup truck rattled into the parking lot outside the stately brick office building that housed Josephine's law practice. As he maneuvered into an open spot, I couldn't help but notice the ostentatious luxury car interspersed among the other modest vehicles. The Porsche stood out like a diamond among stones. It must belong to Josephine's high-profile client.

Landon didn't even glance at it, perfectly content with his trusty vehicle that had logged so many miles over the years. The glitz and glam of overpriced status symbols meant little to the calloused carpenter—whose only business concern was getting the job done right.

Stepping into the lobby, the muffled sound of raised voices echoed from down the hall. Though the words were indecipherable, Josephine's strident tones carried clearly even through the closed conference room doors. Her voice rang out like a judge's gavel—sharp, authoritative, and brooking no argument.

"Please have a seat," her receptionist, Marsha Borden, said warmly. "Ms. Reynolds's meeting is running just a bit over."

Marsha Borden, Josephine's paralegal/office receptionist, embodied a unique blend of warmth and professionalism. Her welcoming smile could put even the most anxious visitors at ease, and her voice carried a soothing quality that made people feel instantly comfortable.

As opposed to Josephine.

"I won't stand for these trumped-up allegations against my client!" we heard her yell. "Your so-called evidence is circumstantial at best. My team will tear it to shreds!"

"Can I get you something to drink?" Marsha asked, her neatly styled auburn hair framing her face gracefully as her hazel eyes sparkled with genuine kindness.

I shook my head. "No, thank you, we're—"

The muffled yelling was suddenly punctuated by the sharp crack of something hard slamming against wood, and then the eerie creak of a door. Landon and I exchanged wide-eyed glances, both clearly taken aback by the sound.

A man's voice responded, far meeker than Josephine's but easier to hear now that the door was slightly open. "Now, see here, Ms. Reynolds, there's no need for such dramatics. If you review the documentation I've provided, you'll see—"

"The only thing I see is a feeble attempt to cast aspersions without adequate proof," Josephine cut him off sharply. "If this is the quality of your supposed proof, I remain wholly unconvinced."

"Really, Ms. Reynolds, please—" the man tried again desperately.

Another loud thump resonated, and we heard papers scattering.

"I'll thank you not to patronize me, Mr. Johansen," Josephine snapped. "Unlike you, I came prepared for battle, and I am fully prepared to annihilate your flimsy claims. Are we clear?"

"Yes," the man responded weakly.

A moment later, the conference room door flew open, banging loudly against the wall. A disheveled man in a rumpled navy suit came hurrying out, clutching his leather briefcase tightly to his chest like a shield. His eyes were wide and movements jittery as he hastened for the exit, looking like he couldn't get out of there fast enough.

"Let me know if there's anything else we can do for you, Mr. Johanson!" Marsha, the receptionist, called out in a honey-sweet voice as the disheveled man shot out the door without so much as a backward glance.

A moment later, Josephine emerged from the conference room, smoothing down her sleek dress and looking utterly unruffled despite the prior shouting match.

"Wretched ambulance chaser," she muttered under her breath as she clicked into the lobby in her stiletto heels. Then she turned to us with a broad, dazzling smile, her entire demeanor transformed.

"Ellie, Landon! Do come in," she greeted us warmly, beckoning us toward the conference room. It was like a switch had been flipped. Her frustration at the unfortunate Mr. Johanson now vanished without a trace.

Sharing an amused look, we followed Josephine inside the conference room. "Okay, we can talk freely in here as long as no one shouts. What's going on with the Alice situation?"

I quickly filled her in on everything we had learned from Ginger and then Mario. Her eyes went wide, and she sank down into a chair next to us.

"A fruitcake? Who gets killed by a fruitcake?" she said. "What on earth?"

"That was our reaction, too," Landon said.

"And Ginger was certain Alice was involved in all this criminal activity?" Josephine leaned forward, steepling her rings together. "How absolutely wild."

"We're still trying to make sense of it all," I admitted.

"Well, in that vein, I have something rather interesting to share with you both," Josephine began, standing up and strolling around the large mahogany table, heels clicking on the tile floor as she moved away from us. She let the statement hang in the air for a moment, looking at me and then at Landon from her place at the opposite end of the room. "It seems, my dear friends, that we may find ourselves on inverse sides of this little mystery."

Landon and I swapped a bewildered look over the polished tabletop.

My friend Josephine had a flair for drama and suspense and clearly she was intent on drawing out her revelation like we were a jury she needed to impress. Her brown eyes glinted with what I could only describe as mischievous glee as she watched our reactions.

"Well?"

"Well, indeed," Josephine said to Landon. "In the tangled web of Tablerock's affairs, it appears you and I have become entangled despite ourselves."

Landon scratched his head, giving me a bewildered shrug.

Josephine's coy act was trying even my patience.

"Would you just spit it out already? I'll be collecting social security by the time you get to the end of this reveal. What do you mean, inverse sides?" I asked.

Josephine lowered herself into the high-backed leather chair at the head of the table, propping her feet up casually. "You're no fun. Fine—I've just received a most fascinating document. Alice Grey's last will and testament." She let the words hang dramatically in the air.

Leanne Leeds

"And?" I prodded.

"And it appears the sole beneficiary is none other than my client, Henry Davis."

"What?"

"You heard me."

Landon looked equally shocked.

"But how did they even know each other?" he asked.

"An excellent question." Josephine tapped her fingers together contemplatively. "One I'm afraid I cannot speculate on, given my duty to protect my client's privacy."

Oh.

Oh, that's what she meant.

Darn it.

"What does it say about her cat, Ginger?" I asked.

She shook her head no.

"Nothing?"

"No, nothing."

"So you're saying Henry Davis, the man whose rare book was stolen, inherits everything from Alice, the woman who supposedly masterminded a theft ring?" My eyes narrowed. "That seems an awfully odd coincidence."

"Does it?" Josephine held up a manicured hand. "I cannot make any accusations. I can't even speculate on the why and wherefore of it all. I'm bound by attorney-client privilege. You understand?" She smoothed an imaginary wrinkle from her skirt. "I merely share the public facts. Any inferences about motives or guilt will have to come from other people this time."

Landon's glance shifted in Josephine's direction. "You sound like you're implying your own client is involved here."

"Oh, Landon." Josephine laughed airily. "You know I am the very soul of discretion." She mimed zipping her lips. "I couldn't imply anything. I could be disbarred for breathing a word to you on the subject."

I knew pressing Josephine further right now would be pointless. As a lawyer, she took confidentiality extremely seriously—sometimes to an aggravating degree. Her coy teasing was likely just her theatrical way of making her straight-jacketed position seem more entertaining than it was.

"Well, this has been illuminating, if not exactly help-ful," Landon said.

Josephine simply shrugged, still smiling. "I'm sure the police will uncover the truth soon enough." She stood once again, straightening her blazer. "Now, I hate to rush you out, but I have clients to attend to."

With that, she ushered us politely but firmly from her office. I looked back to see her waving cheerfully before the door swung shut between us.

Landon shook his head as we walked to his truck. "Leave it to Josephine to drop a bombshell like that, then clam up."

"Honestly, I don't know that she had a choice," I

said. "But if Josephine becomes our adversary on the other side of this thing, I don't really like our odds."

Back at the cat shelter café, I quickly gathered Evie, Darla, and Matt into my small office, shutting the door firmly behind us. The spacious lobby still bustled with activity as we crammed into the cramped room.

"We just came from Josephine's and found out something you all should know," I said, and motioned for the three of them to take a seat as I settled behind my cluttered desk.

Darla perched on the edge of the vinyl chair, her brow furrowed curiously. Matt leaned back in his seat, long legs sprawled out casually as he gave me an affable grin. Evie stood beside him with arms crossed.

"Josephine has Alice's will," Landon said. "Turns out the sole beneficiary of Alice's will is Henry Davis. If it's her will at all—Alice made no mention of Ginger."

Evie frowned and looked at Matt. "She left everything to the dude with the pinched pricey tome?" She looked back at me. "The one that hired Matt's office to find it?"

"The same," I confirmed.

"But I've seen them together at the library. It was like they barely knew each other," Darla said, bewildered. "Why would she leave everything to him?"

Landon shook his head. "We have no idea. But it seems mighty suspicious."

"There's more." I hesitated. "Josephine made it clear she can't discuss the case further with us because Henry Davis is her client."

Stunned silence met this revelation. Then Evie spoke up uncertainly.

"So Josephine is representing the chief murder suspect? The man who inherits from the victim?"

"We don't know that he's even a suspect," Matt pointed out.

"But if he is, we'd be working against her."

"Seems that way," Landon said.

Matt frowned. "She's not a criminal defense attorney, though. This is out of her wheelhouse. Maybe that matters."

"Right, because she's so terrible at this when she works with us," Evie told her boyfriend.

I raised my hands. "Hold on, we're getting ahead of ourselves here. We have no actual evidence Henry killed Alice. All we know is what Ginger claimed about her supposed double life, and we have no proof any of that is true." I met each of their eyes. "We're operating on speculation and assumption."

"Good point, Mom," Evie said.

"While that's true, Henry's name keeps coming up in all this," Matt said thoughtfully, scratching his stubbled chin. "Maybe I should go talk to him, ask about the stolen book, and see if he lets anything slip. I could pick up on something useful. I mean, he did hire us and it is my assignment."

Darla perked up at this idea. "Can we all go?"

Matt chuckled. "Probably not a good idea for us all to just show up at his doorstep. But..." He tapped his fingers on his leg, thinking hard. "I do have some fairly fancy hidden body cam equipment. If we set it up right, you all should be able to watch and listen in real time from here."

Darla was practically bouncing in her seat now.

Evie just shook her head, though I could see a hint of a smile playing on her lips at her friend's enthusiasm.

"I might even have an earpiece I can wear so you guys can chime in while I'm talking to Henry," Matt continued.

"Only if you're sure there's no risk to you," I told him. "If Henry is wrapped up in this, he could be dangerous."

Matt nodded. "I'll keep my guard up. I always do."

I had to admit, I was intrigued by the plan. With Matt's surveillance expertise, we could essentially question Henry together without rousing his suspicion or even letting him know we were looking into anything.

It was certainly worth a try.

Chapter Five

I watched with quiet amusement as Evie expertly fussed with the wires and cables of the surveillance equipment Matt brought, explaining each component to an enthralled Darla. Evie's slender fingers worked adeptly, checking connections and adjusting settings with practiced ease.

Clearly, this wasn't her first time handling such spy gear. I probably should have found that concerning, but mostly I was just impressed by her technical proficiency.

I could barely work the television remote.

Darla peppered her with wide-eyed questions about microphones and frequencies and backup batteries. Evie answered each one patiently, seeming to enjoy passing on her knowledge. There was a new lightness to my daughter that I hadn't seen in some time as she talked animatedly with her hands.

Matt really was an excellent influence on her. His

new job as a private investigator had opened up many opportunities that brought out this brilliant, resourceful side of Evie I hadn't known existed—well, no, that's not true. I'd always known it was there. She just hadn't been confident enough in herself to shine.

"This is a... it's a..." She held up a wire toward Darla as her brain "hitched" on the word. Instead of getting upset like she used to, my daughter just patiently waited for it to come. About ten seconds later, she said, "BNC Cable. We're not using it today, though."

Darla nodded.

Between Matt's practical P.I. field experience and Evie's technical know-how from taking online detective courses, the two made quite the formidable team.

"Are we live yet?" Darla asked eagerly, leaning over Evie's shoulder.

"Just about." Evie clicked a few keys and nodded in satisfaction. "All set. We'll be ready to go as soon as Matt activates the camera."

"Nice work, Evie," I said. "You've really gotten the hang of all this high-tech stuff."

Evie smiled up at me, clearly proud of her handling of the sophisticated gear. "It's pretty fun, actually. Kind of like we're spies in an action movie or something." Her eyes were bright, and I could see how much she was enjoying getting to put her technical skills to use. "I feel very James Bond sometimes."

It was nice to see Evie feel less like a victim of trauma, and more like an agent in her own story.

Landon leaned closer to me on the sofa. "This isolation room is getting more use than I ever could've imagined when I built it."

"No kidding," I said with a muted laugh. "It's come in handy more times than I can count."

The small room we gathered in was simple—just a ten by ten foot room on the second floor officially designated as the quarantine area for new cat intakes at the shelter. But with its thick foam-padded walls designed to limit café noise, it also served as the perfect makeshift headquarters for our private discussions.

When the door sealed shut, the room became an oasis of silence in the normally chaotic and noisy shelter. Outside, cats still meowed, volunteers chatted and phones rang, but inside not a whisper could permeate the soundproof barriers—and, of course, we (or the cats standing on the magic plate) could talk freely without fear of being overheard.

"It definitely gets cramped at times," I admitted. "But it's not that bad."

Landon chuckled. "Reckon I could expand it some. Wouldn't take much to knock down the south wall and add a few feet. I think you have a storage room on the other side."

I considered the idea.

More space would be nice... but there was something cozy about our motley crew of friends crammed in that room trying to solve mysteries. That, and expanding it might seem suspicious—there were usually just one or two cats in the room. Why would two cats need a room larger than ten feet?

"I think it's perfect how it is," I told him.

As I glanced up, I met two pairs of unblinking feline eyes staring back at me. Ginger was perched on one of the tall cat shelves lining the quarantine room walls, raven-colored Belladonna glued to his side.

They watched our huddled gathering, no doubt puzzled by the unusual electronics and heightened sense of anticipation in the room. Belladonna's dark face was tilted curiously, taking in the computer and wires with subtle interest. Ginger seemed ready to bolt at any sudden movement, his gold-and-white body tense.

Looking at him closely, I did notice he seemed a little calmer than when he first arrived, with some of the raw grief and anger dimmed in his intelligent eyes. Having Belladonna by his side appeared to have a truly soothing effect on the scrappy cat.

At first glance, the two felines made for an unlikely pair. Belladonna moved with elegant poise, her sleek panther-like form the epitome of refinement. Ginger, by contrast, was rough around the edges—thick, scrappy, outspoken.

Yet as I watched them now, their growing closeness was undeniably touching.

Belladonna tenderly groomed Ginger's rumpled fur as he nestled against her with absolute trust. She seemed to provide a calm steadiness to his restless spirit, and his need of her appeared to draw hidden empathy out from behind her own prickly shell.

"Those two sure have hit it off quickly," Landon remarked.

"They really have."

They reminded me of an offbeat sitcom couple—the straight-laced lady and the lovable rapscallion.

A notification pinged on Evie's laptop. "We're live," she announced.

All of us gathered closely around the laptop as the screen suddenly sprang to life, showing a crisp view of an ornate study. Heavy wooden furniture, shelves crammed with leather-bound books, and cozy reading chairs created an atmosphere of old-world charm and erudition.

A moment later, Henry Davis shuffled into view. The retired lawyer seemed small and shrunken at over eighty years old. His slight frame drowned in a wool cardigan as he leaned heavily on a carved wooden cane. Watching his hesitant, shuffling movements, it was hard to reconcile this elderly man with a cunning killer.

"Thank you for agreeing to speak with me today, Mr. Davis," Matt said politely off-camera.

"Of course, young man." Henry's voice was refined, with the gentle cadence of a lifelong attorney. He clasped his hands together, gazed directly at the hidden camera lens, and said solemnly, "I don't have much hope that Lodestar can find my book, but I haven't given up all hope yet. Let's sit by the fire. Even the mild Texas winters chill these old bones."

"Lead the way."

As Henry settled slowly into an armchair by a fireplace, I studied his worn face intently for any hint of malice. His eyes seemed kind, if sad, and his manner warm despite the circumstances that had brought Matt here. Certainly not the demeanor of a cold-blooded killer.

Yet... looks could be deceiving. If Ginger was right about Alice's secret life, who knew what secrets this man might hold?

"They seem friendly enough so far," Darla commented.

Landon nodded. "Henry's putting on a good show if he's guilty."

"So, when is the last time you saw the stolen book?" Matt asked.

Henry's brows pinched together. "Yes, I reported the theft last week. Just dreadful timing that it was a holiday week, I suppose. That book was quite valuable, passed down through my family for generations." He shook his head. "I can't imagine how someone even knew about it."

I frowned. He didn't say who he reported it to. Lodestar Investigations? The Tablerock Police? The insurance company?

Matt didn't ask him to clarify, but pulled out a notebook, pen at the ready. "Can you walk me through everything you remember about the day it disappeared? What day was that?"

As Henry recounted the timeline, Darla leaned closer to the screen. "He does seem genuinely upset about the book being stolen. Like, that doesn't look faked, right?"

Evie nodded thoughtfully. "Right. But I'm not sure that means anything."

It was frustrating not being able to ask questions directly. But Matt seemed to pick up on our doubts.

"When you say you reported the book as having been stolen, who did you report it to?" he asked. "The police? Your insurance company? And I have to ask—if there was no evidence of a break-in, are you certain someone took it? Perhaps you just moved it yourself." Matt pointed toward the books on the wall. "Shelved it in the wrong place?"

Henry bristled at Matt's question, adjusting his wire-rimmed spectacles irritably. "Young man, I assure you I know how to keep track of my own library," he huffed. "That book was precisely in its place on the shelf when I left for my club. And gone without a trace upon my return. No one else had access to this study."

It was clear Matt had made a tactical error by combining his questions about the missing book. The rookie move provided the old man an easy opportunity to dodge the first question, and Henry Davis took the out without hesitation.

Matt held up his hands apologetically, trying to keep things casual. "Right, of course. Didn't mean to imply otherwise, sir. Just figuring out the timeline here," he said smoothly. "What club was it that night you were out at, if you don't mind me asking?"

Henry's frown eased as he reached over and caressed the worn leather cover of a notebook sitting on the table next to him, his lips quirking into a faint smile. His fingers traced over its frayed edges and weathered binding, as if the touch comforted him somehow. It seemed...oddly intimate.

Weird.

"Why, my book club at the library, of course. We meet every Tuesday evening without fail. I returned around nine to find the book gone. I read a little of it every night."

"Terrible tragedy, what happened to Alice," Matt said as Mr. Davis provided the opening, his voice softening. "How well did you know her?"

"Awful business," he murmured. "Just dreadful. Alice was a lovely woman, always kind to me whenever I visited the library." He dabbed at his eyes with a handkerchief. "She reminded me of my own granddaughter."

Evie gave me a skeptical look. "He *seems* really broken up about Alice."

"Did you notice anything odd on Tuesday with Alice?" Matt asked.

"Now that you mention it, she did act peculiarly at our book club meeting," Henry mused. "About halfway through the discussion, Alice suddenly gathered up her things in a rush. Said she had forgotten to mail an important package and needed to run it down to the postbox before they closed."

He shook his head, recalling the odd incident. "Wasn't like her to leave in the middle of things. She always stayed for the entire discussion, often chatted with me and a few others as we walked out to our cars afterward. But that night she just hurried off—and since Sarah was fired for that nasty business, there wasn't even a library staffer there with us."

"Oh?"

In his notebook, Matt wrote, "Did Alice steal his book?"

Henry's bushy eyebrows furrowed as he tried to remember details. "Yes, I'd say she was gone for at least an hour before returning. We were nearly done for the evening when she came slipping back into the room."

"Just one more question, sir, if you don't mind," Matt said. "Could you show me where that missing fairy tale book was kept in your library?"

Henry nodded slowly. "Of course, of course." He pushed himself up from his armchair with effort, leaning heavily on his polished wooden cane as he shuffled toward one of the towering bookcases lining the study walls.

"There's no way this guy is a murderer," Landon said. "I doubt he could lift a fruitcake, much less bring it down hard enough on someone's head to kill them dead."

Coming to a stop, he gestured to an empty space on a middle shelf with a gnarled hand. "There. That is precisely where it sat. Rather unremarkable spot for such a valuable book." He shook his head, looking wearily bemused by the entire affair.

As Henry gestured to the space on the shelf, Matt subtly shifted closer. The angle of his concealed body cam swept over the barren spot where the missing book had been, as well as the aged volumes surrounding it.

The rich mahogany shelf contained a mix of cloth and leather-bound books, their titles embossed in fading gold leaf: "The Red Fairy Book," "East of the Sun and West of the Moon," "One Thousand and One Nights." They looked old but well-read, with cracked spines and pages edged in yellow.

There was another prolonged camera-sweeping look over the shelf and surrounding bookcases, documenting the shelf and surroundings from every angle. Matt finally stepped back.

After exchanging goodbyes, the screen went dark.

"So, what do we think?" Darla asked uncertainly.

Landon exhaled. "Hard to say. He seems innocent, but..."

"But that could be an act," Evie finished. She looked up at Ginger. "You lived with Alice. Did she ever mention Henry?"

The orange tabby slowly padded down to the cubby

with the magic plate. He stepped on it and meowed sharply. "My human trusted me, and I don't trust people that talk to cops. Belladonna told me about your buddy Mario. I don't know who you think I am, but I'm no snitch."

"Now just hold on a minute," Landon began, but Ginger cut him off with an irritated lash of his tail.

"Don't bother trying to deny it. I know you've been talking to the cops behind my back," he growled. He flicked his eyes over to Belladonna, who was perched serenely on a ledge watching the exchange. "She told me everything. About you spilling Alice's secrets to the police. Secrets I trusted you with."

Belladonna simply blinked her wide golden eyes slowly in response, neither confirming nor denying the accusation.

Ginger turned his gaze back on us, eyes blazing. "I've got nothing to say to any of you police lapdogs. You think just because Alice is gone, I'll turn traitor and rat her out?" The cat's tail swished angrily. "Not a chance. I know how to keep my mouth shut. Well, now. Maybe I didn't before. But I do now."

"Whoa, take it easy," Landon said in a calming tone, palms raised. "No one's asking you to betray any confidences here. We just want to understand what happened to Alice. Don't you want justice for her?"

At this, Ginger faltered, his bluster diminishing slightly. He glanced down at his paws.

"Of course I do," he admitted gruffly. "Alice deserves justice. But I won't sell her out either. She was always loyal to me, so I'll do the same for her." He hoisted his chin defiantly. "My loyalty is to my human. You can stop fishing, because this cat's no snitch. I'll take what I know to the grave."

Loyal to a fault, it seemed.

I could understand not wanting to tarnish his beloved owner's reputation, but at what cost?

Shielding her secrets certainly wouldn't bring her killer to justice.

Darla leaned forward, her eyes kind. "We don't want you to say anything Alice wouldn't have wanted, sweetie. But if she trusted you with parts of herself she hid from everyone else, maybe it's because she hoped you would share her full truth one day."

Ginger bristled again at this. "How convenient, putting words in the mouth of the dead," he hissed. "She didn't know about this plate. You never told her your secrets, did you? Nope. Then how would you think she would think I would tell anyone? Huh? That's ridiculous. You're just trying to manipulate me."

But beneath the bluster, I sensed his resistance wavering. Darla had struck a chord.

I followed her lead. "Alice can't speak for herself anymore about what she would've wanted. But Darla's right—maybe, in her heart, she hoped someone would someday understand the parts of herself she felt she had to conceal. That's all that we all want, Ginger. Isn't it?"

I moved closer to the plate, meeting Ginger's uncertain gaze.

"No, you're right—we can't know that for sure," I said gently. "And yes, only you can decide where your loyalties lie and what secrets you'll tell. But without the full truth, we may never get justice for Alice."

Ginger said nothing, staring down at his paws. The room fell silent as we watched the battle play out on his face, defiance warring with doubt.

"Ginger, no one thinks badly of Alice," Evie added softly. "Whatever secrets she had, she's still the kind librarian we knew and cared about."

The cat remained frozen, clearly conflicted. His golden eyes flicked between each of us uncertainly as we tried to gently persuade him. I could see the battle waging internally—loyalty to his beloved human versus a desire for justice.

After a long, tense moment, he looked up and met our hopeful gazes one by one. "I hear what you're all saying," he said. "But it doesn't change anything. She was my human, and I loved her. And that means I take her secrets to the grave no matter what."

He lifted his chin. "I'm sorry, but I am no fink. I am not spilling Alice's private business to anyone that talks to cops. That's it. The end."

The finality of his words hung in the air as we exchanged disappointed glances. As frustrating as it was,

I had to admire Ginger's steadfast devotion to his human. But...

I had no clue what the cat was bellyaching about, or why he was so defensive just because we'd shared information with the police. Alice was dead—how could her past crimes cause any more harm at this point?

Alice made some questionable choices—so what?

She couldn't exactly be arrested now.

I felt a flare of frustration as I looked up at Belladonna. If she hadn't gone and told Ginger about us talking to Mario, we might have gotten some useful information from him. But now the stubborn cat refused to budge.

The sleek black cat paused her grooming to fix me with an inscrutable golden stare. Then, tail swishing lightly, she gracefully leaped down from the ledge and padded onto the platter. "What?"

I didn't answer. There was no point.

But one way or another, Ginger would open up.

I would just have to be more clever than a cat.

Chapter Six

MATT STROLLED INTO THE ISOLATION ROOM, jingling car keys in hand. "Hey guys, sorry that took a while. Traffic getting back into town was surprisingly bad."

I raised an eyebrow. "Let me guess—you took a 'scenic route' that just happened to go by Dale's Donuts, where they just so happen to have the best apple fritters in the county?"

Matt's eyes widened in faux innocence. "What? No, of course not!" He paused, failing to suppress a grin. "Okay, fine. I may have made a quick detour for a fritter. But can you blame me?" He rubbed his stomach. "They're legendary! I left a bag of them behind the counter downstairs."

Evie gave him a quick kiss on the cheek. "No problem. We were just discussing what we learned."

"And debating if we should even be involved anymore, frankly," Darla added.

Matt looked at us curiously. "Oh? Why's that?"

I leaned back against the wall. "Ginger refuses to talk about Alice's criminal history. Josephine can't work with us because she's representing Henry Davis. I know that this stolen book thing is your case with Lodestar for your Uncle Javier, but I don't see what help we can be here."

"It feels a little like we're spinning our wheels," Darla said with a sigh, ticking the points off on her fingers. "Like your future mother-in-law said—"

"Whoa, hold up," I interrupted, raising my hands in surprise. "His future what?"

"You heard me," Darla said matter-of-factly.

I turned to Evie with an exaggerated look of shock. "Do you have some news you'd like to share with the class, young lady?"

Evie's face flushed crimson. "Oh, uh, we haven't... I mean, nothing's official..." she stammered, flustered. "No. Nothing."

Matt stood silently with a smile.

"Not yet anyway," Darla added with a wink, clearly enjoying Evie's discomfort. She cleared her throat. "Anyway, as I was saying, between the lack of cat info and Josephine being benched, I say we leave this to the professionals for now. I just don't see how we can help."

Landon scratched his chin thoughtfully. "I don't know. We've cracked tough cases before. And we know things the police don't, like what Ginger said about Alice's double life."

"But we told the police what we knew," I said.

"And that's why Ginger refuses to elaborate on any of that, so what we know is all we're ever going to know unless he changes his mind," Evie argued. She turned to Matt with a conflicted expression. "What do you think, hon? Should we back off and let the police investigate?"

Hon.

She called him hon.

How adorable.

I suppressed a smile as I watched the two.

Matt considered for a moment. "I don't think we're entirely empty-handed here. Henry was oddly evasive about that missing book when I asked who he reported it stolen to. Dodged the question completely."

"I noticed that," I said. "I thought you made a mistake when you gave him the opportunity to dodge."

"No mistake. I gave him an easy out not to answer, and he took it—the question is why he wanted to avoid answering that question. If it was really stolen, why not just say he filed a police report or insurance claim? Why not say he only called my uncle?" Matt pointed out. "Something doesn't make sense."

Darla's eyes widened. "Oh wow, good catch! I can't believe I missed that."

"And think about the timing," Landon added. "That rare book goes missing right before Alice turns up dead. Just one day before, I think."

Evie's brow furrowed. "You're right, that is quite a coincidence."

"What I don't understand is why was such a valuable book just left out in the open like that?" I wondered. "The book is supposedly worth thousands. Don't they keep old books sealed and in temperature controlled rooms like they had in that StreamFlix series? The one about the bookstore serial killer?"

Matt nodded. "Maybe he's hiding something about what really happened."

"But why wouldn't he tell you? After all, he hired you."

"I don't know. Did Ginger mention anything useful when you talked to him earlier?" Matt asked hopefully.

At the mention of Ginger, I grimaced. "Belladonna told him we're friends with Mario, and we shared what he told us. Ginger got defensive about the police being involved and refuses to tell us anything more about Alice's supposed criminal activities. Claimed he won't betray her confidences even after death."

Matt let out a frustrated huff. "Ay Dios mío. That complicates things."

"Exactly! Like I said—the cat won't talk, we can't work with Josephine, the cops are stuck. I say we stay out of this mess before we just make things worse," Darla exclaimed, throwing up her hands.

Evie bit her lip uncertainly. "I don't know... there are some awfully suspicious things going on here."

"Suspicious, yes, but with no actual evidence of a

perpetrator and no real way to get any, what can we do?"
Darla countered.

Landon tugged on his scraggly beard hairs contemplatively. "She raises a fair point. We're grasping at straws with no solid leads to go on here."

"Well, I need to keep digging," Matt said firmly. "I think the missing book has to do with Alice's death. I have no evidence to support my gut, but my gut tells me it's related."

Landon's eyebrows shot up in surprise. "And how many cases has your gut handled so far on its own?"

Matt shifted on his feet, looking embarrassed under Landon's intense scrutiny. "Um. One," Matt answered a little sheepishly. "This one, I mean."

"I can lend a hand," Evie said.

"Look, I'm not trying to be a party pooper or anything here." Darla still looked uncertain. "I just think maybe this is over our heads. The police really should handle it from here."

It wasn't like Darla to give up so easily.

It was she and Evie that came up with this whole "amateur investigations led by talking cats" thing in the first place after all, and I'd have expected more determination from the usually tenacious young woman.

But her point of view was clearly having an effect. The others murmured both agreement and dissent, launching back into debate about whether we should pursue this further, using the same points that had been repeated several times already.

I held up my hands for silence. "This isn't getting us anywhere. Clearly, we all feel a little differently about this." I met each of their conflicted gazes. "I think we should pump the brakes and concentrate on our duties for today. The shelter is overflowing. We have a packed holiday schedule at the café, and there are cats who need our help. Arguing in circles won't move us forward."

I straightened, adopting a brisk, businesslike tone. "Matt, you've got your P.I. assignments to work on. Darla and Evie, the shelter staff could probably use you. Landon, those custom catios won't build themselves." I looked around at the group. "Let's table this for now and do what we do—help cats and bring some holiday cheer to this community. After Alice's death, they sorely need it."

"You're right, Ellie. One case isn't worth arguing about," Matt conceded.

"And you know I'm always happy to see more cats find homes," Evie agreed, brightening a bit.

"Exactly. That's the spirit." I smiled and ushered them toward the door. "It's supposed to be the most wonderful time of the year, folks. Let's try to make that a reality."

The Silver Circle Café bustled with holiday cheer and the rich aroma of freshly brewed coffee. Christmas tunes played merrily over the speakers as customers laughed and chatted at the counter and clustered tables. Twinkling lights lined the windows and festive garlands hung along the cat perch shelves, adding to the warm, festive atmosphere.

I handed an eggnog latte to a smiling customer. "Here you go, Sadie. That should get you in the Christmas spirit."

"Oh, thank you, Ellie! You make the best holiday drinks in town," Sadie said. The elderly lady clutched her woolen shawl around her shoulders. "It's so nice to be able to sit down and have Estella's Chamuco with a great cup of coffee. And I love the green and red sugar for Christmas!"

Estella—Matt's grandmother—has been baking her oversized Mexican Chamucos for Garcia's Corner Market for years. They're circular pastries with generous cream cheese or fruit fillings overflowing from the center.

When you bite into one of Estella's Chamucos, the sweet, dense bread gives way to a lush interior exploding with tangy cream cheese or vibrant jam. They are truly decadent—and constantly sold out each morning, both here and at the market.

"Happy to help get everyone feeling jolly this time of year." I waved as she headed off with her festive beverage.

Glancing around the cozy shelter café, I felt a swell of holiday joy despite the lingering shadow cast by Alice's tragic death. The rescue cats lounged contentedly on top of Christmas scarves, the volunteers chatted amiably with patrons and potential adopters, and delicious aromas filled the air.

Maybe focusing on all this would lift our spirits after the grim events of late.

I bustled behind the counter, refilling pastry displays and taking orders. Darla breezed by with a tray of lattes, her ponytail swishing.

"Table nine needs more napkins when you get a second," she told me over her shoulder.

"On it!" I called back, grabbing a stack from the side cabinet. It felt good to be in my element again, keeping busy with the work I loved.

As I dropped off napkins and cleared empty mugs, snippets of conversation reached my ears.

"Simply tragic about Alice."

"Awful timing right before Christmas."

"I hope they catch whoever did it."

The talk in the café inevitably centered on Alice's shocking murder and the pall it had cast over the normally merry season. I sighed and kept moving, focusing on each small task at hand, eventually swinging by the counter where Old Carl sat nursing his customary black coffee.

"Morning, Carl. Can I get you anything else?"

"Nah, I'm all set, Miss Ellie," he replied, the brim of his worn cowboy hat casting a shadow over his craggy face. "Say, did I hear right that the library's closed up tighter than a tick?"

"I believe so. It's closed for now while the police investigate, but I imagine they'll reopen soon, though."

Carl harrumphed. "A crying shame about Miss Alice. She always did love that Christmas read-aloud for the tykes. Doubt they'll do it now, God rest her soul." He shook his grizzled head mournfully.

Annie, a computer programmer that stopped by every morning on her way to work in Austin, chimed in. "Do you really think they'll cancel story time? The kids look forward to it all year."

Carl took a long sip of coffee, then set down his mug with a clunk. "I bet they'll just up and rehire that Sarah lickety-split now that Alice is gone. Mark my words, she'll be back there shelvin' books before the crime tape's gone."

I paused wiping the counter, intrigued despite myself by Carl's gossip. "I don't see how. I heard Sarah was fired."

He waved a hand dismissively. "I tell ya, it was always Alice what had a problem with Sarah, not the city. Alice went and got the poor girl fired over some nonsense or another and the old mayor just gave in because that's what Jessa would do, right? But now Alice is gone and we have a new mayor with more than half a brain, so nothing stopping 'em hiring Sarah back."

"I thought she was let go for more serious reasons than a personality conflict," I said carefully.

"You can think a lot of things, but it's all gossip. I'm not gossiping. I'm telling you what's what. Sarah got on well enough with the patrons. Only person she didn't get on with was Alice. Mark my words. With Alice gone, I bet they already took down that caution tape and stuck a 'Come Back, Sarah' sign in the window quicker than a jackrabbit. Girl always did her job."

Old Carl sat back in his chair, clearly satisfied with his rambling assessment of the situation. The other patrons murmured among themselves, both intrigued and confused by Carl's words.

Which was the usual reaction to Carl.

Annie chimed in. "You know, Carl has a point. There was that big to-do about Sarah getting let go, but it did seem rather sudden. And it was only after that one disagreement she had with Alice."

"Which disagreement?" someone asked.

"That's right, I do recall people saying Alice demanded she be fired even though the city wasn't fully convinced," another customer named John added.

"Well, in my experience, where there's smoke, there's fire," Carl declared ominously, clearly warming up for another one of his long-winded soliloquies. "You mark my words, there was more going on there between those two ladies than meets the eye."

I'd lost track of how many of the old man's words he expected me to "mark" since I'd moved to Tablerock. My mental notebook dedicated to his ramblings was overflowing at this point. We all knew the drill with Carl's monologues—smile, nod, and wait for him to run out of steam.

Still, I made a mental note to ask Mario if he had followed up with Sarah yet. After her odd behavior when Alice was mentioned, looking into her full alibi that night certainly couldn't hurt.

As for Carl, I kept smiling and occasionally murmuring in agreement whenever he paused for breath. With any luck, Darla would swing by with a slice of pie from the back to distract him soon.

That usually helped speed these speeches along.

The bell above the café door jingled merrily as Laurie breezed inside from the front hallway mantrap entrance. "Afternoon, ladies," she greeted Darla and me cheerfully. "It smells absolutely delicious in here, as always."

Laurie was wearing a festive red Fair Isle Christmas sweater dotted with prancing reindeer and snowflakes under her white doctor's coat. With her rosy cheeks and short, blond hair peeking out from a jaunty Santa hat, she looked like a walking personification of the holiday spirit.

"Hey you," I said, coming around the counter to hand her a coffee. "We've missed you around here the last few days. I thought once you moved in next to the shelter, we'd see you more. Busy?"

"I know, sorry—I've been wrapped up over at the clinic." Laurie leaned against the counter, looking over the baked goods temptingly displayed in the case. "It's just been nonstop juggling patients and paperwork. You would not believe how many people still don't know chocolate and dogs don't mix—and there's tons of chocolate at Christmas." She frowned. "But I'm taking a proper lunch break today—I'll take my usual spinach salad, please."

"Coming right up!" Darla said brightly, grabbing a container of spinach salad with chicken from the refrigerated case. "The vinaigrette dressing on the side?"

Laurie nodded. "You know me so well. And could I get a cinnamon roll too, please? One of the big gooey ones."

As Darla packaged up her order, Laurie jerked her chin toward my small office off the lobby. "Want to chat while I eat? Feel like I'm overdue for a catch-up."

"I'd love that. Darla, you okay holding down the fort for a bit?"

"Absolutely!" Darla said as she added dressing to Laurie's salad, closed the top, and slid it across to her. "You ladies go talk. I've got this."

I led Laurie back to my office and closed the door. It was a small, cluttered space, but it afforded a bit of privacy from the bustle of the café.

Laurie settled into one of the plush chairs, taking a big bite of cinnamon roll. "Mmm...pure heaven," she mumbled through the mouthful.

"You're supposed to eat the salad first."

"Didn't you see 'Pretty Woman'? The salad comes at the end of the meal."

"I did. And it does not."

"I'm a grown woman, *Mom*, and I eat what I want. So, what's new?" she asked before opening the salad and spearing a forkful of spinach. "I feel like I'm woefully out of the loop lately. The last thing I heard was the cat's confession that Alice was really a criminal mastermind. I would have come by this morning for an update, but I had to dive into the belly of a rambunctious German Shepard's stomach to retrieve the Baby Jesus he ate."

I blinked.

Laurie laughed. "I know. The glamorous life of a small town vet, let me tell you."

"Well... okay, stop me if I'm telling you something you already know," I said. "Josephine's been representing Henry Davis, who is also the only person named in Alice's will. At least according to Josephine."

Laurie nodded, looking intrigued. "Right. She mentioned that when she called me earlier. But she couldn't say much else because of attorney-client privilege."

"Yeah, that's what she told me and Landon, too. That she's not going to talk to us while this entire case is going on. What that means, exactly? No idea."

"That's why she was calling." Laurie speared another bite of salad. "She wanted to let me know why she was putting some distance between her and us for the holidays. Though I have to admit, even with her explanation, I don't get the wall of silence that's come down. It seems a little excessive, don't you think?"

I leaned back in my chair. "You should have seen her, Laurie. She was cagey with us. And it's a shame, too, because we could really use Josephine's help to try to sort through all of this."

"I know. I do understand she has to protect her client, as annoyingly tight-lipped as it makes her." She smirked, then grew thoughtful as she ate another forkful of salad. "But the distance she put between us makes me wonder if she knows something about her client's guilt that we don't," she mused after swallowing. "If he was just some old man named in a will, would she be doing all this? Maybe we *should* just let this one go."

I sat up straighter, surprised. "What do you mean?"

Laurie set down her fork and met my gaze. "I mean, it sounds like you've got nowhere to start. The cat refuses to tell us anything. Josephine can't help. And it's nearly Christmas, El. Maybe we should just take a step back this time and let the professionals do their job."

"Darla said the same thing."

"I don't see the point in getting involved here," Laurie said. "Like, what's spurring you on? Ginger made it pretty clear he's not going to give us any help investigating. And last I checked, you run a cat café, not a detective agency. If you have information from an animal that can help bring a bad guy to justice, I get it. I even get we may be obligated to help. But that's not this situation."

I shifted in my seat, struggling to counter her points. "Well, yes, but—"

Laurie held up a hand, a knowing look crossing her face. "Don't tell me you've gotten a taste for this amateur sleuthing business."

"What? No, of course not." I avoided her skeptical gaze, feigning intense interest in a scratch on my desk.

"Mm-hmm." Laurie clearly wasn't buying it. "So you aren't just a teensy bit thrilled every time you get to piece together clues and catch a killer?"

I chuckled reluctantly, finally meeting her amused eyes. "All right, fine. Maybe I'm enjoying this more than I should. I really feel like this 'hobby' of ours has helped Evie quite a bit. That and it's an interest we—me and Evie—share as adults, you know?"

Laurie nodded as she finished her salad. "Hey, no judgment here. I get the appeal of amateur sleuthing." She leaned in conspiratorially. "But hasn't this little crime-fighting hobby of yours nearly gotten you killed every time? If you don't have any info, why risk it?"

I rolled my eyes. "Oh, come on, not every case ended with a gun in my face."

Laurie fixed me with an incredulous look, one eyebrow raised.

"What?"

Laurie just kept staring at me, shaking her head in amusement. "If you say so, Nancy Drew," she chuckled.

Chapter Seven

Strands of twinkling lights illuminated the town square and appeared to bravely resist the darkness. People milled about beneath the glittering glow, though the crowd was noticeably more sparse than the ill-fated tree lighting ceremony held the night before.

Though the decorative lights twinkled on, the murder had obviously dimmed the brightness in people's eyes. Whispers and glances demonstrated the underlying unease that gripped the town—even so, the familiar carols still floated on the crisp air.

Tablerock, Texas, would celebrate this Christmas, refusing to let one tragedy ruin the joyful season.

I stood chatting with Evie, Matt, and Laurie near the elaborately decorated tree that towered over the town square. Lights ready to twinkle and glittering ornaments adorned its soaring branches, while an ornate wooden manger scene had been set up at its base—it still had its

Baby Jesus, so I assumed Laurie's German Shepard had eaten a different one.

Across the square, I could see Landon deep in conversation with Pastor JD Lance and Dale Haberman. The carpenter and the donut shop proprietor looked intently at the retired pastor as he leaned on his cane and spoke about something with an animated exuberance.

Nearby, Mayor Waldo Monroe stood reviewing note cards for the evening's ceremony, his sharp-featured face set in its usual stern expression. Though he exchanged the occasional brief word with a passerby, an aura of standoffish preoccupation surrounded Tablerock's new leader.

Once again, here we were.

Despite the tragedy, the square was rapidly filling up once more with families unloading lawn chairs and blankets to claim prime viewing spots. The rich scent of cocoa and roasted nuts filled the air again as vendors handed out treats. Children darted about, giggling, their cheeks flushed from the nippy air.

"It's just not the same without the cats," Evie said wistfully, hugging her jacket tighter against the chill. "Darla was so disappointed, but we just didn't have enough volunteers to move them here again on such short notice. I hope people still stop by the shelter after."

Laurie nodded. "I'm sure they will. Nothing spreads Christmas cheer like giving an animal a loving home."

Just then, I noticed Estella Garcia, Matt's grandmother, navigating through the crowd toward us. Her salt-and-pepper hair was tucked under a knit cap and she carried a tray of steaming cups.

"Abuelita, qué tal?" Matt greeted her with a quick hug.

"Bien, bien." Estella smiled warmly at our little group as she passed the cups around. "Thought you all could use some hot chocolate on this chilly night. Extra marshmallows. The covers are on the corner there."

"You're too sweet. Thank you, Estella," I said, gratefully clasping the hot beverage.

She waved a hand. "Anything to lift spirits after the tragedy. But we will get through this together, sí?"

Before we could respond to Estella, an ear-piercing feedback squeal erupted from the speakers set up around the square. All heads turned as Mayor Waldo Monroe took his place behind the microphone on the central dais, tapping it to test the sound.

A hush quickly fell over the murmuring crowd as the mayor held up his hands for silence. His solemn gaze swept over the gathered townsfolk, his expression somber. I wondered how he would address the recent troubles plaguing Tablerock.

"Friends and neighbors, welcome once more to our annual lighting ceremony," the mayor began, his deep voice booming through the speakers. "I know many of you have awaited this evening, signaling as it does the start of what should be a joyous holiday season."

He paused, a heavier gravity overtaking his tone.

"But this year the festivities are darkened by sorrow. As you know, we recently lost one of our own."

The mayor spoke about Alice's vibrant spirit and called for unity in the face of darkness. I noticed people dabbing their eyes and leaning on one another.

Evie slipped her arm through mine, sniffling.

"No one embodied the spirit of Christmas more purely than Alice," Mayor Monroe continued somberly. "Her joy and generosity during this season were unmatched. Even during her own troubles, she devoted herself to bringing holiday cheer to others."

He paused, surveying the rapt crowd. "And so because Alice loved Christmas so dearly, I ask you all not to mourn her passing, but to celebrate her life. Honor her memory by keeping your hearts open and sharing kindness, the way she always did."

"Without the burglary," Laurie murmured.

I elbowed her in the ribs.

The mayor's firm voice rang out earnestly across the silent square. "Fill your days with light and laughter, as Alice would want. Let the spirit of the season she helped create here in Tablerock live on through each of you. That is the greatest memorial we can offer someone who gave so much."

He stepped back, nodding slowly as if affirming his own advice. A solemn hush held for a moment longer before a smattering of applause broke out in appreciation of his poignant words.

Following a contemplative silence, Mayor Monroe

announced they should illuminate the massive Christmas tree to remember Alice. He walked to the electrical box at the tree's base and, with a somber nod, he gripped the large switch. In one swift motion, he flipped it upward.

The towering pine instantly blazed to life with hundreds of dazzling multicolored lights. They gleamed against the dark inky sky, illuminating the square in a kaleidoscope of festive colors. Tinsel garland and ornaments glittered and twinkled, creating a vision of holiday magic.

The crowd began softly singing "O Christmas Tree."

The familiar carol took on a mournful, haunting tone as people crowded closer beneath the glowing tree with arms wrapped around shoulders and voices blended together in bittersweet tribute to a woman our town may never have truly known at all.

After flipping the switch to light the huge holiday tree, Mayor Monroe concluded the lighting ceremony and wished the crowd a meaningful season. As cheerful carols began playing over the speakers, the mayor made his way over to where our group was standing.

Up close, the toll of recent events was clear on the mayor's face. His eyes looked heavy and underscored by dark circles. His shoulders slumped slightly under his coat, lacking their usual authoritative posture.

"That was a beautiful tribute, Waldo," Laurie said kindly.

"It really was," I said. "How are you holding up?"

The mayor sighed, his shoulders slumping even more. "It's been a tough day. I struggled with whether to even go forward with the festivities after... well, after what happened." He shook his head sadly. "But the town has a whole two weeks of holiday events planned. I felt we had to carry on as best we could, for everyone's sake. I really believe this was what Alice would have wanted—carrying on with joy, despite the sadness."

Especially if it meant someone's home was empty, so she could burgle it, I thought.

"At least that's what her friend Sarah said."

Laurie's eyes narrowed. "Her friend Sarah? Sarah Black, you mean?"

Waldo nodded.

I tipped my head, studying Waldo curiously. "When did you speak with Sarah?"

"Just this morning, in fact, when I rehired her. I felt it was important to get the library back up and running during the kids' winter break. Too many families rely on it staying open. Jack Jones assured me it's what Alice would've wanted—not to let her tragedy derail the joy of the season."

Jack Jones? "Who's Jack Jones?"

"He's a local thriller author," Laurie told me. "Not a best-selling dude or anything, but his books are pretty popular around here. He writes about—"

She paused, looking hesitant.

"What?" I prompted. "What does he write about?"

Laurie shifted, lowering her voice. "Oh, just... you know, stuff. Crime rings, mysterious codes in books, that kind of thing."

I raised an eyebrow. Her cagey response made me suspicious there was more to these books than regular thrillers. I turned back to Waldo. "I'm just curious—when you talked to Sarah, she told you she and Alice were on good terms?"

"Well, no." Waldo looked mildly surprised by my questioning. "She admitted they'd had their difficulties, though she wouldn't go into detail. But Alice is gone, Ellie, and Sarah cares deeply for the library and the community."

Evie crossed her arms, frowning. "Didn't Jessa fire Sarah pretty abruptly, though? Seems odd you'd just ignore that and rehire her so fast. How do you know it wasn't for a legitimate reason?"

"I asked Jessa for the full story about why Sarah was let go. She was rather evasive with specifics, but I gathered it was merely a personality conflict that got overblown," Mayor Monroe explained. "I'm choosing to give Sarah another chance and take her at her word that she'll uphold the library's values now. Everyone deserves an opportunity to redeem themselves and turn over a new leaf, don't you think?"

I nodded along as the mayor spoke, but something didn't sit right with me.

Former Mayor Jessa Winthrop was many things, but truthful wasn't high on the list. Would she really have given Mayor Monroe—the man who defeated her in an election she'd told everyone who would listen was rigged —an accurate account of why Sarah was terminated?

My bet was no.

"I appreciate you wanting to see the good in people, Waldo," I said carefully. "I really do. But are you sure Jessa gave you the real, unvarnished story about what happened with Sarah?"

Mayor Monroe looked taken aback, clearly not expecting skepticism. "Well, I mean, she was a little evasive about specifics," he admitted. "But what would she achieve by lying to me about it? I'm giving her the benefit of the doubt that it was just a clash of personalities made bigger than it was. If she lied to me, there's nothing I can do about it now, but we'll know soon enough."

I shook my head, unable to match the mayor's willful naivete for Jessa's manipulations.

I hoped I was mistaken, for the library's sake.

But where Jessa was concerned, my cynicism was rarely misplaced.

The crowd began to disperse after the lighting ceremony concluded. As we turned to leave, I caught sight of a familiar figure standing near the empty stage. Josephine was chatting with a tall man wearing a long coat whom I recognized as her husband, though I hadn't seen him in quite some time.

"Josephine!" I shouted, waving eagerly, as if hailing a taxi in a downpour. "Josie! Hey, Josie!"

That ought to get her attention.

Let's see her try to ignore that.

"You really know how to respect boundaries, don't you?" Evie said, eyeing me like a disapproving parent. "Just ignore her."

Fat chance.

"If Josephine doesn't want to see us, she can ignore me," I said.

Josephine shot me a hesitant, almost wary glance when I called out to her. I waved more insistently, beckoning her over. "Josie, c'mon! Come, say hello!"

"Right. Ignore you," Evie breathed.

With slow reluctance, the lawyer murmured something to her husband and then started making her way through the dispersing crowd toward our group as I grinned triumphantly at Evie—who just shook her head.

"Happy holidays, everyone," Josephine greeted us when she finally reached us. Her tone was cordial but missing its usual vivacious energy and warmth. She certainly seemed more subdued and distracted compared to her normally exuberant self.

"Hi Josie." Laurie gave her a brief hug. "Good to see you out and about."

"Yes, well, just a quick appearance before heading home. Busy time of year for attorneys, you know." Josephine punctuated this with a brittle little laugh. Her gaze darted away evasively.

"Hey, Josie, you know anything about Jack Jones?" I asked, keeping my tone casual.

I studied Josephine carefully, searching her face for any hint of recognition at the name. But her expression remained impassive, her expertly painted red lips fixed in a polite smile that didn't quite reach her eyes.

"Who?"

"Jack Jones. Local author?"

At the repeated question, Josephine's dark eyes sharpened, her casual facade slipping for just a moment before the genial mask snapped back into place. "Jack Jones?" She repeated the name once more in a light tone, as if trying to discern why I had brought him up. One precisely shaped eyebrow arched ever so slightly. "Why do you ask?"

Her response was evasive, guarded. I sensed her mind racing to ascertain my motives and determine how much I knew about whatever was causing her to react the way she was.

"Oh, just something the mayor mentioned in passing after the ceremony," I said with an airy wave of my hand, intentionally vague. I watched her closely for any reaction. "The name sort of rang a bell for some reason, so I was curious if you knew of him."

I lied.

It rang no bell.

Josephine studied me for a long moment, her dark brown eyes unreadable. I could almost see the wheels turning behind them, considering her next move in this game of casual interrogation.

"The name does sound somewhat familiar," she said at last, slow and thoughtful. "But I couldn't say where from. A client perhaps, or someone I've run into socially over the years." She gave a graceful shrug. "I'm afraid I can't recall who exactly this Jack Jones is. Should I know him?"

Her gaze remained inscrutable, giving nothing away. But the subtle tension in her frame told me she was not being entirely forthcoming.

Josephine knew more than she was admitting.

Despite the good-natured teasing and eye rolls my friends and family had given me for so insistently summoning Josephine over, they all watched with rapt interest as the two of us now stood beneath the towering Christmas tree, its twinkling multicolored lights casting a soft glow over our faces.

Josephine clasped her hands casually in front of her, standing tall and elegant even in her obvious evasiveness. Her piercing brown eyes bored into mine, silently daring me to press her further. "Are you entirely sure this is the path you're called to walk for the holidays?" she asked me. "There's no turning back once you start down this way."

With a smooth, flawless veneer of polite interest, she mildly delivered a congenial warning.

"I just asked a simple question, Josephine," I said, keeping my voice light despite the growing tension.

Josephine's gaze remained inscrutable. "I have no answers for you, Ellie," she responded. "The name means nothing."

I studied her closely, searching for any little tell, any crack in her composure. But Josephine stood as still and unreadable as a statue.

"Mom, maybe we should go," Evie interjected gently, taking my hand in hers. I could tell my daughter was uncomfortable with the strange dynamic and wanted to diffuse it, but I was like a dog with a bone.

I wasn't ready to let this go.

Not when I was certain Josie was hiding something.

"I don't enjoy being on opposite sides of this," I told Josephine pointedly, holding her gaze. "I thought we were trying to do good in the world, Josie—not protect people that do evil."

At that, emotion finally flashed across Josie's face.

Regret.

Sadness.

Her stiff shoulders slumped ever so slightly.

"You think I like this?" she responded, weariness seeping into her voice. "Believe me, this situation is the last thing I would have wanted. I don't have a choice. I wasn't given a choice."

She looked away with a heavy sigh, the twinkling

Christmas lights reflecting in her eyes. For just a moment, her composure seemed to crack.

But then she took a breath, straightened her shoulders, and resumed the inscrutable mask. "Attorney-client privilege binds me."

With that, she gave us a polite nod before pivoting on her heel and disappearing into the dispersing crowd, the sound of her heels clicking across the pavement echoing behind her as she made her way back to her husband.

Landon turned to look at me, his brow furrowed.

"She was cocky and sort of amused by this whole thing when we were at her office, almost playing it like a game," he said. "But her entire demeanor has changed."

"You're right. She went from casually evasive to downright cagey."

"She even sounds different from when she called me," Laurie said. "And it wasn't just her evasiveness," the vet went on. "She seemed... I don't know. Rattled, maybe? Like something has really put her on edge."

Landon slowly stroked his rough chin. "I've seen Josie redirect and deflect with the best of them while keeping that sly twinkle in her eye. But this time, that twinkle was out. She shut right down and left."

I crossed my arms against the night air, gazing in the direction Josephine had gone. "You're right," I murmured. "I could see it in her eyes. Whatever she knows, it's shaken her. And that author—was it just me, or did it seem like she couldn't get away fast enough once I mentioned him?"

Around us, families laughed and strolled through the festive square, reveling in the glittering lights and holiday music. But a heavy cloud of unease now hung over our own little group.

"I don't like this," Evie murmured, turning to Matt with a worried crease between her brows. "Something weird is going on here."

Matt didn't immediately respond, his handsome face pensive as he continued staring off into the distance.

"You're awfully quiet," Evie prodded, squeezing his arm.

Matt finally glanced down at her, though his brown eyes still had that faraway look. "Sorry, I'm just thinking," he muttered absently, clearly distracted.

"About?"

Matt exhaled heavily, his breath fogging. "I'm thinking we're missing something big here. Some connection we're not seeing." He turned his gaze to me. "Josephine isn't telling us everything she knows. That much is obvious, and she warned us that would be the case. But what could have happened today that would have frightened Josephine Reynolds?"

I shook my head, just as perplexed.

"I wish I knew," Laurie said. "Josie's never been afraid to bend the rules before, and we've been in countless pickles already that she's always handled with a confidence I envy—I've never seen her like this."

"I've got a really bad feeling about this," my daughter said. "There's no way we can just walk away from this now."

Josephine's cryptic reaction had turned an unsettling situation into something far more ominous. But until we understood her motives, we were fumbling in the dark.

Chapter Eight

I slowly combed my fingers through my damp hair, working to untangle the ends after my shower. Wrapped in my terrycloth robe, I sat perched on the edge of my bed, lost in thought about the strange encounter with Josephine. Her cryptic warning and tense evasiveness replayed over and over in my mind.

A soft knock at my cracked bedroom door drew me out of my musing. I glanced up to see Evie standing in the doorway, already dressed for bed in checkered pajama pants and an oversized t-shirt.

"Hey Mom, got a minute?"

"Of course, sweetie. Come on in." I patted the spot next to me on the quilt.

Evie padded over and sat cross-legged on the bed, facing me. She picked at a loose thread on the blanket, not quite meeting my eyes.

"Everything okay?" I asked.

"Yeah, I just..." Evie trailed off, her gaze lowered shyly. She finally glanced up, a faint blush creeping across her cheeks. "I wanted to talk more about what Darla said earlier. You know, about Matt."

"Ah, right. The mother-in-law joke," I said with a smile. "Is it more truth than joke? Have you two talked about getting married?"

Evie fidgeted with a thread on my bedspread, the rosy glow on her face deepening. "We have, a little. I mean, we're still pretty young. It's not like we're rushing to the altar next month or anything." She dropped the thread. "But we are on the same page that marriage makes sense for us, eventually. I think, anyway. We've talked through the practicalities of it."

"The practicalities?" I arched an eyebrow.

"Yeah." Evie tucked a strand of hair behind her ear. "Look, I know most people my age don't sit around analyzing the financial and legal benefits and drawbacks of marriage." She gave a self-conscious little laugh. "But we both know I'm not most people. I can't afford to be a naive romantic about relationships."

I nodded in understanding as I watched her speak. My daughter's congenital heart defect had forced her to confront realities about life that no one should have to face so young, and her pragmatic outlook had developed out of necessity.

"I mean, I want to enjoy just being a couple, too. But Matt and I have to have open, honest talks about the future, for both our sakes." My daughter's voice softened. "Especially with my medical stuff always looming over everything. It's not exactly romantic pillow talk."

I felt my heart seize up as my daughter casually dropped the phrase "pillow talk" to describe private conversations with her boyfriend.

Though she was in her midtwenties now, my mind still pictured her as my little girl, far too young for such intimacies.

As a parent, there were some realities I was not quite ready to confront yet.

"But he needs to fully understand my situation if we're going to keep moving forward. And I think he does, Mom. Matt's been so amazing about it all."

I reached across and gave her hand a supportive squeeze. I was unspeakably grateful Matt had entered our lives. From what I could tell, he truly embraced every part of Evie, medical worries and all.

My daughter deserved that unconditional love and support.

Yet... her words sent an anxious pang through me. No mother ever wants to be reminded of the fragility of their child's life, that threat forever lurking in the background. I wished more than anything that Evie could simply enjoy falling in love without those worries weighing on her.

"I'm so glad you have someone you can be open with," I told her. "Matt is a wonderful man. It's very clear how much he cares about you."

Evie smiled, some of the tension easing from her

face. "He really is. I honestly never imagined I'd find someone like him." She picked up the discarded thread she'd plucked nervously from the blanket and began rolling it between her fingertips. "I just feel so lucky, you know? Which almost makes me more worried about messing this up somehow."

"Oh, sweetie, you couldn't," I assured her, squeezing her hand again.

"I know rationally that's not true." She sighed. "But I guess there's always that little irrational fear when you come across something real. That you'll lose it."

I wished I could protect her from all the uncertainty.

"It's only natural to feel nervous when you find something special," I said. "That vulnerability is part of being in love. But you and Matt are building something beautiful. Focus on communicating openly and enjoying each moment together. The rest will fall into place on its own."

Evie nodded, the worry line smoothing from her brow. "You're right. We just need to keep talking and take things one day at a time."

"When the moment's right, you'll know."

"Thanks, Mom." Evie leaned over and hugged me. I held her tight, grateful she might have found someone to walk beside her on her uniquely challenging life's journey.

Pulling back, Evie wrinkled her nose. "When Darla finds out we talked about this, she's going to combust."

I laughed.

With a mischievous grin, Evie mimed zipping her lips.

I knew her medical worries would always lurk, threatening to dim that light I saw in her eyes every day now. But for the moment, I reveled in seeing her so full of vibrant life and possibility.

I was deep in an enjoyable dream that involved a shirtless Jason Momoa hand-feeding me a delicious low-calorie ice cream sundae. I was just about to take a bite of rocky road when a sudden heavy weight pressed down over my nose and mouth.

My eyes flew open with a start, heart hammering. As my blurry vision adjusted to the darkness, I could just make out Belladonna's fluffy form looming over me, her furry paw planted firmly on my face to squash my nose.

"Stop!" I cried out, opening my mouth and gasping for air as the smothering cat made me swat at it in a panic.

Belladonna nimbly jumped away, landing with a soft thump on the floor.

I bolted upright, flipping on the bedside lamp. "What the heck, Belladonna?" I asked, clutching my chest as my pulse slowed back to normal. "Are you trying to kill me?"

She blinked her luminous yellow eyes slowly, as if asking what my problem was—and I didn't care what the cat experts said. That was no "I love you." Bella turned and quietly exited the cracked bedroom door into the dark hallway beyond.

"I wonder what I did to rile her up," I grumbled, shaking my head. I settled back against the pillows, about to turn off the light, when Belladonna sauntered back in. Before I could react, she leaped onto the bed and began repeatedly swatting at me with a barely sheathed paw.

"Are you kidding me? Stop that!" I sat up quickly and roughly pushed her away.

Belladonna dropped to the floor with a thud and stared up at me, tail swishing expectantly.

"What has gotten into you?" I muttered blearily. "It's..." I squinted at the glowing digits on my nightstand. "It's three in the morning, for heaven's sake!"

The sassy cat turned and trotted out into the hall again. Framed in the doorway, she glanced over her shoulder at me before continuing on.

"You can't be serious," I sighed. "You want me to follow you?"

She flicked her tail in response, and then meowed.

Well, I was awake now anyway.

With a groan, I slid out of bed, the hardwood floors cold under my bare feet.

"This better be good, Belladonna," I muttered, shuffling after the cat through the dark house. I followed the faint sound of her claws clicking against the floor, using my phone's flashlight to avoid bumping into anything.

Belladonna led me to the isolation room. Pushing open the already-ajar door revealed an empty room—no sign of Ginger. I crossed my arms, looking down at her. "Let me guess. You let Ginger out, didn't you?"

In response, Belladonna nimbly leaped up onto the glowing magic plate inset on the floor of the second-level cubby. It illuminated her sleek form in a soft, golden glow.

"Oh, indeed, I did grant that little scamp, Ginger, the privilege of exiting our cozy quarters this evening. They are my quarters, after all," she declared imperiously. "He's fine. The poor thing is taking his beauty rest downstairs with that brutish Digby."

"Digby is not a brute." I blinked groggily, trying to keep up with her pronouncement. "Why on earth would you do that?"

"So that we could have a little tête-à-tête," she said, languidly raising a hind leg to attend to an itch just behind her ear. "I had it in mind to discuss the prospect of inviting him to join our household on a more enduring basis."

"To join—"

"At least until I decide the moment has arrived for him to take his leave," she added with a haughty flick of her tail.

I shook my head, struggling through the mental fog. "Wait, are you saying you want us to adopt Ginger? Keep him here for good?"

"Indeed." Belladonna's gaze locked onto mine,

unyielding and stern. "It appears we have established a connection, he and I. If you need motivation, I think—given sufficient time—I can extract the truth about Alice's transgressions from him and pass those on to you. Consequently, it would be in your best interest to keep his company as well."

I snorted in disbelief. "Bella, are you bribing me to adopt your boyfriend?"

Belladonna's eyes constricted into thin slits. "I am not some giddy schoolgirl with a 'boyfriend,' as you so inelegantly articulated," she retorted, her tone icy. "Our companionship is one of mutual enjoyment, and I can assist him in overcoming his sorrow while providing you with something you need. That is all."

I stared at Belladonna in bewilderment and tried unsuccessfully to stifle an enormous yawn—it was too late at night for this conversation.

"Mutual enjoyment. That's the most dispassionate way I've heard someone say they like a man in my entire life," I replied.

"I don't need your opinion." Belladonna slowly blinked her luminous eyes. "Do we have an agreement?"

I studied her in the magical glow, debating.

On one hand, we had a shelter. One cat, more or less, really didn't matter at all. On the other, adopting every talking witness cat seemed extreme.

The core of it, though, was this—no matter how cold Belladonna sounded, it was clear she liked the scruffy orange cat.

I gave a weary sigh. "If he wants to stay, and he's allowed to, that's fine with me. Bella. I'll need to talk to him about what he wants to do, and if he wants to stay here—"

"No. You do not need to discuss this with him." Belladonna tipped her head. "Remember, if you and I agree here and now, I will share with you the tidbits Ginger reveals in confidence, and I will do so without his knowledge. A clandestine quid pro quo, if you will."

My exhausted brain snapped to alertness. "Wait, really? You'd report secrets he tells you in private?"

She drew a paw over her ear casually. "I believe your human idiom is 'pillow talk.'"

I winced.

"I don't like this, Bella." I hesitated. This felt wrong, but... "Look, obviously, if you learned anything relevant about the case, we would want to know," I conceded. "And if Ginger confides in you freely, and you're okay sharing that privately, I don't see anything wrong with that. But I'm not making his home contingent upon—"

"Then we have an accord." Belladonna swished her plumed tail. "See that adoption papers for Ginger are drafted promptly."

"That's not what I said—"

"I shall leave you to your rest."

With that, she delicately stepped down and slipped out the door, disappearing silently into the darkened mansion. I stood staring after her, marveling at the unexpected twist.

"What the heck just happened?" I asked the empty room.

No answers bubbled up from the shadows.

Maybe Belladonna's unorthodox proposition could provide information where we were currently stuck. I felt uncomfortable about the twisted ethics of it, and justifiably so. Using a new romance—even a cat's—to extract secrets did cross some moral lines for me.

But with Alice's murderer still free and Josephine twisted into a knot we had no idea how to undo, could we afford to be selective?

Belladonna volunteered the information.

I didn't ask her to betray Ginger.

I sighed, running a tired hand through my hair as I made my way back to bed. My jumbled mind kept going back to Josie's cryptic tension and evasiveness earlier that night.

Clearly, she feared something or someone.

And her caginess at the mention of that author...

If snooping into Ginger's private confessions would shed light on the deepening mystery, so be it. My conscience would just have some catching up to do later.

Right now, we needed answers.

And if Belladonna could get them, I wasn't going to stand in her way.

The next morning, I sat at the kitchen table cradling a steaming mug of coffee in my hands. Weak sunlight filtered in through the windows as I stared outside at the little grassy cat enclosure behind the shelter, lost in thought.

A nudge at my elbow drew my gaze down to Digby, the scrappy brown tabby with one eye and half a nose. He was one of the permanent residents of the shelter because of health issues that made adoption unlikely. I'd grown quite attached to the affectionate little cat over the months.

"Morning, Digs," I murmured, scratching under his chin. "You ready for breakfast?"

Digby replied with a raspy meow, nudging a bowl toward me. I chuckled and got up to fill it, returning to my own coffee as he munched away happily on top of the bistro table.

My thoughts soon wandered back to the previous night's encounter with Josephine beneath the glittering Christmas tree, and then Belladonna in the isolation room. In the clarity of morning, I felt a twinge of guilt over how I'd pressed Josie so insistently for answers.

"I was too hard on Josie last night, wasn't I, Digby?" I mused aloud.

The cat glanced up from his food, blinking his one good eye at me.

"I mean, she didn't choose who her client was or get roped into this mess," I went on. "She was just honoring her duties, and I put her on the spot."

Digby meowed around a mouthful of food.

"You're right, I should apologize." I took a sip of coffee. "Josephine's in a tough spot. I should have respected that, and I didn't. She's usually so bold and unflappable. If something has rattled even Josie..." I trailed off, worry gnawing at me.

The back door suddenly swung open, jolting me from my thoughts. Landon's large frame filled the doorway, the chilly morning air swirling around him.

"Morning, beautiful," he rumbled, ducking inside and giving me a quick kiss. His beard, already trying to grow after his morning shave, tickled my cheek. "Talking to yourself again?"

I laughed. "Just chatting with Digby about last night."

Landon poured himself some coffee and sat down across from me as Digby politely shifted to move his butt so it was facing another direction. "Figured I'd find you brooding in here."

"I'm having a side of guilt with my coffee," I admitted. "I feel bad for pushing Josephine so hard."

Landon nodded slowly, taking a sip. "Maybe so, but seems to me she's in that tough spot by choice. She started out making it a joke at the beginning. Don't blame yourself for taking her up on her game."

"I suppose you're right," I conceded. "I just wish I understood what has her so on edge now. It's really not like Josie to be intimidated by any situation, Landon."

"I don't know." He reached over and gave my hand a

comforting squeeze. "We'll figure it out. Oh, by the way, I talked to Waldo. He still wants me to set up those cat trees in the library's lobby."

I raised my eyebrows in surprise. "Really?"

"That's what he said. He hired Sarah, and the building is open. Thought you might want to tag along when I head over with them."

"Definitely. I want to hear from Sarah herself what the situation was between her and Alice." I drained the last of my coffee and stood. "Just let me get dressed real quick."

I headed upstairs to my bedroom and changed into jeans, a green sweater dotted with tiny Christmas trees, and brown boots. After running a brush through my hair, I swiped on some mascara and lip balm.

On my way back downstairs, I popped into Evie's room. She was still bundled under the covers.

"Hey sleepyhead, Landon and I are headed to the library to drop off the cat trees he built for the lobby display," I told her. "Want to come along?"

Evie yawned loudly and stretched, not moving from under her covers. "Sure. In two hours," she mumbled.

"Nope, we're leaving now."

She lifted her mussed head and squinted at the clock by her bedside. "It's seven in the morning," she groaned.

"That's the start of the day for most people, lazy-bones," I said breezily, sitting down on her bed and smoothing her messy hair back gently. "Everything okay?"

She nodded. "Yeah, tired. Go on without me."

"Okay, sweetie. See you soon." I headed back downstairs to find Landon waiting by the front door, truck keys in hand.

"Ready when you are," he said.

Minutes later, we were driving across town toward the library. I gazed out the frosty window as shops and houses decked out for the holidays flashed by, but my thoughts kept returning to Josie.

There were so many puzzling contradictions swirling around.

But my closest friend's uncharacteristic behavior troubled me the most.

Chapter Nine

LANDON'S TRUCK TIRES CRACKLED OVER THE ICY road surface as we pulled up outside the quaint redbrick Tablerock Library. Despite the early morning hour, cheerful holiday lights twinkled in the frosted windows of the humble building, making it seem a warm, welcoming refuge from the bitter cold outside.

As we climbed out, I paused a moment, struck by nostalgia.

I could almost see Evie as a kid again, bounding up the concrete steps, racing excitedly to be first through the heavy wooden doors. I smiled at the memory. We had spent so many Saturday mornings scouring library bookshelves, reading side by side.

When money was tight after Evie's surgeries (not even a six-figure job can easily pay for multiple open heart surgeries) and then after my divorce, I would bring my daughter to the Austin library for free entertainment.

We must have checked out every children's book on the shelves multiple times from multiple branches.

"C'mon, dreamer. Let's get these inside before my fingers freeze off," Landon said, lifting one of the holiday-themed cat trees from the truck bed.

I grabbed the other end, and we maneuvered toward the entrance beneath the carved wooden sign reading "Tablerock Library."

Stepping through the heavy wooden doors, the familiar smell of books—old parchment, the faint scent of worn leather bindings—mingled with the aroma of holiday decor. The rich fragrance of cinnamon potpourri and fresh balsam wreaths swirled around us in a comforting blend.

My gaze swept over the cozy one-room library that was so beloved by our community. Well-worn carpet the color of cranberries muffled our footsteps while recessed lighting cast a warm glow over the rows of shelves packed tight with books of all colors and sizes.

The corner play area with miniature plastic furniture sized for little readers was empty this early in the morning, and across from it, the computer station with three outdated desktops had a single patron. At the back, I could see the study rooms for tutoring sessions or community meetings were empty.

And of course, the focal point—a stately circular circulation desk Landon's company had made, a rich mahogany wood that anchored the space as if it was from another time. Beside it, a giant bulletin board burst with flyers for community events, programs at the library, advertisements for local businesses, and more.

We carried the cat trees toward the front where a cleared space had been cordoned off beside the circulation desk.

You'd never know a murder took place here just a few days ago.

As we set down the first tree, movement at the desk caught my eye. A petite woman with a short pixie cut and cat-eye glasses stood up.

Sarah Black.

"Well, hey there!" she chirped, scurrying around toward us. "You guys are really early! Well, everyone's really early during the holidays, I guess. Right?"

I studied the woman who now stood beaming before us. Dressed in a yet another cheerful holiday sweater, she seemed surprisingly upbeat given the circumstances. Her grin stretched unnaturally wide across a pleasant, round face.

She appeared flat-out delighted to have assumed supervision of the library under such grim conditions. Her cheer seemed... excessive.

Off-putting, even.

"Nice to see you, Sarah," Landon said amiably. "I'm sure you know Ellie."

Sarah turned her mega-watt smile on me. "Of course! Everyone knows the crazy cat lady, right? Mayor Monroe said you'd be bringing these by." She gestured at the cat trees enthusiastically. "They're absolutely perfect for the cat-themed holiday book display. Thank you! It's going to be such a fantastic exhibit—my first since I'm back!"

I narrowed my eyes at the librarian. Sure, she was probably thrilled to have her job back after being fired—but she got it because someone was murdered. Her unapologetic, exuberant joy was rubbing me all kinds of wrong.

Where was the grief? The shock or unease at returning to the scene of such a gruesome crime? If it were me, I wouldn't have set foot in here just two days after her death.

Sarah Black seemed utterly unfazed by it all.

I managed a polite smile in return. "Happy to help brighten up the place during such a hard time."

"Oh, yes, right! Aren't you sweet!" Sarah said. "With Alice gone, being back here is so bittersweet. But I worked with her, and I know she'd want us carrying on with holiday cheer. We always have, even when times are tough!"

As she babbled on about the library's stalwart history of facing local catastrophes with uninterrupted book circle schedules, my attention wandered to a gathering happening in the meeting corner of the large room.

A small group of around ten people sat in a circle of chairs facing away from us. I recognized a college-aged young man that worked at the local donut shop, as well as a few other vaguely familiar faces from around town.

Leading them was a scruffy-looking man gesturing

animatedly in front of a whiteboard propped on an easel. On it was scribbled "Tablerock Christmas Scavenger Group with your host: Author Jack Jones" in red marker.

I nudged Landon discreetly and nodded toward the group. Jack Jones. The local author Mayor Monroe had mentioned played a large role in encouraging Tablerock to rehire Sarah Black. What did Laurie say he wrote? Thrillers? Mysteries?

"Oh, sorry, did you want to go to the meeting?" Sarah asked us.

At that, Jack turned.

His unkempt stubble covered sharp features and his shaggy dark hair hung to his eyebrows. The looks tried to be messy, but it seemed to me Jones put a lot of effort into looking so disheveled. His gray t-shirt had some faded graphic, and it paired with expensive, professionally ripped jeans. Early thirties, if I had to guess.

"You should join us! It's okay, come on over," Jack called with a wave of his hand. "We haven't assigned teams yet."

Ugh.

There was a palpable energy in the room, a buzz of anticipation for the bibliophilic quest about to commence.

"Happy to have you join us. We're still doing introductions," Jack told Sarah amiably before turning to his group with a polite smile. "And since we are, I'll start. I'm Jack Jones. You are all here for the library scavenger hunt group? It should be fun—I don't know if you're aware, but it's being led by a *USA Today* bestselling thriller author." He gave a light chuckle. "That would be me, of course."

Well, isn't he humble, I thought sarcastically.

"I've put together a bunch of fun clues and challenges related to books here in the library, as well as spots important to the town's literary history. It'll be a great way to get into the holiday spirit, explore the town, and explore books in the library at the same time," Jack explained.

His voice was pleasant, with a smooth, deep timbre. He had an easy affability about him that I could imagine would draw people in.

Aside from coming off a bit too slick, Jack seemed harmless.

So far.

Sarah turned to us with an almost adoring expression as she gushed about the local author.

"We're so lucky to have him lead the scavenger hunt! I've read all of Jack's books and he's just the best thriller writer. So much better than Dan Brown! I don't know how Alice convinced him to run this event for us, but I'm so glad that she did," Sarah said enthusiastically.

My eyebrows went up a little.

"Oh, that's great," I said politely. "What kinds of books does he write?"

Jack's face fell. "You don't know?"

"Small town thrillers mostly, with really creative puzzling twists," Sarah explained. "They are so clever and unpredictable. You never can guess the endings! The clues are always hidden in the craziest places!"

"Well, thank you for the compliment, Sarah," Jack said. He made no effort to bring her praise to an end or get the meeting back on track. "I'm glad someone here knows a little about what I do." He glared at me.

Well, that was a little snotty.

Especially since Sarah's praise was effusive, bordering on fangirling. She clearly had a bit of hero worship going on when it came to this guy, but that didn't seem to be enough for him.

Landon shook Jack Jones's hand. "Nice to meet you, Jack. Landon Rogers, and this is Ellie Rockwell. We didn't mean to interrupt—just dropping some things off. Mayor Monroe is a friend of mine, by the way. He mentioned last night that he spoke to you about reopening the library."

Jack grinned. "Yes, as the town's only living famous author—"

Wow, this guy was full of himself.

"—Waldo tends to give my opinion on anything having to do with books considerable weight." Jack went on to explain he would've had to cancel the scavenger hunt without the library to meet in.

"Why would you have to cancel?" I asked, frowning.

"There's only ten people here. You could have met almost anywhere. The cat café—"

"Dale's Donuts would have given you a corner," Landon told him.

"The Tablerock Inn would have worked," I said.

Landon nodded. "Pepper Jalisco's. I think they host a book club."

Jack waved a hand casually. "Oh sure, we could've made something work. But we really needed to hold it here at the library," he said smoothly. "Many of the scavenger hunt clues I created have to do with specific books or locations here."

"I see," I said.

But I didn't.

Why not just change the clues and leave those out?

"In any case," he said, gesturing to the whiteboard. "We have the space. The library has reopened, and we can move on. Next, we'll form teams."

"This does seem like a wonderful idea. Is this scavenger group one that happens frequently?"

"Nope. First time," Jack told me.

"Really. Do you all know each other?" I asked the group.

"Oh, it's a good mix of folks," Jack answered for them. "Some I know from around town, some are new faces. But we posted on SocialBook and made sure everyone knew that anyone is welcome to join the hunt. I hoped we'd get more than ten, but I imagine with the situation here, some folks are avoiding the library."

But not you.

One man raised his hand. "I know we didn't get to finish introducing ourselves, but my name's Devin. Just moved here a few months ago from Dallas."

An older woman nodded and said, "I'm Betty. Grew up here but just got back after living out west. Excited to do something social!"

After everyone introduced themselves, Jack turned to us again.

"So what do you say? Care to join our merry band of misfits?" He flashed a grin full of even white teeth. His smile was Colgate commercial worthy.

"We'd love to, but I have a pretty busy holiday schedule with the shelter," I demurred politely. "If you'd like to hide something on the—"

"Oh, I don't know, Ellie, I think we have time," Landon interjected, giving me a meaningful look.

"No, I'm sure we don't, what with the holiday fundraiser coming up..." I trailed off lamely, trying to signal to Landon that I didn't think joining was a good use of our time right now.

But Landon brushed off my protest and turned back to Jack. "Well, maybe I can convince her. Could I get a list of the scavenger hunt clues and details? That way, if I can get her on board, we can just jump right in without delay."

Jack nodded agreeably. "Of course, no problem." He grabbed a stapled packet of papers from a nearby table and handed it over. "Here's the instruction sheet and a list of clues to get you started. I tried to come up with some good brainteasers. You have to have it all solved by Christmas Eve to get credit, and the first to solve all of it wins."

Landon and I finished setting up the cat trees around the circulation desk. Sarah fluttered about the display, oohing and ahhing over the handiwork like a hyper hummingbird.

"These are just perfect!" she gushed once again as we positioned the last one. "You are just so talented, Landon!"

I tried not to visibly cringe at her excessive praise, but Landon just chuckled good-naturedly.

"Well, glad you like 'em," he said.

"It really makes such a difference." Sarah clasped her hands, gazing around. "I can't thank you enough for your contribution to getting the library looking cheerful again so quickly. And Jack has been just amazing too, getting everything organized and the rare collections back in order. I don't know what I'd do without him!"

There was that fawning over Jack Jones again.

I resisted the urge to roll my eyes.

"Of course, happy to help," I said evenly. "It must be difficult getting things up and running again so quickly, and with no help."

Sarah's smile faltered slightly. "Yes, well... it's a

terrible shock, just awful what happened to Alice." Her voice took on a bitter edge. "I mean, don't get me wrong. I didn't like her, and it really makes me angry that she fired me—but even so, she didn't deserve to go the way she did."

I studied her face, searching for any deeper emotion behind her words. But her expression smoothed over quickly.

"Anyway, at least Mayor Monroe was kind enough to give me my job back right away," she went on. "I was so thrilled when he called. And Jack has been a godsend, too. He's been here for hours yesterday and today helping me shelve books, organize displays after the police messed everything up. Just doing anything I needed him to do to reopen the place without asking for anything in return. He's so selfless!"

I raised my eyebrows slightly at that.

Jack certainly seemed to have taken an unusually active role in getting the library up and running again.

"That's very kind of him," I said. "But don't you usually have volunteers that help out?"

Sarah waved a hand dismissively. "Oh, he was happy to pitch in. And actually, I gave all the regular volunteers time off for the holidays this year. Jack insisted we didn't need them with the two of us here, and it would be a nice thing to do to start my tenure. Giving them holidays off."

I nodded politely, but internally I found that rather odd.

If Sarah was newly returned and Jack had his own event to organize, why turn down volunteer help with shelving and displays right before the holidays? It seemed an illogical decision.

I filed the inconsistency away to ponder later.

"Well, it looks great in here," Landon said. "Seems like you've got things under control. We'll let you get back to it."

"Thanks again for all the help, both of you." Sarah's gaze turned to me, her tone softening. "I know you and Alice were friendly. I'm just so sorry about what happened. Please let me know if there's anything I can do, anything at all."

Her words sounded well-meaning enough. But something about her mournful expression came across as forced, like bad acting. It didn't seem to reach her eyes.

"We appreciate that. This has been a difficult time for everyone who knew Alice," I responded carefully.

Time to dig deeper.

"I have to admit, I was a little surprised to see you back here at the library," I said, keeping my tone light. "Evie mentioned you had left a while ago?"

I posed it as an innocent statement rather than a direct question, hoping to catch her off guard.

It worked.

Sarah's friendly expression instantly hardened, her cheeks flushing. Her hands closed into tight fists on the circulation desk.

"Oh, did she?" Sarah asked sharply. "Well, I'm sure

Evie mentioned how unfair it was that I was asked to leave."

I blinked, surprised by her sudden shift in demeanor. "I don't believe I got all the details, no."

Sarah crossed her arms. "It's funny how people are perfectly happy to gossip about the bad parts of what happens to people, but the circumstances just get left in the dust if they don't make a good story." Her voice dripped with bitter disdain.

I resisted the defensive urge to snap back at the slight insult toward Evie. "As you know, my daughter can have issues with her memory sometimes, Sarah—it could have been an innocent overlook. Why don't you tell me what happened? That way it's not gossip."

Sarah scowled, anger brewing in her eyes. "I caught Alice claiming extra hours on her timesheet. Which was ridiculous, if you ask me. She was always watching me like a hawk, and she was the one skirting the lines. Oh, whatever. Honestly, I'm pretty sure she had it out for me from day one."

My eyebrows shot up in surprise at the bold admission.

"So she fired you for accusing her of falsifying her timecard?" Landon asked.

"No!" Sarah spluttered. "I mean, that makes it sound... She wasn't..." She huffed out a frustrated breath. "Look, I caught her working well into the evening and those extra hours had nothing to do with the library. But her overtime took all the money in the budget, so I could never get a raise. I mean, I worked through my breaks sometimes and just rounded up a little, but after I caught her doing it, Alice dramatically called it 'stealing from taxpayers' and fired me for the same thing I caught her doing far worse than I ever did." She crossed her arms, lips pressed thin. "Anyway, it was just an excuse. She wanted me gone because I was on to her little racket."

"What racket?" I asked.

Sarah leaned forward, dropping her voice. "Alice had something going on in the back that had zero connection to the library. I'd find hidden books, and then a week later they'd be gone. Maybe she was siphoning off a little money from the annual allocation for her own pocket. Or maybe they were donations that she never logged that she wanted to keep. I don't know. But something was going on."

"Why didn't you report her when you found out?" Landon asked.

"I never figured out what she was doing." Sarah let out a bitter laugh. "Besides, who would've believed me over Little Miss Prim and Proper? She framed me as incompetent and let me go before I could dig deeper." Her lip curled in contempt. "Alice pulled the wool over everyone's eyes with that squeaky clean act. But I think she was dirtier than anyone knew."

"Did you ever find any kind of proof or see anyone else in the back around where Alice kept those books? She might have been working with someone," I said.

Sarah shook her head. "Just me and the volunteers in the back. Jack's been there because he does so much work for the library. Oh, and I saw Henry Davis back there a few times, but he's a patron, so that's not weird.

"It sounds like you're not really sure what Alice was doing," Landon said. "If anything."

Sarah shrugged. "Believe what you want. I know what I saw. Jessa was fooled by Alice, too, but at least Mayor Monroe realized I got a raw deal and did right by giving me my job back. And anyway, whatever she was doing, it doesn't matter now. It obviously got her killed."

"Maybe."

"Well, I'm glad you're back." I wasn't sure what else to say, and I wanted to keep the lines of communication open with the new librarian.

The compliment softened Sarah slightly. "Me, too." She gestured around. "I should get back to it."

"Yep. Thanks, Sarah. And let us know if you need anything." Landon gave her a parting smile and corralled me toward the exit.

Back in the truck, I shook my head as we pulled away from the curb. "That was a lot of nothing... but also kind of a whole lot," I said, trying to make sense of the encounters. "Nothing majorly suspicious jumped out, but at the same time, there were a lot of little things that felt... off. Jack's insistence on using the library and the dismissal of the volunteers. Sarah's incredible, over-the-top praise of him."

Landon nodded thoughtfully as he drove. "Yeah, I agree. A lot of puzzling behavior, but hard to pinpoint exactly what it means."

"It's like trying to assemble a jigsaw puzzle while missing half the pieces," I said with a sigh. "We can't tell what the full picture looks like yet."

"Sarah clearly has an axe to grind over being fired. But if she was fired for stumbling onto something shady Alice was mixed up in—which we already know from Ginger seems likely—it might explain her behavior."

"But Jack Jones?" I sighed. "Just when I think we're gaining clarity, new layers of mystery emerge. We need to see what we can uncover about those books Sarah mentioned without raising suspicion."

"Roger that, Nancy Drew," Landon said with a chuckle. "We'll get to the bottom of it. But for now, I'd say we've done enough sleuthing before coffee."

My stomach rumbled an agreement. I patted it absently, my mind already racing ahead to the next steps in unraveling this convoluted case.

Chapter Ten

THE MOUTHWATERING SCENT OF FRYING EGGS AND spicy chorizo sausage greeted us as we stepped into the warmth of Pepper Jalisco's restaurant. Despite the early morning hour, the cozy Mexican eatery already bustled with patrons chatting amiably over steaming plates of food.

After our puzzling encounter at the library, Landon and I were both ready for the comforting respite of a hearty breakfast.

We slid into a vinyl booth near the front windows, the red pleather cracked and worn soft from years of use. A bubbly waitress named Lupe soon arrived to take our order, her curly hair bouncing as she recited the specials.

"Sounds great, Lupe. And it looks like we got here just in time to beat the rush," Landon commented, scanning the crowded room.

"You did! Happy holidays, y'all! Take a minute to

look things over," she said in a bubbly drawl tinged with a Spanish lilt.

My mouth watered as I perused the menu filled with spicy breakfast options. Ever since our shelter took in the litter of Jalisco kittens last spring, I'd become a regular at Pepper's and eagerly anticipated my fix of their savory migas or fluffy huevos rancheros.

"Ooh, everything looks so good," I murmured. "I can never decide here."

Landon chuckled. "I know what you mean. But I'm leaning toward the chorizo con huevos. That's some good stuff."

When our server returned, I went with the veggie burrito stuffed with refried beans, guacamole, pico de gallo and Pepper's signature spicy salsa. Landon ordered his chorizo and eggs, smothered in melted cheese and salsa.

"And coffee, yes?"

Before we could finish nodding, two large mugs of dark Mexican coffee appeared promptly at our table. As I doctored mine up generously with cream and sugar, I expected the jolt of caffeine would hopefully begin reviving my still-slightly groggy brain.

As we waited for our food, Landon pulled the scavenger hunt packet from his pocket and held it out. "Figured we may as well look at these clues while we're waiting. Something about that author fella seemed a little hinky."

"Hinky?" I asked.

"Can't explain it. Just... something off about the fella."

I flipped through the stapled sheets.

Jack had created numbered clues that involved piecing together things like book titles, author names, and well known places in Tablerock from cryptic-sounding puzzles. Nothing stood out as suspicious upon first glance. But toward the end of the extensive list, one clue gave me pause, and I read it out loud.

"Number thirty-seven," I said, my voice lowered. "*In the shadows of Tablerock's secrets, where tales of old reside, follow the hush of whispered words to the place where the first of the grim meets the last brother of time. The treasure shall reveal itself under the watchful eyes of knowledge.*" I looked up. "What does this have to do with Christmas?"

Landon shrugged. "Does any of it have a Christmas theme?"

I scanned. "Not really. And *first of the grim*—that sounds an awful lot like a first edition of the Grimm book," I told Landon. "I have no idea what a brother of time is, though. Or the watchful eyes of knowledge. You?"

He shook his head, perplexed. "It could be about the stolen book, but there are dozens of books with the word grim in the title. Dozens of books about time travel, too."

"What does Jack Jones write, specifically?" I pulled out my phone and searched. "Laurie acted kind of sketchy last night when he was mentioned, and I totally forgot to ask her what that was about."

"Thrillers," Landon said.

"Yes, I get that, but what kind of thrillers?" I scanned the covers of Jack Jones's books for a moment and skimmed through the synopsis. "Well, according to this, Jack Jones is an author of thriller books featuring mysteries and conspiracies. He's got one series, The Librarian's Last Tome, that features a ring of book thieves." I looked up. "That can't be a coincidence."

Landon's eyebrows shot up. "Book thieves? That's definitely an odd coincidence, considering what Ginger said about Alice."

"Right? And here's another question I have—how was Sarah so sure Alice was the one doing something shady involving the library's rare book collection? It sounds like Jack was in and out of the back. Henry Davis took a spin there, too. Lots of volunteers. Why assume it was Alice? And it could be Sarah, right? And she just told us that to throw suspicion off herself."

He chuckled. "You're turning into a very paranoid woman, Ellie."

"Maybe. You have hard evidence none of those things are true?"

Landon didn't have an answer.

I scanned down the list again and tapped my finger on another strange clue.

"Twenty-nine. *The author's dark early work holds the next puzzle piece in its pages. Look in the cellar, six through nine.*" I looked up. "The library doesn't have a basement. This is Texas. Nothing has a basement."

Landon sipped his coffee, then nodded thoughtfully. "You know, might be Jack's way of snooping for something without drawing suspicion to himself."

"Snooping for what, though?"

"Alice's stash of stolen books?"

I set down the papers with a sigh. "I wish we knew more specifics about those books she supposedly stole. And if he is looking for a hidden stash, does that mean he killed Alice?"

Before Landon could respond, our plates arrived aromatic and piping hot. The burrito smothered in rich green chile sauce made my mouth water.

"I don't know that we need to jump to that conclusion just based on some scavenger hunt clues, Ellie." Landon swallowed a bite of chorizo and eggs, and then continued. "But something definitely seems off with that author. Could just be I don't like people that are full of themselves, but whether clues point to Jack, Sarah, stolen books, or something else entirely, I can't tell yet."

"Same here." I dabbed my mouth with a napkin.

Landon gave a rueful chuckle. "Well, we've cracked tougher cases with less to go on before. We'll figure this one out, too, Nancy Drew."

"Would you stop calling me that?"

"No."

As we finished up our meal, I glanced around the homey restaurant, soaking in the warm chatter and clatter of dishes that filled the space. Despite the lingering questions from our visit to the library, it felt good to relax—sort of—and enjoy a hearty breakfast.

As we were finishing, I noticed Deputy Markham and Mario Lopez entering the restaurant together. Mario glanced around the nearly full dining room, and a look of recognition flashed across his face when he spotted us. The two uniformed men headed straight for our booth instead of waiting for an empty table.

"Well, fancy running into you two here," Deputy Markham greeted us as they slid into the seats.

"We seem to keep bumping into each other lately," Mario added with a friendly smile.

I returned their greetings politely as Landon shook hands with both men, though I sensed this was no coincidence. The lawmen signaled the waitress for coffee as they made idle small talk.

"Best breakfast burritos in town." But he didn't get one. Mario gestured to the server for an order of huevos rancheros. "Don?"

"Same for me," the deputy told Lupe.

"We were just finishing up ourselves," Landon said, wiping his mouth with a napkin. "I actually have to head out soon to work on some holiday decorations for the city. Waldo asked if I could build a few wooden reindeer and toy soldiers to put up by the town square display to replace the ones that got broken last night."

I raised an eyebrow. "I didn't hear about that. Are you talking about the ones behind the tree?"

Landon nodded.

"Someone had a bit too much egg nog last night," Mario explained.

"Not just someone. Jessa Winthrop," Markham said. "She drove her Cadillac right up on the lawn in front of city hall and took out half of Santa's reindeer. It's real nice of you to donate your talents, Landon," Deputy Markham said appreciatively. "You do good work."

Landon gave a modest shrug. "Happy to help however I can."

"So what brings you two out and about this morning?" I asked.

"Just eating breakfast. We were out a few hours ago, actually." Mario lowered his voice. "We had a break-in at Alice's apartment last night."

My eyebrows shot up in surprise. "Really? Was anything taken?"

"Doesn't appear so, but the place was completely ransacked. Drawers dumped out, furniture overturned. Whoever it was made a real mess of things."

"Any idea what they could've been looking for?"

"No telling," Don Markham said. "With Alice gone, we don't have an inventory to compare it to. Whatever the intruder was after, they were pretty determined, though. Tore the place apart. Excuse me for a moment. I need to step away and wash up before the food arrives," he said casually.

What could someone have wanted badly enough to break into Alice's home just days after she was murdered? Sure, she could have a stash of money or books, but even all things considered, it was an incredibly risky move.

As soon as the deputy was out of earshot, Mario glanced at me. "Think you could bring Ginger to the apartment later? I'm the lead on this case, so I let the cat in, and no one else should be there after ten or so."

Bringing Ginger there did make sense—he was an indoor cat, and that apartment was his entire universe for most of his life. Cats know their own territory. He may pick up on something no one else would.

Even so, I hated bringing the magic plate out of the shelter...

I met Mario's hopeful stare and nodded. "All right. I'll bring Ginger by around eleven just to be safe," I agreed.

Mario's shoulders relaxed. "Good, thank you. I know it's asking a lot, but he may find leads we've overlooked. Any advantage we can get tracking down what's going on here—and proving it with evidence—is worth trying at this point," he said.

"Probably," I said. "And I appreciate you letting us know about the break-in."

He gave a solemn nod. "Open communication, right?"

"Right." I looked up. "I think this is yours."

Mario thanked Lupe as his breakfast platter arrived. "Aye, Lupe, you're my favorite person right now."

"Just right now?" the cute waitress said, and she winked at him as she put down the salsa. "I'll be right back with the deputy's order."

Landon and I made small talk as Don Markham wove his way back through the crowded diner. We slid out of the booth, trading spaces with Don, who plopped down heavily across from Mario just as Lupe lowered his breakfast, the table now laden with heaping plates of hot food.

"You two enjoy," Landon said.

Neither man looked up as they mumbled, waved, and tucked in.

At the counter, Landon paid for all four meals, dismissing the cashier's questioning look. "I know you all usually don't charge them. If you don't, then keep it as a tip, and Merry Christmas," he said with a smile.

The cashier's confused expression transformed into a warm, beaming smile in response. "You are such a good man, Landon," she said sincerely. "We need more people like you."

Landon gave a polite nod as he tucked away his wallet and dropped a hundred-dollar bill on the counter. "It was our pleasure. Please wish everyone in the back a Merry Christmas from us."

The cashier gasped and snatched up the crinkled bill. "And a very Merry Christmas to you both!"

Back outside in the dimly lit parking lot, I turned to Landon and wrapped my arms around him in a tight embrace. "You really are a good man, Landon Rogers," I said, my voice muffled against his coat. "Sometimes I forget to tell you. But you are, and I'm so lucky to have you."

Landon chuckled softly as he enveloped me in his sturdy arms. "Well now, Ellie, you're going to make me blush with all this high praise," he replied, though I could hear the smile in his voice.

I leaned back to look up at him, his kind face illuminated by the glowing sign behind us. "I mean it, though. And I know I don't tell you enough."

Landon gently brushed a windswept hair from my face, his eyes crinkling at the corners. "Well, I suppose we're both people who believe in service and doing right by others," he replied. "That kind of moral compass, it's the glue that binds us together. Through all of this, you and me, we're in it for reasons beyond us."

I squeezed him tightly once more before reluctantly pulling away.

"So, I didn't want to say it in there, but I don't know about taking the cat and the plate to Alice's, Ellie. Seems awfully risky taking that thing into an active crime scene. Maybe we should stick to just having you walk through and see if you notice anything off. Or taking a video and showing it to the cat."

I pondered his hesitation, understanding his caution. If Don Markham or anyone else other than Mario saw that enchanted platter in action, it would raise some eyebrows, for sure.

Still...

"Ginger is our one shot at an inventory of items from the apartment," I pointed out. "There's no other way we'll know if the killer was looking for something specific and found it."

I put a hand on Landon's arm.

"It's a risk, I know. But Mario said he's the lead—he can let me in, and he knows we can't do anything with anyone else there. You're right that we can't parade the magic platter around. But if we're strategic, I think I can get Ginger on it long enough to ask if he notices anything missing."

Landon slowly nodded, though he still looked uneasy. "Okay. But we'll have to be really careful. In and out, as quick as we can."

"Absolutely." I gave his arm a grateful squeeze.

The aroma of freshly brewed coffee enveloped us as a chorus of meows and purrs greeted our arrival. Cats of all fur lengths and colors wound eagerly around our ankles, their tails curling up in greeting. I couldn't help but smile as I scratched a few fuzzy heads, eliciting louder rumbles of contentment from the affectionate felines.

After giving a last pat to a playful ginger kitten, I

made my way past the displays of flaky croissants and fresh danishes toward the back stairwell leading up from the bustling café. "I'm wondering why we call this the isolation room," I joked.

"So people think whatever's inside needs to be isolated. Which, technically, isn't wrong."

Inside, I found Belladonna perched imperiously on her usual second-level cubby, glancing over at me with a slow blink of her luminous golden eyes. Ginger—Alice's orange-patched longhair cat and possibly Belladonna's new boyfriend—was curled up in a patch of morning sunlight on the carpeted cat tree, his tail swishing lazily.

As I entered, Ginger lifted his head and gave a little "prrp?" of greeting, his yellow-ish eyes bright and attentive. He stretched, back arching, before padding over to rub against my legs. I smiled and gave him a few affectionate strokes along his sides before he meandered back to his sunny spot.

Belladonna observed Ginger with mild disinterest, remaining poised in her cubby like a regal lioness surveying her territory. "What is it you seek?" she asked, her voice tinged with suspicion. "Given the hour, I am inclined to believe your presence here bodes ill."

I quickly briefed the cats about the break-in at Alice's apartment.

"So we were hoping Ginger could go back with us and the platter and let us know if anything seems off or missing," I said.

With a graceful leap, Ginger landed in the cubby, his

copper coat glimmering in the ethereal light cast by the crystal platter invisible beneath them. Belladonna exuded an air of haughty indifference, even as Ginger inched closer, his fluffy tail twitching back and forth.

"As long as you don't expect me to betray Alice, I will go with you and see if I know what this burglar was looking for," he said. Ginger's golden eyes blinked slowly as he regarded Belladonna, whose gaze remained fixed on some indistinct point on the far wall. "Only if Belladonna can come as well."

"Now, wait a minute—"

Ginger's luminous eyes darkened as he hissed at me, and he kneaded the platter with his claws extended. "I said what I said."

I opened my mouth to assure him we'd have him back as quick as we could and that he wouldn't be apart from her for long, but Belladonna spoke up first.

"Be reasonable," she purred, running her tail along his back.

"I am being reasonable. They want something. I want something."

"This presents an optimal chance to provide information that might be vital to the investigation," Belladonna said. She nuzzled his neck, her tone softening. "I understand your desire to have me there, but I will only be a distraction. The sooner this villain is caught, the sooner your mind may be at ease."

The orange cat still looked uncertain, his ears flattening. I felt a pang of sympathy for what we were asking of him. Going back into a home he'd lost couldn't be easy to contemplate.

"She's right. I know you don't like them, but this could really help the police," I added gently. "It's going to be hard enough dragging a crystal platter into the apartment and hiding it from the people that don't know about it, Ginger. I have no idea how we'd explain what Belladonna was doing there."

"Oh, all right," Ginger sighed. "For Alice. Though I have to admit, the idea of going back there rattles my nerves." He turned his eyes up at me. "Will you be nearby the entire time?"

I nodded. "Absolutely. You won't be alone for even a moment. We'll make this quick and painless."

Belladonna delicately licked his ear in a comforting gesture, and Ginger noticeably relaxed under her ministrations. "Very well. When do we go?"

"In a few hours," I said. "Mario wanted to make sure the rest of the police cleared out of the apartment, so we're shooting for eleven."

Chapter Eleven

THE SMELL OF DEAD LEAVES HUNG IN THE AIR AS WE trudged up the stairs to Alice's apartment. When we reached her scratched white door, Landon gave three sharp knocks.

The door swung open, and there stood Mario dressed in relaxed weekend clothes—dark washed jeans and a tan cable-knit sweater—instead of his uniform. His usual stern expression was softened, his brown eyes missing their normal piercing gleam.

He gave us a nod. "Come in."

"No uniform?"

Mario half-smiled at me. "You mentioned Ginger was uncomfortable with law enforcement. I thought this might put him more at ease."

Stepping into Alice's apartment, I gawked in sheer amazement. If the police had disordered the tidy, cozy home in their initial search, the intruder had upended it with the efficiency and destructive power of a Category 5 hurricane.

Drawers hung crookedly open, contents spewed across the hardwood in haphazard piles. The sofa cushions gaped with stuffing, bursting out like cotton entrails, peppered with loose change and TV remotes. Craft cabinets stood agape and shattered dishes littered the granite counters in sharp, jagged fragments.

Even the refrigerator had been savaged, expired produce and smeared condiments dripping down the shelves, leaving trails of waste on the linoleum below.

"How could the neighbors not have heard this and called the police?" I asked Mario incredulously.

"Well... they did hear the commotion," he admitted. "But when they realized it was coming from Alice's place, they didn't call it in."

I looked at him sharply. "What? Why wouldn't they report something like this?"

Mario shrugged. "People around here have seen cops coming and going from Alice's a lot since she was killed," he said. "They just assumed it was us tossing the place again, not an actual break-in."

I turned back and surveyed more of the damage.

It was as if no surface had been left unsearched, no container left unopened. The intruder had torn through everything with ruthless determination, leaving absolute destruction in their wake. I stepped gingerly through the debris, disbelief rising in my throat at the violation of this once welcoming home.

What were they searching for with such frenzy?

Ginger's carrier thumped softly as I set it on the cluttered floor. Unlatching the metal door, the long-haired orange cat tentatively emerged, nose fluttering as he surveyed the chaos. His tail ballooned to twice its size, the fur standing on end, and distress radiated from his tense body.

"I know, buddy. I'm so sorry," I murmured, my heart aching for the shocked cat. Ginger turned his wide eyes up at me, pupils dilated pools of anger.

Poor guy—this upheaval was the last thing he needed.

Rummaging in my oversized purse, I retrieved the enchanted platter and placed it on the least cluttered patch of carpet. Ginger wasted no time stepping onto the glowing surface.

"They broke all my human's things!" he yowled, eyes flashing with outrage. His yellow eyes almost seemed to glisten with angry tears as he surveyed the wreckage of his former home. Tail lashing, he turned to me. "Who would do this?" he demanded, pink nose twitching, whiskers quivering with each indignant breath.

I stroked his back gently, feeling helpless to console the grieving cat. "We're trying to figure that out," I told him gently. "Is there anything you notice missing that seems unusual?"

Ginger's eyes roved over the ransacked space, tail thrashing. "Are you kidding me?" he huffed. "Do you see this place? It's like trying to find a fly in a backyard.

Which I can do, by the way." He plopped down on his hindquarters, pupils narrowing to slits. "But it would take some effort."

"I understand."

His nose twitched as he scanned the room intently. "Give me a second. If anything major got taken, I'll sniff it out."

"What about the glass? You can't—"

"There's not that much. I can avoid it."

I frowned. "Be careful."

Ginger lowered his nose to the jagged shards of the shattered lamp, nose twitching purposefully while he canvassed the chaos. He stalked past the overturned bookshelf, scanning the strewn novels and scattered knickknacks. I followed in his wake, stepping over debris as he led the way.

Mario trailed at a distance, respectfully giving the distressed cat space to investigate. I glanced back to see Landon lingering in the doorway, his sturdy frame leaning against the front entrance, ensuring no one could walk in.

Ginger wove skillfully through the mess, nose hovering just above the wreckage. His ears swiveled and rotated like tiny radar dishes, tuned for any clue. Aside from the occasional swish of Ginger's tail against my leg as he searched for something amiss amid the upheaval, he communicated little.

Several times, Ginger froze, eyes widening as he scented particular items—a hairbrush, a silk scarf. He swiveled his ears back, pressed flat against his head, and emitted soft distress mews. Other times, he would tilt just one ear back while leaving the other perked forward intently.

Mario watched the cat's inspection, frowning. "He doesn't seem very concerned by anything, just upset in general about the mess."

I shook my head. "His expressions are subtle, but cats show emotion in different ways than we do," I explained. "See how his ears go back when he smells something familiar? That shows grief and stress. Both ears forward means focus or interest."

I pointed to Ginger's tail. "His puffed up tail means he feels threatened, or he wants to threaten. They do this to make themselves look bigger and more intimidating. It's not that he lacks feelings, they're just displayed differently through ear position, tail movements, eye movement. It seems tenuous, but it's not, really, once you know what to look for."

Mario's eyebrows shot up, clearly intrigued by my interpretation of Ginger's nonverbal cues. "Huh, good to know. I always thought cats looked pretty stoic and unconcerned about everything."

I smiled. "Nope, their emotions just get lost in translation sometimes."

"Belladonna seems pretty stoic, though."

"Belladonna can be difficult. An apathetic and entitled little twit sometimes, to be honest," I said bluntly.

"That's just her personality, though, not because she's a cat."

Ginger's head snapped up, eyes narrowing to emerald slits. A raspy hiss slipped through his bared teeth.

"Sorry," I offered, taking a small step back.

Mario raised an eyebrow.

"They're involved."

"With what?"

"Each other." I lowered my voice. "I think they're seeing each other. You know, in a relationship?"

"They're... okay, then," Mario replied after a beat, though his brows remained furrowed. The cop didn't seem fully convinced that a romance between two cats was something he needed to understand.

We followed as Ginger crept into the bedroom, picking his way through the debris. The bedroom had equal damage—dresser drawers had been dumped out, contents scattered across the carpet like the aftermath of an explosion in a fabric store. The mattress was stripped bare, with only a few twisted blankets remaining around the edges.

Ginger hopped up and began anxiously kneading and circling on the bare mattress, his paws working furiously at the exposed padding. His ears flattened back against his head once again as he surveyed the violation of Alice's inner sanctuary. I could hear him murmuring upset little meows under his breath as he took in the extent of the damage.

With a plaintive mew, Ginger moved to the night-stand and nosed open the drawer. He stuck his entire head inside, sniffing intently as he rifled through the contents. After a thorough inspection, he sat back on his haunches and glared at me, eyes narrowed in accusation.

"Oh shoot," I muttered, immediately grasping the problem. I dashed back to the living room, retrieved the magic plate and set it down gently on the stripped mattress.

"Here you go," I said breathlessly.

Ginger stepped onto the platter, his paws pressing into the crystalline center. A flare of brilliant green glowed, tendrils of enchanted light radiating outward across the surface. For a moment, Ginger's fur seemed lit from within by the illumination.

"The book's gone!" he cried, his distressed yowl echoing through the ravaged bedroom. His tail lashed violently.

"What book, Ginger?" Mario asked.

Ginger's eyes narrowed, pupils constricting to slits. "You know, you can take off the uniform, but I'm no chump," he replied, whiskers twitching. "I know you're still a cop."

"What book, Ginger?" I asked him.

The cat turned to me as if he'd immediately forgotten Mario was there. "The leather one where Alice kept all her important information written," he explained. "Her business ledger, contacts, everything!

She was always scribbling in it on Sundays and then hiding it away in the drawer."

"Why Sundays?" Mario asked as if that was significant somehow.

Ginger's glare sharpened, eyes narrowing to slits. "Did you say something, cop?" he spat. The platter flared brightly.

"Why Sundays, Ginger?" I asked.

The cat turned his penetrating gaze to me, body language softening a bit. "That's when Alice would come home from her night out," he explained, tail swishing. "She'd pour herself some wine, take out that leather book, and write stuff down. Private stuff. Private stuff that cops"—he hissed at Mario—"don't get to hear about."

I reached down to stroke his head. "This information helps a lot, Ginger. Thank you. Now the police have a specific item to look for related to what happened to her."

"I didn't tell the police anything," the cat responded, and he jumped to the floor.

After a final disconsolate lap around his thoroughly dismantled former home, I stowed away the platter, scooped Ginger up and secured him in his carrier as he protested leaving his violated domain.

"You can't stay here, sweetheart, and I know it's sad for you—but I'm taking you back to Belladonna. We'll find whoever did this to Alice. I promise," I whispered to the distraught cat. I gave Mario a meaningful look as I stood. The missing ledger seemed a likely motive for the violent ransacking.

Now we just had to find out who took it, and why.

Back at the shelter after visiting Alice's apartment, Landon, Mario, and I sat down in my office to discuss the fresh revelations from Ginger about the missing ledger.

"It's seeming more and more likely everything that cat said about Alice is true," Mario said, running a hand through his dark hair. "I called up a contact I have in the FBI's art theft division, described the situation, and asked if they'd had any major rare book heists they tracked that matched Ginger's claims."

Landon and I leaned forward intently. "And?"

"And it turns out the bureau has been investigating a skilled thief they've dubbed the Bibliophile Bandit for years now. Every weekend without fail, a priceless first edition or rare manuscript would vanish from private collections. Never any evidence left behind."

Mario shook his head in disbelief. "Would you believe over three hundred books worth millions stolen over the past fifteen years? Always on a Saturday night."

My jaw fell open in shock and Landon's dark eyebrows rose high on his forehead, eyes wide with surprise. For a moment, we just stared at each other.

"That lines up awfully well with Ginger's descriptions of Alice's double life," Landon said. "I'm not surprised, but... I'm kind of surprised. If you get my meaning."

I nodded slowly. "I have to admit, it's getting hard to deny she was up to some shady business. But if Alice was stealing and selling hundreds of rare books, where's all the money? She lived in a modest apartment, drove a modest car. She certainly didn't flaunt wealth."

"Excellent question." Mario flipped open his notebook. "And you're right, she didn't seem to have money. My team tossed her financials. No massive savings account, a minimal retirement fund, no property under her name other than the car."

"If she was this huge international book thief, the money had to be going somewhere," I pointed out.

"You're right, but I don't think this is an if anymore. We found fake passports, IDs in multiple aliases, burner phones, disguises hidden in the back of her closet behind a fake panel. She was definitely traveling under assumed identities."

"You found this after her place was tossed?"

He nodded.

My eyes widened. "But why wouldn't she put the leather book in there with the rest of the stuff from her life as the Bibliophile Bandit?"

"I don't know. From what we can piece together, her routine was apparently to work at the library until Saturdays in the early afternoon. Then she'd fly out to a different city in the late afternoon or early evening every weekend using fake credentials, break into a rare book collection late at night, and fly back early Sunday morning in time to get home before the library reopened Monday morning."

I sat back, blown away by the extent of Alice's hidden activities.

Landon let out a low whistle.

"That's bold, I'll give her that. She must have had her routes down to catch flights without arousing suspicion," Landon said. "How did no one ever see her?"

"Austin's not a small place now," I said.

"No kidding." Mario rifled through his notes. "Looks like she booked a lot of last-minute fares that got her to major hubs—New York, Chicago, Seattle, San Francisco—always gone Saturday, back Sunday."

I shook my head in disbelief. "In a way, I still can't believe it."

"Yep. Right under everyone's noses all this time," Mario murmured. He sank back heavily into his chair, the wood creaking under his weight. "Looks like that cat wasn't lying or making up stories after all. I think we had a bona fide criminal mastermind on our hands here in Tablerock for years and never knew it."

"Well, someone knew it," I said, my brain trying to reconcile the sweet, polite librarian with this shockingly sinister hidden life. "That money is somewhere. And if it's not in her name or one of her aliases—"

"Well, we haven't checked all her aliases yet. I bet we'll turn up something."

"The big question now is, was she double-crossed by a partner that was part of the scheme, caught by someone she stole from, or was she targeted by someone who wanted to get their hands on the proceeds?" Landon said. "It's clear from that apartment someone is desperate to find things she hid there, and my question is whether all that damage was really over a ledger that was sitting in a drawer by the bed." Landon looked at Mario. "Maybe they were looking for those identities, and they didn't find what they were looking for."

"You know, with everything going on, I feel like we've all been so focused on Alice's secret life that we're forgetting the most basic part of this case," I said.

Mario looked at me. "What do you mean?"

"Well, Alice was murdered in the library, where she worked every day. A public building, right in the thick of downtown. There had to have been witnesses around who saw something that night." I leaned forward. "Were there any security cameras that might have caught footage of who entered or left the library before or after the murder? Or eyewitnesses on the street who noticed someone going in or coming out?"

Mario smacked his forehead dramatically. "Dios mío, I'm such an idiot," he said with an exaggerated eye roll. "Here we are obsessing over some missing book when the murder happened at the library surrounded by witnesses and security cameras. Cameras!"

He was making fun of me. Okay, maybe it was silly. Of course he thought of it already.

"Okay, Mario, I get it. I just thought—"

He shot me a glare that would make a nun proud. "No, no, really—I'm grateful you are here to state the obvious for me and get me back on track. However would I manage without you?" he asked, his voice dripping with sarcasm. "We're clearly incapable of basic police work without someone holding our hands. Cameras. On the street? Brilliant!"

I crossed my arms, unamused by his dramatic, patronizing tone. "All right, all right, no need to be a jerk about it," I muttered.

Mario chuckled and flipped through his notebook. "There are no exterior security cameras at the library itself. We've requested footage from surrounding shops to see if it captured anyone around the time of death. As for eyewitnesses, unfortunately everyone we've spoken to so far says the same thing—with the tree lighting attracting so many people downtown that night, there were crowds everywhere. Tons of folks coming and going all over the square."

Landon sighed. "So in other words, yes, there were potentially witnesses around, but too many to pinpoint anyone specific doing something specific."

"Everybody saw everybody," Mario agreed. "So nobody saw nothing. We do still need to investigate every identity Alice had. Maybe something will shake loose there."

Evie poked her head into my office, an uncertain look flashing across her face. "Um, Mom? Jessa Winthrop is here asking to see you," she said.

I raised my eyebrows in surprise. Jessa Winthrop rarely made personal appearances these days unless something was seriously wrong, or she seriously intended to draw attention to herself by unleashing her awful personality on someone undeserving.

Mario and Landon exchanged concerned glances.

"It's fine. What's she going to do in the shelter's lobby?" I assured them, though my shoulders had tensed at the sound of her name. I stood. "I'll go see what she wants."

"I don't think you should go out there, especially in the middle of all this—that woman is nothing but trouble," Landon said.

"I know how to handle Jessa," I said with confidence.

Though, in truth, our past encounters had been relentlessly thorny.

Jessa Winthrop—the former mayor of Tablerock, mistress of the late (and corrupt) Beau Blackwell, and mother of murderer Joel Winthrop—rarely dropped by to see me. Though her son Joel was safely behind bars and she was no longer in charge of the town, Jessa continued haunting Tablerock like a specter clinging stubbornly to a realm she should have departed from long ago.

On one occasion, she had hinted that she knew about Fiona's enchanted cat communication platter. Her possible knowledge meant I could not afford to ignore her requests, veiled as they often were behind a polite veneer.

When she commanded attention, it was safer to provide it.

"Well, look who finally showed up," Jessa said, her words dripping with disdain. She looked me up and down with a sneer as the lobby Christmas tree twinkled merrily behind her.

I said nothing, refusing to take the bait.

I could see the hint of a smug smile playing on Jessa's artificially glossed lips, the pursed pucker ready to pounce on any reaction I gave her. Everything about the woman oozed entitlement, from her ostentatious jewelry to her self-important tone, but I kept my expression neutral and my gaze focused straight ahead.

This may be her game, but I wasn't going to play by her rules.

"Hello, Ms. Winthrop," I said evenly. "To what do we owe the pleasure?"

"Oh, Ellie. Always so formal." Her tone oozed false congeniality. She clasped her hands together. "I simply wanted to stop by and see how things were going. And check in on Belladonna, of course. You know, Beau always thought highly of her."

If that were true—and I doubted it was—it was a one-sided affection.

Belladonna despised him.

"She's doing well, thank you," I responded politely.

She waited for me to continue.

I waited silently for her true purpose to emerge, refusing to make idle small talk. No need to indulge Jessa's pretense of caring one whit about the cat. When it became clear I would not fill the tense silence, Jessa adjusted her posture, looking irritated. She idly examined her manicure.

"I also wanted to discuss a delicate matter with you," she began casually. Too casually. "It's regarding a certain... let's say, *involvement*, that you keep having with the Tablerock police department."

I stiffened, immediately on guard. "I'm not sure what you're talking about."

"Oh, I'm completely sure you are, in fact, fully aware of what I am talking about." Jessa examined her cuticles. "I wouldn't want to cause any alarm by speaking about it here, naturally. But—like I said—you and I *both* know what we're talking about." She finally lifted her gaze to mine, eyes glinting. "Don't we?"

I didn't know how much she actually knew about the magic talking cat platter drink tray thing, but I suspected Beau had told her things about Fiona's magic item during their affair—not the full truth perhaps, but enough to make Jessa aware that Fiona had something special.

Jessa's knowledge was dangerous, but the full scope of it remained unclear.

I folded my arms casually across my chest, clinging

to nonchalance. "I still have no idea what you're talking about, Ms. Winthrop."

Jessa pursed her lips, looking unconvinced. Her shrewd gaze bored into me. "I see. Well, if we're going to play it that way, then we'll play it that way. Keep in mind, Ellie, that knowledge you shouldn't have can be dangerous."

"Okay." I maintained a polite, impassive expression.

Jessa stepped closer, eyes flashing. "Do you really think this ignorant act works on me?"

"I'm not following, Ms. Winthrop," I told her in a measured tone. "Nothing in my life has anything at all to do with you, and I'm pretty sure nothing in your life has to do with me. Now, unless you'd like a coffee or a pastry, I don't think we have anything to say to one another."

Jessa lingered a moment longer, as if hoping I'd crack. Finally, she exhaled sharply. "Very well. Do give Belladonna my regards."

With that, she pivoted and swept imperiously out the front door in a waft of cloying perfume.

"What was that about?" Ellie asked after Jessa had stormed out.

"You know, an hour ago I would have said it was just Jessa being Jessa," I replied, still staring at the door through which the former mayor had departed. "Now?" I shook my head, disturbed by the gnawing unease Jessa's visit had provoked. "Now I'm not so sure."

Chapter Twelve

THE SILVER CIRCLE CAFÉ BUSTLED WITH PATRONS seeking refuge from the chilly December air outside. The rich aroma of roasted coffee beans mingled with the sugary scent of frosted gingerbread cookies as I scrambled around behind the checkout, filling orders for holiday shoppers.

Despite the cheerful atmosphere, snatches of conversation revealed that Alice's shocking murder—and now the break-in at her apartment—still weighed heavily on the both town's collective conscience, and the visitors that came from out of town.

"Simply dreadful, that burglary," Sadie Taggart murmured to another elderly patron seated near her usual table by the window, a tabby cat between them. "As if the poor woman hasn't endured enough from her murder, then to add insult to injury? They trash her place. Horrible."

The other woman clucked her tongue in agreement, absentmindedly stroking the cat. "Oh, I know, it's just awful. I heard they turned the whole apartment upside down looking for something. Made an absolute mess of it."

Gossip did not take long to make the rounds in Tablerock.

I half-listened as I prepared a triple-shot peppermint mocha for a waiting customer, my mind wandering to the revelations we'd uncovered. We'd learned so much about Alice's secret life as a skilled thief. I felt her posthumously uncovered criminal activities likely explained why she was murdered—but none of it explained who whacked her with a fruitcake, or why.

"Order up, Miss Ellie!"

Marcos's cheerful voice at the pickup counter jerked me from my thoughts. I hurried over to retrieve the finished drink.

Every time I heard someone call me Miss Ellie, I thought of Ellie Ewing, the well known character from the popular TV series "Dallas." I'd get a mental image of myself in a Southern hairdo and flowy dress, sashaying around some ranch, barking orders like a cattle boss.

Well, it could be worse.

They could still be calling me Mrs. Rockwell.

"One peppermint mocha for Carol!" I called out, setting it on the counter with a smile. The blond woman grabbed her steaming beverage, already paid for, and bustled off into the crowded café.

The nonstop flow of patrons kept me occupied, but nagging questions refused to leave my mind. Like Henry Davis—why hire Matt's detective agency when he apparently never filed a police report about the missing book to begin with?

Well, I didn't know that for sure.

We forgot to ask.

I made a mental note to follow up on that with Mario later.

Just then, Evie hurried over. "Mom, you need to see this," she said, angling her laptop screen so I could see. "Someone snapped pics of Jessa and Henry Davis together at Dale's Donuts," she explained, keeping her voice low. "Look at the time stamp—it looks like it was right after she came here. And look who's in the background." She tapped the screen to make the image bigger.

I leaned closer, squinting.

There, seated at a corner table behind Henry and Jessa, was a familiar shaggy-haired figure.

"Jack Jones," I breathed.

Evie nodded. "Hard to believe that's just some random coincidence, right?"

I met my daughter's troubled gaze, my own uncertainty reflected in her eyes. Between Jessa's icy "visit" to the café and her sudden connection to the man who stood to inherit everything from Alice...

No, I didn't believe in coincidences anymore.

Well, I did.

Just not with anything having to do with Jessa Winthrop.

"We need to get that to Mario and Matt," I murmured.

"I already sent it to Matt. Can you text Mario?" Once I nodded, Evie frowned. "Something weird is definitely going on with those three. This feels too sketchy."

"We'll figure it out, sweetie. Let me finish up this rush with Marcos, and then I'll send the link to Mario. I think Darla can use your help with the adoptions."

Evie nodded and hurried off to help Darla as a large group walked in the front door. I turned back to the bustling counter, determined to power through the holiday crunch.

As I whisked about frothing milk and doling out pastries—two things I never thought would have to do with cats and my rescue—my eyes kept drifting back to Evie's laptop sitting open on the back counter, the incriminating breakfast photo glaring at me from the glowing screen.

What were Jessa and Henry meeting about?

Why was Jack there?

He was close enough to eavesdrop on their conversation... wasn't he?

"Miss Ellie!" I hurriedly prepared a tray of lattes and delivered them to a crowded table. As I turned back toward the counter, Old Carl flagged me down from his usual spot at the front.

"Say, Miss Ellie, what's the word on that break-in

over at Alice's place?" He leaned forward expectantly, woolly white eyebrow tufts arched. "Police turn up any clues yet?"

I paused wiping down the table, debating how to respond. Carl meant well, but he did have a penchant for gossiping. "I'm not sure, Carl," I hedged. "I know they're following up on some leads, but these things take time."

Carl huffed out an indignant breath. "Well, if you ask me, those police fellas are chasin' their own tails on this one," he declared, jutting out his scruffy chin. "Wouldn't know a clue if it up and bit 'em. Mark my words, they're sniffin' down the wrong trails as usual."

I smiled politely as Carl launched into one of his rambling monologues about the general incompetence of local law enforcement, and as the animated old-timer built up steam, I resumed working, keeping half an ear tuned to his diatribe like a parent enduring a child's tantrum.

Carl's confidence in Mario, Deputy Markham, and their team's detective skills was clearly not high.

As I handed Carl a fresh black coffee refill, I noticed the holiday lunch crowd was finally thinning out. I quickly texted Mario—and Landon—a link to the incriminating photo, and hoped they had more ideas than I did.

I sank into the plush office chair behind my cluttered desk and glanced at the clock. Nearly time for my standing afternoon coffee chat with Laurie during her break from the vet clinic.

Right on cue, a brisk knock sounded at the door.

"Come on in!" I called.

The door swung open and Laurie breezed inside, the scent of antiseptic and wet dog preceding her in her white lab coat. "Hey you," she greeted me warmly, collapsing into the seat across from me. "I've been running nonstop all day. I think next year we should do some huge presentation on dogs and chocolate. At this point, I should just keep a hose at the ready." She held out a steaming cup. "Brought you a salted caramel mocha."

"Thanks." I took a grateful sip of the rich, sweet coffee concoction, sighing as the warmth spread through me. "You know, I never thought of myself as a coffee shop owner, and this whole thing has just been more wildly successful than I would have ever thought."

"Everybody always wanted to see the Wardwell mansion. I think you struck on a magic combination with the mansion, the cats, and great coffee. If you add puppies, you'll need a reservation to get in."

"No puppies."

Laurie smiled, seeming to relax as she settled back into the plush chair. "I'll get you yet. You just need the right puppy to convince you. So, what's the latest around here? Feel like I've been out of the loop."

I quickly filled her in on the incriminating breakfast photo of Jessa, Henry, and Jack together at the diner, and my vague theory that it implied they were connected in Alice's murder. "How? No idea. Alice was fantastic at keeping secrets, and none of her secrets directly points to anyone."

"Ginger still won't say anything?"

"He's said a little more, but no, not really."

Laurie looked thoughtful as she absorbed this information, idly stirring a rock sugar swizzle stick in her coffee. "I mean, it is an interesting coincidence," she said. "But don't you think you might be reading too much into it? Tablerock's not that big—there's only so many places to grab a bite."

I shook my head. "It was right on the heels of Jessa basically threatening me, Laurie. The timing can't be an accident."

"Maybe, maybe not." Laurie didn't seem fully convinced. "What about Jack's scavenger hunt thing you texted me about? You said some of the clues seemed suspicious, and I'm telling you, I feel like the guy basically wrote stuff just like this. He's a Dan Brown wanna-be, sure, but the book seems to be prophetically ripped from the current headlines—stolen books, a female book thief."

"Well, randomly reading over the scavenger hunt clues at breakfast before being fully fed or caffeinated this morning, sure." I leaned forward. "They seemed odd. I don't know. Landon thinks I might just be paranoid, but I think they might be some way for Jack to snoop around undetected looking for something."

Laurie arched an eyebrow. "Like what?"

"The books Alice stole? Her money from selling the stolen books?"

Laurie pursed her lips, mulling this over as she sipped her coffee. "I don't know, El," she said after a moment. "That seems awfully speculative."

"Well, can you think of a better explanation for why a thriller author would create a cryptic scavenger hunt based in the library where Alice was just murdered only a few days after she was killed?" I challenged.

"Are you saying he decided to have it only after she was dead?"

"Well, no." I pursed my lips. "Huh. That would be weird if he did."

Laurie chuckled.

"I don't know when he scheduled it, actually. If it was after Alice was killed, that's crazy suspicious."

"And if it was before, it's not?" Laurie held up her hands. "Hey, you know I love a good conspiracy theory. I just think we need something more solid before making accusations."

I blew out a frustrated breath.

Laurie had a point.

Just then, the office door creaked open, and Darla poked her head in. "Laurie, your assistant just called," she said. "Wanted me to let you know Mrs. White is here early for Socks' appointment, but no huge rush."

Laurie nodded. "Got it, thanks, Darla. Tell her to do the intake and I'll head back over in a few."

As Darla left the room, Laurie turned back to me, idly peeling the paper sleeve off her cup. "That's my cue to get going. Look, I hear you, but maybe just give it some time, see if anything more concrete emerges?" she suggested. "Could be you're making connections that aren't really there."

Laurie's level-headed perspective was balancing out my own dog-with-a-bone determination to find answers. While I didn't want to jump to conclusions, something was, as Landon would say, hinky.

"Here's a thought," Darla said as she stuck her head back in the room. "Why don't you just *do* the hunt? Then you'll know whether it's shady or not."

I groaned. "There were like fifty clues on the list, and some were pretty cryptic, like that one mentioning a cellar—we don't really have basements around here, so how would I even know where to look?"

"Actually, we do," Laurie said matter-of-factly. At my surprised look, she shrugged. "I mean, not in houses, but quite a few buildings in town have basements or cellars."

Darla nodded in confirmation. "It's true. Remember, you and Laurie got trapped in a basement together back during the whole honey fiasco. So, yeah, they're around here and there. Usually in government buildings. Wineries definitely have them, and we have a few."

"Yep. We can help tonight, I'm sure." She stood and

smoothed her lab coat. "Let me know if you find anything before that. But for now, duty calls."

After they both left, I drummed my fingers on my desk.

Basements, cellars... those underground spaces could easily hide secrets.

I bustled behind the counter and filled a seemingly endless stream of holiday drink orders. Despite the cheery atmosphere, my thoughts kept straying to Landon.

I missed having him around today.

He'd been gone since early morning, busily resurrecting Santa's reindeer in the display that Jessa had plowed into outside city hall. I smiled to myself, picturing Tablerock's burly carpenter carefully crafting new handmade wooden reindeer to replace the damaged ones quickly, before Christmas was passed.

Everything about our town's holiday celebrations came so late.

Here it was December 21st already, with Christmas just a few days away, and we'd only just lit the tree in the square. Most places were decked out for the holidays weeks earlier. But that was Tablerock for you.

Always a day late and a dollar short.

"Order up, Miss Ellie!" Marcos called again, sliding two steaming mugs onto the pickup counter.

I hurried over and delivered the lattes, then wiped down a newly vacant table near where Old Carl sat—still—sipping his usual black coffee.

"Say, Miss Ellie, whatever became of that visit from Jessa Winthrop yesterday?" the elderly man asked, bushy white eyebrows raised inquisitively. "What'd she want, stoppin' in here like that?"

I shrugged, collecting discarded napkins and stirring sticks from the table. "I'm not really sure, Carl. I didn't exactly roll out the welcome mat."

Carl harrumphed. "Well, now, everyone in town knows that woman don't make social calls without an angle to work. Stoppin' by just to chat? Hogwash." He thumped his hairy knuckles on the table for emphasis. "What'd she claim she wanted?"

I stacked the empty mugs onto my tray and turned. "She claimed she just wanted to check on how Belladonna was doing. Though you're probably right—I doubt that was her real motivation."

"Darn right, it weren't."

Carl sounded like a professor lecturing passionately to a captive classroom.

"We *all* know that fancy cat's just fine, sittin' pretty over here in the mansion. Heck, that cat's got more money than most folks in this town, I reckon, with that inheritance from Fiona Blackwell. She took care of that cat, I'll tell you what." He shook his scruffy chin. "Nah, Jessa weren't here about no cat. She had some other angle. We both know it."

I paused wiping the table, intrigued despite myself by the old gossip's speculations. "What makes you say that?"

Carl leaned forward eagerly, clearly warming to the subject. "Now, I ain't claimin' to know Jessa's business," he began in a conspiratorial rumble. "But way I hear it, she's been cozyin' up somethin' fierce to that Henry Davis fellow lately."

Henry Davis certainly hadn't seemed like Jessa's type during our brief encounter at the tree lighting... but then again, he supposedly had money, which—let's face it—was probably all it took to be Jessa's type.

Money enough to hire Josephine.

And she wasn't cheap.

But still...

Carl must have read my skeptical expression, because he quickly elaborated. "Oh, I know, I know—he don't seem her speed on the surface. But consider the facts. Man's the wealthiest widower 'round these parts." He jabbed a crooked finger at me. "Mark my words, Jessa's got her eye on seducing that old coot into marriage. She's strapped for cash since Beau up and croaked in the wrong order to take Fiona's money, and she's sniffin' out her next sugar daddy."

I stared at Carl. "You really think Jessa and Henry are dating?"

"Can't say for sure they're properly dating, but they's been spotted together an awful lot lately," Carl said knowingly. "Puttin' their heads together and whisperin' over at Dale's Donuts, for one. Your little Evie showed you the picture. You mark my words—she's sunk her claws into that man, same as she done with poor Beau."

I grabbed my now-full tray, mulling over this potential development as I moved back toward the counter. If Carl's gossip was true, maybe Jessa's visit to the café really did have to do with Alice's murder somehow.

Could she have come to intimidate me into backing off whatever I knew about her new beau's—pun intended—connection to Alice's murder?

No...

Well, maybe.

It was a stretch, but then again, everything about this case felt tangled in knots.

As I deposited the empty mugs and slid the tray onto the dish rack, I reminded myself to ask Landon for his take on Jessa and Henry's potential romantic entanglement when he got back from reindeer duty.

In the meantime, I had coffee to serve and holiday drink orders piling up.

"Order up, Miss Ellie!"

Coffee and cats demanded my attention.

The rest could wait.

Chapter Thirteen

THE CAFÉ CLOSED AT SIX P.M. SHARP, EVERY SINGLE night.

We had a cozy back area where the cats could retreat from the bustle up front during the day, but even so—the whole place hummed with energy whenever the café filled up and those doors opened.

Josephine kept urging me to stay open later—till nine, she insisted. A few extra evening hours could boost profits. Her eyes would light up as she described local musicians playing for patrons beneath dimmed lights, like my cat shelter would be the next Armadillo World Headquarters.

But I didn't budge.

Nine to six was plenty for me—and for the cats. The daily blur of serving coffee-customers and cat-wrangling left me more eager for that closing bell than I used to be, and I was grateful when those last lingering patrons reluctantly shuffled out as I locked the door.

Despite Josephine's dreams of bustling evenings, I relished the quiet settling over my home.

Time to unwind.

Well... normally, it would be time to unwind.

The front door swung open, allowing a blast of icy air to swirl into the shelter. Landon lumbered through the doorway right on cue at six fifteen, his oddly lumber-jack-looking coat dusted with wood shavings.

"Hey there," I said, unable to keep the smile off my face.

Landon stomped his boots and tried to brush the leftover sawdust from his sleeves in the front lobby. "I just finished up with the reindeer cutouts for the holiday decorations. But you'll never believe who showed up at the workshop while I was working."

I raised an eyebrow. "Who was it?"

"It was Jessa Winthrop herself," he replied, a hint of annoyance in his tone. "She came snooping around asking all sorts of nosy questions about what we were talking about at your place yesterday with Mario."

I tensed, immediately on alert. "That woman has some nerve."

Landon nodded emphatically. "I know. It was unbe-lievable."

"Hold that thought." I held up a hand. "I think I just heard Matt and Evie pull in. Let's wait until they're inside so you don't have to go over anything twice."

While we waited for the kids to come in, I tidied up the café, wiping down tables and collecting stray mugs and plates. The cats lounged lazily over tables and on chairs, their tails swishing. I grabbed the container of cat treats in my hands and shook it vigorously, rousing a calico from her nap.

She stretched with a squeaky yawn.

"Come on, let's go to the hangout room," I called out, ushering the cats toward the doorway with the shaking treats in one hand and a toy with a bell in the other. "Darla, they're coming!"

"I'm ready!" she called from the back.

They raced after me, meowing expectantly, their eyes on the treat container. Once they closed in, a handful of treats thrown into the hangout room managed to clear the café of cats in seconds, leaving only traces of fur behind on the cushions.

A few minutes later, the front door chimed and Matt and Evie hurried in, their cheeks flushed from the cold.

"Brr, it's getting nippy out there," Matt remarked, stomping his boots on the mat. (Back east, he'd be doing it to get rid of snow—here we did it to get rid of dirt.) He unwound the scarf from around his neck and tossed it on the table.

Evie peeled off her gloves, tucking them into her coat pocket. "I can't believe it's almost Christmas," she said breathlessly. Her eyes lit up at the sight of the Christmas tree tucked in the far corner, its lights twinkling merrily.

"I just love this time of year—even with everything going on, it's still so pretty everywhere."

The two of them joined Landon and me at the table nearest the glittering tree, its festive presence warming the cozy café.

"We have some news," I said.

Evie raised an eyebrow. "Oh?"

Once everyone was settled, Landon launched into the details of Jessa's impromptu interrogation. "She didn't outright ask about anything. Kept dancing around it. But she clearly wanted to know what Mario told us about the case, asked if he shared any 'interesting discoveries' about Alice."

I shook my head in disbelief. "Did she mention Henry at all? I talked to Old Carl today, and he swore that Jessa and Henry were dating."

"Nope. But I can tell you something's got her mighty riled up." Landon stroked his chin. "I may not like her, but that woman's sharp as a tack under all that polish and perfume. She wouldn't risk showing her hand unless she knew something for sure."

"Or wanted something," Matt pointed out.

Evie turned to me, her face pinched with worry. "This all feels connected, right? Jessa shows up here practically threatening you, then meets with Henry and Jack at the donut shop?" She bit her lip. "I can't escape the feeling they're in this together somehow."

"Remember, they didn't meet together," I said. "Jessa and Henry were at one table, Jack was at another table.

Laurie thinks we might be making a mountain out of a molehill here, that it could just be a coincidence."

Just then, Darla breezed in from the hangout room, her ponytail swishing enthusiastically behind her. "Hey guys, what's going on over here in this little huddle session?" she asked, head cocked.

I glanced up. "We were just talking about the strange encounters we've had with Jessa today," I explained. "She showed up here."

"I knew that."

"She showed up at city hall today to ask me questions," Landon added.

I pointed. "That, too. It makes me wonder what her game is."

"You don't think she had something to do with Alice, too, do you?"

"We're not sure, but the circle of suspicion seems to get wider instead of narrower. Henry reported a book stolen and hired Matt's firm to look into it, Henry might be dating Jessa, Sarah got her job back and had reason to be angry at Alice, Jack—" I stopped and frowned. "Wait, why do we suspect Jack?"

"Access," Landon said.

"And because he wrote a book about a book thief and Alice was a book thief," Evie added. "His protagonist wasn't a librarian, but I think she was a computer programmer with some EV car company." My daughter scrunched her face up. "That, and Mom thinks he's just weird."

"A little," I conceded.

"She doesn't like him. He's full of himself."

"That may be so, but it's pretty thin on Jack," Matt admitted.

"What about that SocialBook photo today?" I asked. "Though I'll admit that a lot of these things don't seem like clues. They just seem like situations we're not in favor of that may or may not be tangentially related to Alice's secret life."

"But hon, if Alice's secret life didn't get her killed, what did?" Landon asked.

"Hold on." Matt looked at Landon. "Are you saying we need to start from square one?"

Landon's eyebrows shot up, his eyes widening in surprise. "No, that's not what I'm saying—"

"Wow, you guys are really chasing your tails." Darla suddenly looked surprised. "Didn't you say you thought that some of the scavenger hunt clues were a little sketchy? Do that scavenger hunt Jack made up. See if there is anything sketchy about it."

I hesitated.

Sure, some of those clues had struck me as odd... but traipsing all over town deciphering Jack's riddles wasn't how I wanted to spend the Thursday night before Christmas.

I opened my mouth to respond to Darla, but before I could get a word out, Matt turned to Evie.

"You know what, that idea is not half bad," he said, nodding slowly. He rubbed his chin. "We could poke around, chat up some folks, see what interesting tidbits shake loose. A little holiday scavenger hunt could be just the thing."

Evie rolled her eyes dramatically, but couldn't hide a smile. "I'm in if you are." She looked across at me and Landon. "Mom?"

"I suppose it couldn't hurt. Landon and I did wonder if Jack was using this as a cover for something," I said, holding up my hands in surrender. "I suppose the only way to find out for sure is to do the thing."

"I'll bring the shelter van around front so we can all ride together," Matt said, and then looked at me. "If that's all right with you, Miss Ellie."

I nodded.

The shelter's white van idled by the curb, its sliding door thrown open.

Inside, the upholstered benches lining the walls looked worn but serviceable. I hoisted myself up into the van, the suspension sinking under my weight. Landon followed behind me, the van tilting further as he climbed in. Once Darla and Evie were seated, I reached for the sliding door handle and heaved it closed with a metallic clank.

"All right, where to first?" Matt asked, glancing over his shoulder as he backed out of the small parking lot in front of the shelter.

Evie squinted down at the first clue in the packet Landon had gotten from Jack. "Let's see... Okay, here's the first one: *Where laughter rings and childhood dreams once played, seek the keepers of lost youth 'neath the watcher's shade.*"

We puzzled over the cryptic riddle, our brows furrowed, as Matt navigated the busy late rush hour streets. He steered toward Tablerock's center, where we'd be able to reach any part of our small town swiftly.

I muttered the strange words under my breath, trying to wrest some meaning from their ambiguity. Beside me, Landon and Evie wore matching looks of concentration, equally stumped.

"Lost youth, childhood dreams... maybe the elementary school?" Darla suggested. "Kids play there, and the trees kind of watch over the playground, shading it."

I nodded. "You know, I think you might be onto something."

"It's as good a guess as any," Landon agreed. "Worth checking out."

Matt steered the van in the direction of Tablerock Elementary. In five minutes, we were pulling up into the shadowy parking lot, the school a dark mass looming against the night sky. A sliver of moon hung overhead in the dusky sky, and our shoes thumped against the asphalt as we climbed out and made our way toward the playground at the back of the building.

Sure enough, an ancient, towering oak tree spread its leafless branches over the swing-sets and jungle gym below. Evie snapped a quick photo with her phone and texted it to the number provided. Suddenly, she frowned.

"What is it?"

She looked at me. "Did you register your phone number?"

"No, why?"

Evie held up her phone. "How does he know who sent the photo? You're all sending it to the same number. How do you know who got the answer there first?"

"It's only ten or so people," Landon pointed out. "Maybe a particular phone number gets texted they won, and then you know?"

I peered around curiously. "Anything else here seem significant?"

We poked around the play structures, scanned the tree trunk, and checked the wooden sign declaring the playground's construction date. But nothing struck us as suspicious or noteworthy. Just a normal schoolyard, quiet and still at this later hour.

"Maybe this hint was only about finding this location, nothing deeper?" Darla suggested. "It's possible only one scavenger assignment thing is significant, and it's hidden among the other fifty."

"Could be," Matt said. "Doesn't seem like anything to me."

"Let's move onto the next one," Landon said. "What's the second clue say?"

Evie read from the paper again as we climbed back

into the warm van, our frosty breaths fogging the windows. "*Where unwanted treasures await forgotten fates, seek the watcher that guards the back gates.*"

"Hmm, unwanted treasures, forgotten fates..." I mused aloud. "The landfill?"

"That's not technically in town," Landon said.

Darla clapped her hands. "The Tablerock Thrift drop-off area behind the store. People leave stuff back there all the time."

"Okay, heading there," Matt said, already pulling back onto the road toward downtown.

Minutes later, the van bounced as Matt guided it down the alley behind the thrift shop. Matt slowed and pulled up alongside an enormous metal donation bin shoved against the back wall, a security camera mounted high above, its black glass eye peering down at us from the shadows.

"The watcher guarding the gates?" Landon asked. "That's got to be it."

"Is the bin a gate, though?" I asked.

Matt scoped the scene and exhaled heavily. "I can't think of anything else that fits." Matt checked his watch and shook his head. "Let's look around and see if we can find anything that looks more like a gate, but if not, I say we move on to the third one."

The alley itself was utterly mundane once we looked past the slightly creepy looking donation bin. Cracked pavement, overflowing dumpsters, bare brick walls— nothing remarkable caught our eye. Evie took another photo to document our find and texted it to the scavenger number.

"Any response from the number?" I asked.

"Nope."

After a thorough search turned up nothing unusual, we climbed disappointedly back into the van.

"Well, that was another uneventful stop," I said. "Maybe Jack's clues really are just directing participants to random spots, and this really is nothing more than a game."

"Could be," Matt agreed. "But we've visited two. There are over forty more. I wouldn't make any assumptions just yet."

Everyone murmured their agreement as we buckled in. I leaned my head against the window, watching the holiday lights twinkling outside the foggy pane, disappointed our search had seemed fruitless so far but still clinging to a faint hope the remaining clues might yet unravel some aspect of this mystery.

"Okay, where to?"

"Can you tell me the next one?" Darla asked as Matt pulled out of the lot.

Evie angled the paper, squinting in the dim glow of her phone's flashlight. "Number three reads: *Atop stone steps where leaders lie, by those who shaped our history, the next spot waits if you seek the plaque raised high.*" She wrinkled her nose. "No thoughts on that one." She turned and looked at her friend. "Darla? This seems to be your show."

"Maybe the cemetery?" Darla suggested uncertainly. "Where leaders lie could mean dead people?"

Landon shook his head. "I'm thinking city hall. That clue could have a double meaning—where leaders *lie* as in telling untruths. It has stone steps and those historical plaques out front."

Darla tilted her head. "I think I like Landon's better."

"Okay," Evie said. "Let's try there."

Matt turned the van toward city hall square. Within minutes, we were nearing the small but stately building, its limestone facade glowing in the moonlight.

I pointed. "See that plaque up there? That must be it."

Evie captured an additional image to document the find.

A few clues later, our disappointment remained.

"So far, I'm not seeing these scavenger hunt clues as anything suspicious," I said with a frustrated sigh. "A school, an alley, the courthouse steps, city hall, a water fountain, a bakery. Seems like regular spots around town."

Matt nodded thoughtfully as he steered us back toward downtown. "You're right, nothing too out of the ordinary yet. But we've still only found seven out of fifty clues, and we haven't done any of the ones for books in the library. Maybe as we find more, a bigger picture will emerge. Or maybe only the library clues are significant."

"I hope so," Evie said. "Because right now it does just seem like a random game."

I rubbed my temples, trying to fight off discouragement. Could we have been mistaken about Jack Jones?

"Okay, what's the next one say?" Landon asked.

Evie checked the list. "It says: *Where the smoke and ink collide, displayed past truths are revealed on side.*"

We were confounded by the ambiguous phrase. Smoke and ink?

"Oooh, I know, I know! There's a tattoo shop next to a vape store off Carson Street. The small house that used to be a salon?" Darla said.

I blinked. "I think I know just the spot. It has those weird murals painted on it, right?"

"Yeah, yeah, I got it," Matt said. "I know the place you mean."

He looped the van around toward the shop, its artsy walls coming into view beneath the streetlights. Sure enough, colorful spray-painted graffiti swirled together with fragmented newspaper clippings plastered haphazardly across the exterior.

We piled out of the van, moving in for a closer look at the chaotic collage. My eyes darted around anxiously, trying to make sense of the madness. Photos, maps, strange symbols—it was a bizarre mishmash of art painted and varnished across an industrial-looking corrugated metal facade. I squinted, scanning for anything recognizable in this incoherent ten foot grunge decoupage.

One faded newspaper clipping caught my eye.

I leaned closer, pulse quickening.

Suddenly, it clicked.

"Look!" I jabbed my finger at the picture. "It's Jack and Alice."

The others gathered around, peering at the photograph bonded onto the wall with some type of shiny sealer. It showed Jack and Alice smiling together in front of the town library. The librarian's perky, innocent face seemed totally out of place amid the edgy images surrounding it.

"Proof they knew each other," Evie said.

"Or just proof his picture was in the paper about a library event," Darla pointed out. "I mean, of course they'd know each other. She was the town librarian, and he's a local author."

She had a point. Their paths probably did cross fairly often.

"He's not really a celebrity, though, right?" I said. "Sure, he writes books, but it doesn't seem like he's a *New York Times* bestseller or that famous."

Landon nodded. "True, his writing doesn't have huge mainstream success. But even so, he lives in a brand new half-million dollar ranch house out in Bridle Creek Estates, so he must make a pretty good living."

"Wait, really?" I asked.

Bridle Creek Estates was spit-shined and sparkling

new, a luxury development to the core. Sprawling one-acre plots boasted mammoth homes and lavish pools out back. The place just screamed money, and not a single newly built house sold for under half a million there.

Landon nodded. "We installed a custom library in his house before he moved in. It wasn't cheap, either."

"Wow." Evie looked surprised.

Matt pulled out his phone, tapping the screen. "Let me do some quick research on Mr. Jones. See if I can figure out where his money comes from. It could be book sales."

"And he could have been Alice's partner," I said. "Any progress on your case with Mr. Davis and his stolen book?"

Matt shook his head, brow furrowed in frustration. "Nothing yet. I've contacted rare book dealers across the country and no one has seen that particular Grimm fairy tale edition surface anywhere. If someone took it, they're holding on to it."

I frowned.

Before I could ponder further, Matt looked up from his phone. "Well, this is interesting. Jack Jones used to work for a famous antiquarian bookseller named—" His eyes grew wide. "Hallwood and Grey in London."

"Grey" I raised my eyebrows, surprised by this information. "Grey as in Alice Grey?"

"I don't know. It could be," Matt said. "She was from Tablerock, though, wasn't she?"

"Yes," Darla confirmed. "She was."

Still...

It can't be a coincidence.

The thought flashed like a neon sign in my mind.

I glanced around at the others' faces, seeing my own stunned realization mirrored there. They felt it too, the undeniable tangle of the past resonating in the present like a plucked violin string.

Chapter Fourteen

SARAH BLACK EMERGED FROM LIBERTY TATTOOS, plastic wrap around her forearm as she waved enthusiastically to our group huddled on the sidewalk. With a peppy spring in her step, she bounded over and said, "Hey everyone! Fancy running into y'all here." The new town librarian beamed at us, her eyes bright despite the evening hour. "Don't tell me you're all here to get some spur-of-the-moment holiday ink?"

She let loose a bubbly laugh, gesturing at the tattoo parlor behind her. The fluorescent lights within bathed her round, cheerful face in an odd-colored glow.

Well, Sarah's having a great week, I thought.

First, the woman that fired her got murdered, then she got hired back after being fired from the job she'd had for years—a promotion to head honcho included. And now, the cherry on top was apparently new ink from Gil Dexter (who, by all accounts, was very hard to get an appointment with) to commemorate her triumphant moment. Maybe she'll even win the lottery before New Year's Day.

"Gil already closed up shop for the night, though. He's so in demand his shop doesn't have to stay open very late for him to make buckets of money." Sarah told us with a toss of her head.

She was right. Gil Dexter was a big shot, nationally known tattoo artist who'd relocated from hip, liberal downtown Austin to our conservative (and conservatively priced) small town right around when I did. He'd made a name for himself slinging ink to rock stars and celebs back in the '80s, his unique designs sought-after status symbols in certain circles.

I read in the local paper he thought Austin was getting "too uppity" and "bougie" for his tastes. Our "grittier" small town vibe suited him better, he said.

Tablerock was as quaint and wholesome as they come—it wasn't exactly gritty, and it was much more pearl-clutching than a rowdy frat party at the university. But maybe it appeared "western edgy" to some. At least in comparison to Austin's slick and expensive style today.

"Between you and me, I think Gil could make a fortune staying open later and hiring some tattoo apprentices," Sarah continued. "All those impulsive folks out at the bars who get a wild idea to get 'Mom' tattooed on their bicep at two a.m.—he's missing out on a goldmine!"

"The bars?" Matt looked confused.

"What bars?" Evie asked.

"We really don't have bars in Tablerock," Darla pointed out.

"Oh, true. True. But you never know, right? Someday Tablerock might grow big enough that we'll have our own pubs and bars, right? We already have a nationally famous tattoo artist." Sarah's eyes lit up as if she imagined Tablerock transforming into an urban paradise. "Anyway, were you guys here to get some new ink?"

Landon shook his head. "No, no ink for us tonight. We're actually out doing that holiday scavenger hunt Jack Jones organized. The one you got us into this morning?" He jerked a thumb at the collage of painted images and newspaper clippings adorning the brick exterior behind us. "This building is one of the things we need to photograph."

"Oh, how fun!" Sarah clasped her hands, eyes lighting up.

Apparently, she found the idea of grown adults scrambling around town on a Thursday evening searching for random things to photograph exciting.

"It's been interesting," Darla said.

Sarah bobbed her head, but then she paused, looking suddenly puzzled. "Wait, all of you are doing it together?" she asked.

"Yes," Evie said.

"I thought it was supposed to be competed solo or in teams. Not like, half the town working on it at once."

"We're not all officially taking part," Darla said with an airy wave of her hand. "Ellie and Landon just wanted to check out some of the clues for fun, since they seemed intriguing. Matt, Evie, and I tagged along. Kind of a festive group outing, you know?"

Darla smiled.

Beside her, Evie watched Sarah closely, saying nothing, while Matt stood slightly apart from the group, an unreadable expression on his face.

"That makes sense." Sarah visibly relaxed, all cheer once more. "A nice holiday treat before Christmas comes. I bet some of Jack's clues lead you to some really unexpected places."

She glanced down at her phone, frowning.

"Speaking of unexpected places, it's gotten kind of late. I should probably head home." Sarah sighed. "Honestly, I wish I could join you all, but I've got to be up at the crack of dawn tomorrow. You know, to get the library ready for the big holiday reading event."

"By the way, what's that on your arm?" Darla asked curiously, pointing to the plastic-wrapped artwork on Sarah's forearm.

She glanced down. "My new tattoo. It's gorgeous— wanna see?"

She held out her arm, giving us a clearer view of the vibrant, fantastical imagery inked across her skin. Intricate floral patterns twisted, intertwining with the silhouette of a grand castle with a princess astride a galloping horse in the center, frozen mid-charge. The rich details and whimsical fairytale elements drew the eye in, making it seem as if the tattoo sprawled to life across Sarah's arm, conjuring a world of myth and magic.

"Wow," Evie breathed, leaning in for a closer look. "That's beautiful work."

Sarah nodded, admiring the art herself. "I know, isn't it stunning? I can't stop staring at the colors and how they pop. Look at all the tiny flourishes Gil fit in!" She looked up. "Okay, I really have to get home. My days start early now."

"I thought the library didn't open until ten?" I asked. "When Alice ran the place, the library never opened before ten in the morning. I only know because she always popped by the Silver Circle Café at nine every morning for her coffee."

"That may be how Alice ran things, but I never agreed with that. I'm going to open the place at seven in the morning so folks can get what they need before school and work. I never understood why Alice opened so late, especially with us so close to the schools." She looked somber for a fleeting moment before plastering the cheerful smile back on her face. "Not trying to be disrespectful or anything.

"No, we get it," Darla said. "You know, we should all meet up for drinks tomorrow at the Rockside Café after you close up at the library. Say around seven? Celebrate your new job?"

Darla grinned once more at Sarah, who looked momentarily startled by the impromptu invitation before nodding. "Wow, really? That sounds cool. Thanks for being so welcoming!"

"Of course!"

If Darla and Sarah were any more chipper, they'd be two Disney princesses singing together in a forest glade.

The librarian checked the time once more and sighed. "Well, I really must run. See you tomorrow night!" With a last wave, she hurried off toward the parking lot like a racehorse bolting out of the gates.

As soon as she was out of earshot, Darla turned to us.

"Well, we all better get some questions ready for tomorrow. If she gets suspicious or offended, we might only get one shot at questioning Sarah—which means only one shot to casually grill her for info while she's drinking. We need to make it count." Darla gave us a meaningful look. "We need to be ready to read between the lines of whatever she says. Pick up on any nervous tics or odd behavior. The tiniest reactions could end up being key clues."

Evie and I exchanged glances.

"I have to ask. Do we really think that girl could have killed Alice?" I asked.

"Okay, I'm glad you said it, Mom. I honestly don't see it."

"You two think because you like her, she can't be a murderer?" Matt asked.

"Not exactly, but... kind of." My daughter looked up

at him. "I think I'd know. That I'd be able to sense if she was a murderer. Or at least had that kind of darkness in her. She's about as dark as a field of daisies on a sunny day."

Matt nodded, his expression serious. "I understand what you're saying, but I still think she's the only person we've found that gained something from Alice's death. We've also been talking about Alice's murder like it was planned, but we have no evidence of that—the thing that bothers me is who plans to kill someone in a public building with a fruitcake?"

Landon nodded in agreement just as Evie chimed in with a strong disagreement. "So because Sarah seems chipper in general and the murder seems like a flighty, silly one that wasn't planned, she's a suspect?"

"I just realized something interesting," Darla said, tapping her chin as she glanced around at all of us.

I looked at her. "What's interesting?"

"We're split down gender lines here," she explained. "All the women—you, me, and Evie—we don't think Sarah is involved. Because I'm with you. I don't see it. But Matt and Landon are convinced she's at least a viable suspect." Darla raised her eyebrows. "That's interesting."

Evie leaned forward, her eyes brightening. "Then we're right. Because that actually proves Sarah's innocence if you think about it."

I arched my brow. "How's that?"

"Well," Evie explained, "I read somewhere that

sociopaths and skilled manipulators are usually able to win over and fool the opposite sex, but they have a harder time convincing those of the same sex. Like, men are fooled by female sociopaths, but females can see right through them." She gestured around the circle. "If Sarah was truly sinister and trying to play us, the men would be the ones defending her innocence, while we women would be more skeptical that she could have done it. That it's flipped suggests she's probably being genuine."

Evie looked pleased with her logic.

Darla and I glanced at each other, then back at the men.

"Huh," Matt said, brow furrowed as he thought it over.

"Well, drinks tomorrow night will hopefully provide more clarity, and I think you kids should go without us old fogies. You're closer to Sarah's age. She might be more relaxed talking to people she thinks of as peers," Landon said. He checked his watch, exhaling heavily into the frosty air. "For now, I reckon we should call it a night on the scavenger hunt. Ellie and I will pick it back up tomorrow while you three are out with Sarah."

Everyone voiced their agreement, weariness descending on us now that the adrenaline rush of chasing clues through the dark streets had dissipated.

I sank onto the edge of my bed with a tired sigh, dropping my hairbrush on the nightstand. Despite running all over tonight chasing leads, frustration lingered. It seemed to me we were no closer to the truth about Alice's murder, and a voice way back in my mind wondered what the heck we were even doing at this point.

Maybe we just aren't cut out for this mystery-solving stuff.

"Were our past victories just dumb luck thanks to that magical crystal drink tray platter magic device thing?" I asked no one in particular. "I mean, if you think about it, the talking cats are the ones who gave us the biggest breaks in those cases. Without that advantage, are we even halfway capable detectives? Or just dumb amateurs bumbling our way through, getting nowhere?"

Before I could spiral further into my gloomy musings, a soft knock interrupted my thoughts. I glanced up to see Evie peeking tentatively into the bedroom. She was already dressed in her pajamas.

"Mom? Who are you talking to?" she asked.

"Oh, just myself, I guess," I replied, mustering a faint smile. "Are you all ready for bed?"

"Yeah, but I'm out of toothpaste. Can I grab some from the cabinet?" she asked through a barely stifled yawn, pointing toward my bathroom.

"Sure thing. I'll get it for you." I swung my legs over the side of the bed and pushed myself up, padding across the room to the small bathroom off my bedroom suite.

After flipping on the light, I opened the closet and surveyed the orderly shelves, quickly locating an unopened tube of toothpaste. I went back into the bedroom and lightly tossed the tube underhand to Evie, who was now sitting on the edge of the mattress.

She caught it deftly in one hand. "Thanks. Everything okay?"

"It's fine. I talk to myself sometimes. It's a middle-aged woman thing, I think." I waved off her concern. "I'm fine."

"I can tell something's bugging you."

I hesitated, uncertain how candid to be.

Since she was little, I'd always tried protecting Evie from my troubles. Between her heart condition and post-surgery cognitive struggles, she'd endured enough upset. I just fell into the practice of automatically shielding her from anything potentially distressing—though I'm sure all parents do that to some extent.

But she wasn't a child now. She was growing into a thoughtful young woman before my eyes—and she deserved honesty from me.

Even if it meant admitting my own doubts.

"I've just started second guessing this whole mystery-solving hobby of ours," I admitted. "After another fruitless night chasing dead-end clues, I can't help but wonder if we're really cut out for this."

Evie nodded. "No one said it would be easy, though, Mom."

I shook my head, my doubts and frustration bubbling

up. "It's not about it being easy. I have to ask myself—are we honestly helping anyone here? Or are we just getting in the way while the police try to do their job?" I sighed. "I don't know. Maybe it's just the holidays getting to me. That, and I think I feel a little lost without Josephine's help. Well, that and Ginger refusing to tell us what he knows—what are we even doing? We have nothing solid to go on."

Evie nodded again. "I get that. I've felt discouraged, too, sometimes. But Mom—no one else knew the things we did about Alice's secret life. I mean, sure, maybe the police would have stumbled on it, and maybe they wouldn't have—but we knew it right away."

That was true.

She bumped my shoulder playfully with hers. "If it wasn't for us blabbing, the cops would still think she was just a kindly small town librarian who got whacked with a fruitcake. Because of what we shared from Ginger, now they're digging into her past. We're contributing, even if it doesn't always feel like it leads anywhere."

I knew Evie had a point.

If nothing else, we had provided Mario with crucial background to aid his investigation. I just wished I felt we were doing more concrete good (while also not disrupting actual law enforcement procedures).

"And we do have something no one else does," Evie added.

I chuckled. "Yes, we do."

Evie grinned. "I know things seem murky, but have a little faith."

"It is the season for it, I suppose."

Evie gave me a final supportive squeeze before standing. "We've got this, Mom. Try not to stress too much."

I stood up and pulled her into a proper hug. "Thank you, sweetie," I said as we pulled apart. "Now go brush your teeth. Your breath smells awful."

With a chuckle, she disappeared down the hallway toward her room as Belladonna and Ginger pushed their way into my bedroom and hopped up on my bed.

Belladonna was curled in a tight ball of black fur at my feet, her body radiating a soothing warmth. Ginger was draped heavily across my legs, the rise and fall of his belly matching the pace of his rumbling snores. Their soft, familiar presences comforted me as exhaustion seeped into my bones.

My eyelids fluttered closed, sleep reaching up to embrace me...

Until my cell phone on the nightstand blared to life, jolting me alert. I fumbled to grab it, squinting in the sudden brightness as I swiped to answer.

"Hello?"

"Hey Ellie, it's Landon. Sorry to call so late," came the familiar rough voice on the other end.

I sat up straighter, accidentally dislodging a disgruntled Ginger from my legs. "That's okay. I wasn't asleep yet. What's up?"

"I know it's late, but a thought just occurred to me and I wanted to run it by you real quick. About that ledger Ginger said was missing."

"Okay, shoot."

"The police tossed Alice's apartment when she was first killed, right?"

"Yes. There were several officers there when I went to get Ginger."

"But they didn't find that ledger or take it into evidence?" Landon paused, and when I didn't say anything, he added, "That's a question. Maybe I missed something, but when Ginger said it was missing, Mario didn't say anything about the police having it. Right?"

"Right. I just assumed the police missed the ledger in their initial search, or maybe didn't realize it's significance," I told him. "Or, of course, Mario is keeping secrets from us."

I could almost hear the scratching sound as Landon stroked his perpetually stubbled chin.

"Ellie, if the police searched the apartment top to bottom, why wouldn't they have confiscated a notebook full of what's supposedly incriminating information about Alice's shady dealings?"

"But they didn't know she had shady dealings. Not then. And how suspicious would a ledger full of books be in a librarian's house?"

"They knew she'd been murdered, though. I feel like any handwritten book going back years? They'd grab it. Examine it. Wouldn't they?"

I slowly sat further upright.

He might have a point—that ledger probably would have been seized immediately as potential evidence. Wouldn't it?

"So, I'd think so, but Landon—I'm not a police officer. I don't know why they grab what they grab and why they leave what they leave," I said. "If the police had found a ledger, I would think they would have taken it right away—but I'm basing that opinion on watching police procedurals."

"Yeah, well, just because it's on television doesn't mean it ain't true," Landon said. "I think we need to clarify things with Mario. And if they didn't take that ledger the first time they searched the place, I want to know why they didn't."

We were both silent a moment as we turned over the implications.

"Maybe we're assuming too much, Landon. Maybe the ledger was already gone."

"So, that's what I'm thinking. But think about it—if this supposed missing ledger was not in that apartment by the time the police showed up, that means someone grabbed it super-fast after Alice died. And if that's true—."

I gasped. "It means the person who killed her knew to go get it before the police showed up. It would mean the business partner in her theft ring killed her."

"Maybe," he said. "Yeah, I think maybe."

I nodded, even though Landon couldn't see me. "No, you're absolutely right. This makes sense."

"Right now, it's a theory. We need to talk to Mario." We sat in contemplative silence for a few moments, and then Landon added, "Mario, and—I hate to say it—but not just Mario. You know who else we have to talk to?"

"Yeah, I know." I sighed. "We're going to have to press Ginger more for specifics. As much as I hate it, he's holding back information we really need if we're going to sort this out. Belladonna said she'll try, but..."

"I don't like it either, but I don't see another way forward. We've gone nowhere chasing shadows and scavenger hunts."

I absently stroked Ginger's soft fur. The sleek cat purred contentedly as if he didn't understand—or didn't care about—what I was saying. "We'll start first thing tomorrow," I told Landon. "Hopefully, we can get some clarity from them both."

Landon made a noise of assent. "Sounds like a plan. I'll let you get some shut-eye now. Sorry again for the late night call."

"No, I'm glad you called. It was really weighing on your mind, wasn't it?"

"Sure was," he admitted. "My brain just refused to settle down until I talked it through with you. You always seem to help me see things more clearly."

I smiled at the compliment. "Well, hopefully some sleep will help us both gain clarity. Goodnight, Landon."

"Night, Ellie."

I ended the call and set my phone back on the nightstand, mind churning. As I burrowed back under the covers between two softly snoring cats, my mind kept spinning like a hamster wheel, digesting everything I'd just learned.

Chapter Fifteen

THE SILVER CIRCLE CAT CAFÉ BUSTLED WITH holiday chaos and feline commotion. Adopters crowded the tables, eager to give rescued cats cozy forever homes, while playful kittens scampered underfoot. I wove among the bustle, dodging grabbing hands, swishing tails and wayward paws like a running back juking tacklers on the football field.

"Coming through, watch those toes!" I called out as I lugged a twenty-pound bag of kitty litter toward the supply room. "That goes for the humans more than the cats, folks! Look up! Pay attention, very busy today!"

As I waited for a large man to get out from in front of me, a fluffy tabby wound eagerly around my ankles, nearly tripping me. "Easy there, fuzzy butt," I told him. "If I break my ankle, no more extra treats in the evening."

The fluffy cat meowed indignantly, as if annoyed I

commented on his rear end, and then turned away with such a haughty flick of his tail that it would rival any diva.

From the front desk, Darla's voice rang out above the lively chatter. "Excuse me, ladies, but we need to remain calm and orderly, please!" A brief pause. "Ellie? Evie? Can someone come help?"

I dropped off the litter and ran back toward the reception area to find two elderly women in a heated (but careful) tug-of-war over a bemused black and white long-haired cat with an adorably innocent face. The old women grappled fiercely—but gently—back and forth, jostling the poor tuxedo between them.

"I saw Hondo first, Agnes!" one woman shouted, one hand around Hondo and the other pointing an accusatory finger at her friend like a playground tattle-tale. "You can't just cut in line and snatch him like the last slice of pizza at a kids' birthday party! He's a cat!"

Agnes gasped dramatically, pressing the tuxedo kitten closer against her. "How dare you! I fell in love with Hondo the minute I laid eyes on him. That little face just melts my heart. And you wandered off, Myrtle. That means you lost your place! He's mine!"

"It's not my fault. My bladder ain't what it used to be!"

Hondo meowed. The laid back cat seemed to be trying to calm the overwrought women down.

"Now ladies, let's take a deep breath," I said. "I know Hondo is irresistible, but fighting won't solve anything."

To Darla, I added under my breath, "Can you grab Hondo from them before this geriatric cage match gets out of hand?"

The women eyed each other begrudgingly, like contestants in a stare-down competition neither wanted to lose. But they reluctantly nodded as Darla deftly extracted the totally calm cottony cat from the skirmish, handling the poor thing with the calm expertise of a bomb squad professional.

"Ladies, I assure you we have plenty of wonderful cats looking for homes," I said. "No need to come to blows over this little guy."

Myrtle huffed. "But I want Hondo! His dim-witted little face is so darling."

"Well, I think he'd be happier adopted by someone less *grabby*," Agnes shot back.

I sighed.

Customer service during the holidays was no one's forte. Between the endless lines, frantic visitors, and keeping a smile plastered on my face for hours? Well, let's just say my holiday spirit was a little lacking.

Just a little more than a week of mandatory jingle-belled insanity and I'd make it to January, when I could go back to being my normal self.

Speaking of bells, the cheerful jingle announced Evie's arrival as she burst through the door separating the shelter lobby from the cat café, a drink tray laden with lattes balanced in her hands. Her light brown hair spilled out from beneath a jaunty Santa hat, the white pom-pom on the end bouncing with each brisk step.

She hurried into the reception area toward the staff, weaving between visitors and cats with practiced ease. "Coffee delivery!" she called out in a sing-song voice, handing the hot beverage tray to a volunteer behind the front desk. "Extra shot of... of..." She frowned.

"Espresso?" I asked.

"Yes!"

They cheered in relief.

"Thanks." Evie sidled over to me. "Everything okay over here?"

I quickly recounted the tiff over Hondo.

"No problem. I've got this," Evie assured me. She turned to the grumpy women with a peppy smile. "Hi, ladies! I know just the solution..."

As my daughter smoothly defused the situation, I marveled at her ease handling difficult patrons—a skill I definitely lacked at the moment. She was like the Dog Whisperer on television, except with bickering humans instead of unruly pups. I half expected her to make "tsst tsst" sounds and holding out calming hands toward the two old women as she patiently listened to both sides.

I slipped away from the lobby, leaving Evie to manage the crowd of eager adopters like a patient sheepdog herding excitable pups. I pushed my way back into the bustling café, inhaling deeply as the scent of freshly baked goods enveloped me in a warm, sugary embrace and my stomach let out an audible rumble that would put a hungry bear cub to shame.

"How's it going in here?" I asked Keisha, our newest café employee.

She brushed a stray braid back from her face and gave me a wry smile. "Oh, you know, just living the food service dream," she replied dryly.

At 29, Keisha had already seen her fair share of demanding customers and chaotic rushes at several Tablerock establishments, and by all accounts she'd handled it all with grace and humor. When she applied here, I felt lucky to get her.

I chuckled sympathetically. "Well, hopefully it's been smooth sailing so far today?"

Keisha laughed. "Smooth sailing? More like navigating stormy waters with nothing but a broken compass!" She gestured at the overwhelmed counter. "But don't worry, I'll get this place shipshape again soon enough."

I had to admire her unflappable spirit. Our little cat café threw her plenty of curveballs, but Keisha took each one in stride. She seemed to fit right in with the rest of our ragtag crew.

"I'm glad you're rolling with the punches," I said. "Let me know if you need any backup."

Keisha gave me a mock salute. "Aye aye, captain. Now if you'll excuse me, I need to get back to placating the siren call of caffeine-craving customers."

Back in the crowded lobby, I spotted Matt easing his

way inside, navigating through the sea of people like he was trying to sneak out of a movie for a snack.

"Hey," I called out from the café. "We're slammed. Lend a hand if you can?"

Matt nodded. "Absolutely. Just tell me where you need me."

I quickly set him to restocking paperwork at the front desk and tidying the post-adoption counseling area. Within minutes, he had the clutter organized and was efficiently filing the adoption forms.

"Ellie, we've almost got a situation over here!" Darla waved me over urgently, like a frazzled air traffic controller on a busy day. She pointed to where Eloise, a normally docile tabby, was hissing and swiping like an offended society lady. The object of her ire was a young family holding a curious toddler edging too close to her space. "I can't get over there. I have my hands full!"

"On it!"

But before I could intervene, the toddler let out an ear-piercing shriek of delight to my utter horror, and he clapped his hands excitedly. "Kitty!" he cried out, lunging forward to grab a handful of Eloise's fur.

"Oh, little boy, please don't do that!" I shouted.

This was rapidly escalating from drama to crisis, and I sped up, prepared to leap into action hero mode to protect both baby and cat from each other's impending meltdowns. Visions of flying fur and tears flashed through my mind.

But instead of scratching the kid, Eloise froze.

She stared at the toddler for a long moment, as if processing this loud, grabby creature. Then she promptly flopped onto her back, legs straight up in the air, belly exposed. To my astonishment, she started purring like a motorboat while her paws kneaded the air happily.

The parents and I exchanged surprised looks.

Huh.

Well, okay, then.

A little unexpected, but okay.

The husband looked at me. "Where can I—"

"The adoption papers are right over there in the corner," I told him. "That cat's Eloise, and congratulations! She'll make a wonderful addition to your family."

I turned to avert the next crisis.

When would we get a single quiet moment today?

As if on cue, Old Carl's gravelly voice rang out. "Say there, Miss Ellie, you sure got your hands full today! Never seen this place so busy, no, sir."

"Well, it's the holidays, Carl," I said to Captain Obvious.

He shook his scruffy head. "Seems to me Christmas ain't nothin' but headaches and hubbub every which way you look nowadays. It's a cryin' shame, I tell ya."

I bit my tongue.

Carl's grinchy griping was the last thing I needed.

Just then, Fluffy, one of our resident Russian blues, let out a hiss that could curdle milk as her fur stood on end until she resembled an angry bottle brush. Two rambunctious kids chased each other too close to her napping spot, and the elderly cat reached her absolute limit.

I hustled over and gently picked Fluffy up, murmuring "it's okay, I've got you" as she yowled in protest. Her claws pricked my skin like tiny needles as I whisked her away from the chaos.

Quickly up two flights of stairs, I carried the still-hissing fur ball to the third floor quiet room, depositing her on a cozy cat tree in the corner. She scowled at me indignantly but soon settled in, the cries of spirited children now safely muffled two floors below.

"You're welcome," I told her.

She responded by letting out another hiss in my direction, then turned to present me with a view of her butt.

Charming.

I hurried downstairs to my office, seeking my own much-needed breather. I sank into my desk chair with a relief that was almost euphoric. Sweet, blessed silence! No hissing or human bickering could reach me here.

I chugged a forgotten mug of coffee sitting on my desk, now lukewarm and bordering on tar-like sludge. But I sighed blissfully as the hit of caffeine entered my system. After the morning I'd had, this sad excuse for coffee tasted like the nectar of the gods.

A soft knock preceded Evie cracking open the door. "Mind if I join you?"

I waved her inside and she plopped onto the old

couch with a groan. "What a day already. At this rate, we'll be empty by the new year!"

"It's the Friday before Christmas. Did we expect anything less?"

"Good point." Evie yawned. "I just wish we could've talked to Ginger this morning like we planned. But at this rate, there's no way we'll have a minute. I barely have time for this."

I nodded glumly.

Our hopes of pressing Ginger for more details had been promptly dashed by the holiday rush. Questioning the stubborn and bereaved cat required privacy and patience—two things in short supply around here today. I could barely hear myself think over the cacophony, let alone conduct a sensitive interview with a temperamental feline.

"Hopefully tonight things will settle down enough to—" My reply was interrupted by another knock.

Darla poked her head in, ponytail askew. "Sorry guys, I know you're on break, but we've got multiple litter pans that need scrubbing and everybody is helping with an adoption. The poop levels are reaching epic proportions out here."

I stifled a groan and hauled myself to my feet.

So much for a respite.

Evie gave my hand a sympathetic squeeze before trailing after Darla. I followed reluctantly, steeling myself for more chaos.

The front door chimed as it opened, and I glanced up.

Landon stepped inside, his salt-and-pepper hair windswept in a just-rolled-out-of-bed way that always looked oddly sophisticated on him. The corners of his mouth turned up when he caught my eye, and I felt an instant lift in spirits.

Mario followed on his heels, the police badge on his chest glinting under the fluorescent lights. I waved them over, exhaling in relief at the sight of the two familiar faces joining me amid the turmoil.

"Quite a cat-astrophe today, huh?" Landon said, chuckling at his own pun.

"Understatement of the year." I could hear my voice laced with fatigue and it wasn't even lunch yet. "And what wind blew you two in my direction this morning? I would have thought you'd take one look at the parking lot and keep driving toward Dale's Donuts."

"We were hoping to get your take on a recent development," Mario said. He lowered his voice conspiratorially. "But maybe we should talk somewhere more private."

I nodded. "My office is just—"

Before I could finish, Matt hurried over, phone clutched tightly in his hand.

"I've just received a call from my boss," he said in a hushed whisper, as if sharing a secret. "Henry Davis rang Lodestar this morning. He claims the book has mysteriously reappeared in his house. Thinks it wasn't lost to begin with and he just misplaced it himself."

"He what?" Landon's face reflected a mixture of surprise and skepticism.

Matt responded with a solemn nod. "You heard me. You were there, sort of, during my interview with him. Not a single moment did he give me the impression that he might be yanking my chain."

"You were where during what?" Mario looked at Landon.

"Matt paid a visit to Henry Davis to discuss the disappearance of the book he had hired Lodestar to find," Landon explained. "Matt was wired with a hidden camera, so we all got a front-row seat to the interview, right there on Evie's computer."

"Speaking of, I've wondered this whole time but never got around to asking—did Mr. Davis file an official report about the theft with the police?" I asked Mario. "We assumed not, since you never said anything."

Mario gave his head a decisive shake. "There's no police report filed by Henry Davis recently about a stolen book," he said. "But there was a report by Josephine. She mentioned a 'rare, valuable book' taken from an anonymous client not long after Alice met her unfortunate end."

I blinked. "Josephine?"

"Yes."

"*Our* Josephine? Josephine Reynolds?"

"Yes, that's what I said."

My eyes widened in disbelief. "Are you allowed to do that? Hide someone's identity like that in a police report?"

"Not usually, but yes, if the victim requests anonymity and if you're their lawyer." Mario shrugged. "I have to admit, I thought it was odd."

"The anonymous person has to be Henry Davis, right?" Matt asked.

Evie frowned. "Why would Josephine report it anonymously and then Henry himself call Lodestar to have it investigated? If Henry wanted to remain anonymous, he never would have called Lodestar. Right? Especially since Josephine knew darn well Matt and I would eventually talk about it together. She'd have to know we'd suspect it was him."

I froze, Evie's point hitting me like a thunderclap. "Come on. Let's go somewhere more private."

The six of us navigated our way up to the third floor overlook, a snug haven strewn with velvety cat beds, jingling toys, and the tranquil hum of purring felines—a sanctuary where our resident shelter cats could retreat from the apocalyptic level of holiday over-stimulation down below.

The moment the final click of the door latch echoed in Matt's wake, I swiveled around to face my ragtag group of investigators.

"That was the point," I said.

"What was the point?" Mario asked.

"She must have hid the client's name from the official record to make us pay attention to Henry. But *why*? What conclusions can we draw from Josephine deliberately concealing her client's identity in the police report —even though she knew we'd easily figure out it was Henry?" I threw the question out to the group.

Evie, her arms folded across her chest and her brow furrowed in thought, was the first to respond. "I think Josephine was attempting to cast a shadow of doubt over Henry without breaching attorney-client privilege. That's the only logical explanation."

"Whoa, hold up," Darla said, her voice a mix of disbelief and concern. "Are you absolutely certain about that? It seems like a pretty significant ethical boundary for a lawyer to cross."

"Darla brings up a valid point," Matt said. "Pointing toward a client's guilt you're supposed to be advocating for, even indirectly, would breach her professional obligations."

"Maybe she knows loopholes we don't," Landon reasoned. "If anyone could stay on the right side of a line while swimming in a pond of gray paint, it's Josie."

Darla shook her head. "Josephine is way too ethical to intentionally cast suspicion on her own client like that. I don't buy it."

"What do you think, Mario?" I asked.

The police officer tugged at his collar, looking uncertain. "I'm not sure," he admitted. "Okay, yes—this anonymous reporting is suspicious. I'll give you that. But implying Josephine would betray a client in any capacity? Madre mía, that's a bold claim."

"None of us are lawyers," Evie pointed out reasonably. "Josephine absolutely knows loopholes or exceptions we're not considering. I mean, think about what happened the night Mom found out about Fiona's inheritance. She just barreled over everyone. Legal? Probably. But did you guys have a clue what you were signing? I didn't. Maybe what she did is totally legit."

"Maybe," I said. "But *what* did she do?"

"Point at Henry."

"For what, though?" Matt asked.

The room fell silent.

"Look," Landon said. "Only one way to know for sure—we need to talk to Josephine herself, to see if she'll explain the situation."

Mario nodded. "I agree. I'd like to hear her full rationale."

I rolled my eyes. "Right. It will be just that easy. Come on—*if* she went to this much trouble to give us a hint, she's not going to just explain to us how we should interpret it."

"Besides, I thought we wanted to talk to the cat first?" Landon asked.

"Well, 'first' might be stretching it—we were blissfully ignorant of this aspect of the whole mess just sixty minutes ago," I told my boyfriend. "All right, on our agenda: a consultation with Josephine that I think is pointless, a tête-à-tête with Ginger with the drink tray plate thing, and a possible powwow with Henry, I'd assume, once we have a clue what's going on. Am I forgetting anything?"

"The drinks with Sarah? And what about Jack Jones?" Darla asked.

"The scavenger hunt, even though I still think Sarah Black might have done it," Landon added.

In other words, we still suspected everyone.

"Okay, adding that confounded scavenger hunt put on by Jack." I threw up my hands in mock surrender, letting out a dramatic, weary sigh. "Anyone else have another wrench they want to throw into our holiday plans? Someone else we need to look into?"

Landon leaned in. "You forgot the—"

"Yes, yes, drinks with Sarah. Anything else?"

The room filled with a series of loud, frantic meows before anyone could respond. I turned to see Ginger standing in the doorway, his eyes wide and alert and trained on Mario. The cat's tail flicked back and forth in apparent agitation.

"See, he agrees with me. We should talk to Ginger first," Landon joked, attempting to lighten the mood.

Chapter Sixteen

WE TRUDGED OUT OF THE COZY CAT ROOM, THE third floor hallway swallowing us into its warm sunlight. I lingered, propping open the heavy door with my foot until the others had shuffled past in a line.

With a final envying glance back at the cats lounging lazily amid sunbeams and scratching posts, I stepped into the hall. The door shut behind me.

Downstairs, we entered the smaller "isolation" room. I made a mental note that I really needed to rename this space. We were using a different isolation room on the other side of the shelter nowadays for new residents' adjustment periods, and we only brought animals in here to interact with them via the magic plate drink tray thing.

I really needed to give that thing a better name, too.

My gaze swept over the cat trees with plush beds, dangling felt mice, and cushioned cubby holes lining one wall. When I'd designed the renovation of Wardwell Manor, this was meant to be a space for frightened newcomers.

What it had become was Belladonna's private apartment, and she absolutely treated it like her own personal kingdom. And speaking of her highness...

Belladonna glared imperiously at us.

I bit back an amused smile at her regal demeanor. Though I would never admit it out loud, I had a soft spot for Fiona's temperamental old cat. Underneath her prickly exterior, Belladonna could—when she wanted to —really surprise us.

She just rarely wanted to.

The black cat's sleek form sprawled gracefully curled around a suspicious Ginger as they both lay atop the hidden magic platter. When we approached, the orange cat's ears swiveled warily, suspiciously.

"I know, I know," I said, giving him a soothing chin scratch as he bristled. "You've made it clear you won't tell us anything directly, and we've tried to respect that. But, Ginger, we're getting absolutely nowhere. We need to ask you questions about Alice, and we need you to tell us the truth about her."

At the mention of questions, Ginger instantly arched his back, fur standing on end. He turned and hissed at Mario, eyes narrowing to slits.

"I told you no. This is all your fault, isn't it, copper?" Ginger spat angrily. Then he turned his angry eyes on me. "What, you think a few chin scratches are gonna make me turn stool pigeon?" Turning back toward the object of his anti-police ire, he swiped a paw in Mario's direction. "Well, think again! I already told you—this cat's no snitch!"

Mario held up his hands, palms out, as if to halt a runaway train headed right for him. "Whoa, there. Take it easy, little guy. I know you're—"

Ginger hissed. "Did you just call me *little guy*, you oversized buffoon?"

"—protective of your human's secrets, and I respect that. But she's gone now. Anything you can share to help us find who did this to her will avenge Alice's death, not betray her life."

Ginger stopped and blinked. "That was kind of poetic."

"Thank you."

"Shut up. You're still a buffoon."

"I'm sorry that I have to do this. I'm just trying to get Alice justice."

Ginger huffed, turning up his nose. "Oh, please. Can it with the self-righteous act. You don't care about justice, only closing cases and getting pats on the back." He lashed his tail, clearly unmoved. "I wasn't born in a barn, pal. I know good and well once a cat's out of the bag, there's no stuffing it back in."

"That's true," Mario conceded calmly. "You're one smart kitty. But try to see this from my perspective—"

"Oh, I'll see things from your perspective when donkeys sprout wings and take flight," Ginger snapped.

"I don't owe you anything, so quit wasting your breath. It's not my fault you can't figure anything out on your own."

It went back and forth for several more minutes with Mario attempting reason, persuasion, and supplication, speaking in a calm tone to the cat, and Ginger having absolutely none of it. The cat responded to Mario's overtures with nothing but scornful retorts, feline insults, and outright refusal to cooperate.

"Ginger's feisty spirit is really on full display today," Evie whispered.

She was right—the cat seemed to have a bottomless well of snarky comebacks, each one delivered with a flick of his tail and a furious hiss.

"I wonder if he came like that, or Belladonna's been giving him lessons," I whispered back.

"It would be prudent for you to remember that I am not deaf," Belladonna said, an icy edge to her voice.

"Sorry, Bella," Evie told her.

"That remark was intended for your mother," Belladonna responded, her voice still echoing a cold, authoritative tone.

I looked at her and shrugged. "Fair enough, but I said what I said."

When Belladonna didn't respond, the dispute between Mario and Ginger continued.

"Look, Ginger, this isn't about my career—this is Tablerock, Texas. It's not like there are many career trajectories here for me, so this isn't about getting recognition. It's about getting a dangerous person off the streets so no one else gets hurt. It's about getting justice for Alice. It's about understanding her truth." Mario tilted his head. "I mean, she meant something to you once, didn't she?"

"Uh oh," Evie whispered.

Mario was not a cat person.

Ginger's back arched in response, fur standing on end as he puffed up to twice his normal size. His golden eyes were wild, ears pinned back flat against his head, and a guttural growl rumbled from deep within his chest. To add to the final menace, his tail whipped back and forth like a windshield wiper on the highest setting.

"Look," Mario said. "I didn't mean to insult your feelings."

Crouched low, Ginger's muscles tensed as if ready to pounce directly toward Mario's face, sharp claws extended and glinting under the lights. The tough-talking but usually docile orange cat was now the picture of predatory menace.

Belladonna's eyes narrowed toward Ginger with annoyance and she let out an irritated huff, the fur along her spine bristling.

Alarm bells went off in my head. "Bella, what are you—"

Before I could finish my sentence, she lunged at Ginger, clamping her jaws around the scruff of his neck, teeth sinking into fur and flesh. My heart stopped as Belladonna emitted a warning growl.

But then, just as quickly, she released him.

Ginger whirled around with a startled squeak, eyes wide. "What was that, woman?"

"Watch your tone. These humans clearly have no intention of abandoning this endeavor," Belladonna said in a reasonable tone that contrasted starkly with her aggressive maneuver. She sat back primly. "The prudent course is to just provide the relevant intelligence you possess—so we might all return to more worthwhile pursuits. Like lying down in silence without all these people staring at us."

Ginger blinked at her slowly, then glanced around at our expectant stares.

"Oh, all right," he huffed out at last. "I'll tell you what I know about Alice's secrets. But only because my darling Bella has complete faith in your intentions," he added, with a loving nuzzle toward Belladonna.

"You misunderstand me," she told Ginger.

"How?"

"I harbor no absolute trust in their motives. I simply desire for them to cease their interference in our time together," Bella articulated, her voice laced with frosty imperiousness. "Though I also am of the opinion they are *likely* to act upon their proclaimed intentions." She gave him an inscrutable feline look in return. "Enough with this. Tell them what you know."

Finally.

Finally, we might uncover the full truth of Alice's hidden criminal life—straight from the cat's mouth.

Some crowded onto the carpet, others perched expectantly on the edges of cubbies like birds ready to take flight. It was like a tiny amphitheater, with tall cat trees looming over the small room like columns in an ancient ruin. I folded my legs beneath me, leaning forward as all eyes pivoted toward Ginger.

The orange and white cat sat back on his haunches, his gaze drifting over our enthralled faces. He let out a raspy cough, his throat bobbing as he tried to clear it. A slimy glob suddenly shot from his mouth, landing on the carpet with an audible splat.

"Ew," Mario said.

Evie snatched a paper towel from the side table and held it out to Mario, her nose wrinkling at the mess. "Hairball. You get used to it."

He grabbed it, dabbing at the spot as murmured sounds of disgust rippled through the room. Crumpling the soiled towel into a ball, he tossed it into the trash.

"You see, love?" Belladonna said. "They can be useful."

Mario glared.

"Yes, well... I suppose I should start at the beginning," Ginger said. "When Alice first discovered her calling."

The cat curled into a ball, circling twice before settling into the soft curve of Belladonna's side. A rumbling purr vibrated from his throat as he nuzzled his nose into her fur. Belladonna responded with a lazy blink of her golden eyes, keeping them half-lidded.

"Alice always loved books more than anything—more than people, more than life. Not more than cats, of course, but that's obvious," he said. "As a child, she hid away for hours in her room, devouring novel after novel like she was a glutton at an all-you-can-read book buffet. The characters in those pages? She said they were her only friends."

His luminous eyes took on a faraway look, as if imagining his former mistress as a child. I, too, could envision a young, lonely Alice finding solace between pages.

"When she was young, she always loved reading, and as she got older, her passion for books only increased. She aspired to be a librarian so she could be around books all day, every day. She told me she loved running her fingers over the book spines and smelling the old pages. Books were her universe. Besides cats, I mean."

Ginger's tone softened, filled with affection for his departed owner.

"One day in college, Alice was helping organize a fundraiser for the library branch where she interned," he went on. "This wealthy guy offered a really sizable donation—but he would only donate on one condition. He wanted twenty specific books banned from circulation."

"Wait a minute. I want to make sure I understand this." Evie's eyes widened. "He was trying to bribe the library so he could censor what people could read?"

"Basically." Ginger seemed to bob his furry head in a nod. "Alice was shocked, but as just an intern, she kept quiet while the man loudly demanded certain books be thrown out—and one was her very favorite book. He bragged to the head librarian about his own rare book collection, saying he only cared about preserving great literature and wisdom. Not rubbish."

"People with money like to make the rules," Darla murmured.

Ginger lashed his tail. "Alice didn't think he should get to keep such valuable books all to himself. Especially when he didn't seem to understand what books were for."

I pictured a young Alice listening to this pompous hypocrite dictate what literature others could access, and could imagine her eyes blazing with righteous fury, her hands clenching at her sides, barely able to hold her tongue while stories she loved were condemned.

"So, she broke in to his library and stole a few of his precious first editions—and then anonymously donated the money from the sale to the library. You know, to cover his donation," Ginger declared proudly. "When people have tons of books, they don't always miss one, so it was easy at first."

"It sounds to me like this was one person who made her angry," Matt said. "How did she go from anger at this one person to—"

"Well, she hadn't planned on it becoming a calling. But she ran into another rich book banner, and another, and another... The more she met, the angrier she became, and the more it strengthened her conviction that no one had the right to restrict another person's access to books. One day she woke up and realized her youthful crusade had become her life's purpose."

By the time Alice adopted Ginger off the streets, he told us, her weekend theft adventures were routine.

"Did she keep the books?" Evie asked.

"No," Ginger said. "She sold them. At least I think she sold them."

"But then what did she do with the money from selling the rare books?" Mario asked.

"She was fighting censorship and supporting vulnerable libraries across the country," he said. "It wasn't just about taking it from book banners. It was about giving book sharers the ability to fight. She funneled money anonymously to libraries facing closure or censorship threats. It seemed like she had an entire process for distributing the funds. Like the Robin Hood of rare books."

"But how did she sell the stolen books to get that money?" I asked. "Did she have a fence or something?"

The cat sneezed and then said, "She never explained the details of converting books to human money. I am, after all, a cat."

"Are there really that many rich rare book hoarders trying to shut down libraries and ban books?" Landon asked.

"You'd be surprised," Ginger told him.

Despite being extreme, Alice's motivations made an odd sort of sense to me, and though I didn't condone her methods, I understood her compulsion to liberate literature from the oppressive grip of censors. Her methods were illegal, but her motives clearly came from a place of moral conviction.

I felt we were finally glimpsing the full truth of the woman known publicly as a simple small town librarian —but who had secretly led an extraordinary double life.

"So Alice was stealing rare books to anonymously fund libraries and fight censorship," Evie summarized. "That actually makes her sound pretty noble."

"Misguided, maybe," I said, "but coming from a place of principle."

Mario leaned forward. "This is all enlightening background, but it doesn't get us closer to who killed Alice. Ginger, did she ever mention anyone in town she was having issues with?"

The orange cat shook his furry head. "No, she didn't confide town gossip to me. We had better things to do— like sit in silence reading. But I know you have your own theories about the suspects." His luminous eyes narrowed. "I shared. Your turn. Let's hear them."

Evie and I exchanged a glance.

Where to even begin?

I cleared my throat. "Well, there's Sarah Black, the

librarian who Alice fired under what seems like questionable circumstances. She seemed to harbor a lot of resentment, and I find it odd that she was hired so quickly."

"That's true," Matt agreed. "Sarah gained from Alice's death by getting her job back."

Darla shook her head. "I still can't see Sarah as a cold-blooded killer. She's so... perky. I just don't get that 'killer' vibe from her."

"And then there's Jack Jones," I said. "The author who weirdly helped get Sarah rehired. He knew Alice, wrote books about rare book theft rings that seem eerily similar to her actual activities."

Ginger's ears perked up with interest. "An author, you say?"

"Yeah, I don't think so." Darla shook her head. "I've read his books. The book theft ring he wrote about didn't steal to be altruistic. It was just a thriller thing."

"Even so, it is suspicious," Landon said in his gravelly drawl. "And that scavenger hunt of his still seems shady to me. Well, crass, at least. But we have no actual evidence tying him to Alice's murder specifically."

"We have no real evidence tying anyone to anything," I said.

"It's all circumstantial." Evie nodded. "Well, circumstantial, and a vibe. He's just generally creepy. Not necessarily a killer."

I leaned forward. "Ginger, does the name Jack Jones mean anything to you? Did Alice ever mention him?"

Leanne Leeds

Almost imperceptibly, he shook his head. The motion was subtle, yet clear in its meaning. "He'd been over at the apartment a few times. Alice wasn't thrilled about it." His eyes narrowed to slits. "But someone gifted with weaving lies could craft a good alibi."

"I don't know that it's a reason to look at him, but may as well. We have nothing else." Mario jotted notes in his small pad. "I'll look deeper into this Jack Jones fellow and see if any concrete connections to Alice emerge."

"What about Henry Davis?" Darla asked. "The man is named in Alice's will and he *also* reported his rare book stolen around the same time she died. That's suspicious."

At this, Ginger's ears pricked forward, eyes flashing with recognition. "Henry Davis? Oh, yes, that name I do know. Alice spoke of him now and then. He was a patron of the Tablerock Library."

I frowned. "Hold on—he was a patron? As in he donated money?"

"That's what I just said. Did you not hear me?"

"I heard. I just wanted to make sure." I turned toward Landon. "The night they found Alice, we talked to Henry Davis at the tree lighting before it got canceled. He asked if we'd seen Alice Grey because he needed to speak with her about something. We were with Sarah, Josephine, and he came over. Remember?"

"Yes, you're right," Landon said.

I looked at Ginger. "Could he have been Alice's partner in this book theft ring?"

"How would I know?"

"Did you ever see him at her apartment?"

"He walks with a cane. Could he even get up the stairs by himself?" Matt asked.

"Let's say he can." I met Mario's gaze. "Motive and opportunity?"

He nodded slowly. "Well, his alibi is paper thin, since he lives alone. No one to vouch for him until everyone saw him at the tree lighting."

"Maybe he was the one helping her funnel stolen book money to libraries," Matt pointed out. "With Josephine as his lawyer, he'd know how to hide it."

"He was a lawyer," Landon said. "He wouldn't need Josephine for that."

So, motive, means, and opportunity.

Maybe.

"I think we need to pay another visit to Mr. Davis," Mario said decisively. "It's time for more direct questions."

"I think we need to talk to Josephine," Evie added.

"I think we need to find that leather book Ginger said is missing," Matt said.

"I think you're all forgetting that we have a video of Matt interviewing Henry Davis in his library," I pointed out. "And we should probably take another look at it."

Chapter Seventeen

Evie hurried downstairs to retrieve her laptop, leaving the rest of us in the cat room exchanging speculative glances. After a few moments, Mario, Matt, Landon, and Darla turned to me almost simultaneously with questioning looks, as if expecting me to fill the silence.

I cleared my throat. "Anyone want to see cute videos of kittens falling off furniture while we wait?"

"Why do you think we need to watch the video of Matt's meeting with Henry Davis? I haven't seen it yet, yes," Mario said. "But is there a reason you want to see it once more? Do you think you missed something important?"

"Maybe," I admitted. "It's just a nagging feeling I have that we might have overlooked something. I don't know—maybe it's the holidays, but since Alice died and we got involved, I've felt like I was stumbling around in a darkened room. Something's nagging me about the video." I looked at Mario. "Mostly, though, it's that you haven't even seen the footage yet. And neither has Ginger."

"Hold on, back up—what's nagging you about it?" Landon asked.

I thought back to our initial live viewing of the secretly recorded interview. "When we were all watching it, something caught my eye—but I don't remember what. It was just a fleeting moment, but the oddness of something I saw stuck with me. Well, the feeling of it, anyway—but I can't quite recall what it was."

Landon nodded. "Gotcha. It's worth reviewing again with fresh eyes. Could be we were too focused on listening to the conversation itself. Maybe we missed something in the background."

Evie came back into the room, slightly out of breath, with her laptop clutched tightly to her chest. "It's crazy down there," she said.

"Do we need to go help?" I asked.

"No. I think they've got it." She walked over to a low table and kneeled down to prop open the laptop screen. Her fingers flew across the keyboard as she pulled up the video file, then she clicked rapidly to enlarge it until the footage filled the entire display. She rocked back on her heels, glancing up at us. "Can everyone see?"

Nods rippled through the room.

"All right, let's all take a look together," she said. "Let me hit—"

"Wait—I think Landon had a good idea." I said, holding up a hand. "Honey, why don't you turn down the audio so we don't focus too much on the conversation between Matt and Henry for now? Instead, let's really look at the surroundings, the room itself. See if we notice anything that strikes us as odd or out of place." I looked at Ginger. "Especially you. If you see anything of Alice's, say something."

Ginger gave a short head bob of understanding.

Evie frowned. "What about Mario?"

"We can play it with sound again after we do it this way."

"Okay."

My daughter adjusted the volume until no sound emitted from the speakers.

Then she clicked play.

The video sprang to life, showing Matt entering an ornate study behind the elderly Henry Davis. The familiar bookshelves lined the walls behind them, leather volumes packed tightly together.

"I wish we had that leather journal," Mario said. "If you're right and it does list books, we could compare the titles to what's on the shelf."

"Yeah? Well, I wish you people had guarded my mistress's lair better," Ginger told him.

"Fair enough."

We continued watching the soundless interaction, eyes darting around the stylish space on the small screen, scouring every corner. As the interview proceeded, I constantly second-guessed myself, wondering if I had imagined something being off or if it had just been my imagination playing tricks. "Maybe we should get a television and stream this onto a bigger screen," I said, squinting at the small laptop display.

Finally, near the end of the footage, Henry Davis reached out and caressed—

"There!" I jabbed a finger at the screen. "Did you see that?"

Evie paused the video mid-frame, the blurry image suspended on the screen.

"What is that he's touching?" Darla asked, frowning. "Is that... leather?"

"A leather book," Evie said.

"Ginger, is that Alice's journal? The book she wrote in?" I asked.

The orange cat peered closely at the screen, eyes narrowed in concentration. After a moment, he shook his furry head. "It looks like it could be," he said. "I can't be sure, but if I had to fall one way or another, I'd say it is. Probably. I mean, maybe." He paused. "Or not."

"That would be impossible, though," Landon said.

"Are you calling me a liar?" Ginger hissed.

Landon's eyes widened, eyebrows shooting up

toward his hairline. "Me? No, of course not. I said it's impossible because this"—Landon pointed at the computer—"happened on Wednesday morning. But someone broke into Alice's apartment looking for the ledger on Wednesday night. You visited the morning after, and that was Thursday." Landon looked at me. "If that's Alice's journal, it wasn't even there when someone ransacked her house."

Mario's pen scribbled furiously across his notepad. "Okay, if this is all as you say, they—whoever they is—couldn't have been looking for the journal if Henry already had it," he muttered through gritted teeth.

"Or maybe they didn't realize the journal was already—" I tried to say, but Mario didn't seem to register my words and interrupted.

"If not the journal, then what were they looking for?" Mario rapped his pen against the notepad in a staccato beat, leaving a trail of words across the page.

"Henry's book of fairy tales?" I mused aloud. "It was supposedly missing, and then it suddenly wasn't missing. And let's not forget he never reported it stolen to the police."

Matt leaned closer to the screen. "What are we saying, then? Alice stole Henry's fairy tale book, and then Henry stole Alice's leather ledger?"

"You guys are grasping," Darla said.

"Well, maybe that's what happened." I shrugged. "We don't know."

"Exactly. Look, Alice was a professional criminal,

and she never got caught. Someone could have been on the hunt for the Hope Diamond in her house for all we know," Darla said. "We don't have enough information at this point to make a guess. All we know is that Henry Davis probably has Alice's ledger and a book—"

"Not just a book. Technically, he has everything Alice ever owned," Matt said, cutting her off. "I don't think we should underestimate that Henry's her will's beneficiary, that he's hiding behind Josephine, and that Alice's will made no provision for Ginger."

The orange cat's nose wrinkled, and his tail swished back and forth in agitation. "I can take care of myself just fine," he grumbled, his words tinged with annoyance.

"We're all completely ignoring Sarah and Jack. We haven't cleared either of them." Evie said, her arms crossed. "I think we need to circle back to the scavenger hunt, but just as an excuse. The library is one of the locations in the hunt because Jack included hints for books. We could use that as an excuse to snoop around. It's the one place we really haven't examined."

"And it was a sacred place to Alice," Darla added.

"That's true," I told her.

"Maybe we should split up," Mario said. "I could take Matt with me to the Davis house. Tell him Lodestar let us know about the stolen book, that I'd like to see it just to make sure the case is really closed. Or something."

Evie cocked an eyebrow at Mario. "You guys really

do just make up the rules as you go along, huh?" she said, her tone landing somewhere between amusement and judgment.

"I'm not forging legal documents here. If the guy tells us to get lost, we'll respectfully get lost." He leaned back against the wall. "I don't make the rules, I just... bend them a little. When needed."

"Uh huh. Fine." Evie rolled her eyes. "I'll stay here with Darla and monitor Matt's body cam."

"What about Josephine?" Darla asked. "I thought we wanted to go talk to her."

"Let's wait on that. Landon and I will head to the library to scout around," I said. "I know it's not a lot to work with, but maybe we can find some small clue, a loose thread we can tug to unravel this whole tangled mess."

"Okay." Landon nodded, his eyes glinting with renewed motivation. "Let's see where this path takes us."

I sank back against the cracked vinyl seat of Landon's pickup truck as we rumbled our way across town toward the library. My fingertips idly traced the familiar cracks in the worn dashboard. For all its dings and imperfections, the old Ford had a comforting, well-worn feel to it.

Kind of like Landon himself.

He kept his eyes on the road as he navigated the

streets. "You're awfully quiet over there," he remarked after a few moments. "Everything okay?"

I glanced over at him. "Oh, I'm fine. Just thinking."

"About the case?"

"About everything, really." I turned my gaze out the window, watching bare winter trees flash by. "The shelter, the café, this investigation, Christmas. My mind feels scattered in twenty directions. I'm worried we're neglecting the shelter, your business—I really should be working instead of chasing all these loose ends."

Landon nodded thoughtfully. "You and Evie built Silver Circle from the ground up. It's your baby. Only natural to feel anxious stepping back from the day-to-day."

"Exactly," I said, relieved he understood my unease. Then I blinked.

"Wait—I'm not stepping back."

"Sure you are. A little bit. It's the middle of the day, and we're going to a scavenger hunt. And it's okay for you to do that—but it can be hard to get used to."

I am surprised that Landon thinks I am stepping away from work. This is all just because of Alice's murder. I'm not stepping away, I thought to myself, bristling slightly. "Well, this isn't something I do all the time. Once this investigation is over, things will return to normal."

"No doubt." Landon reached over and gave my hand a comforting squeeze. "But Ellie, you hired good people.

Smart, responsible folks who care about the place as much as you do. It'll keep running just fine."

"I guess I just feel guilty being away during the busy holiday season. Maybe I should—"

"Now hold on." Landon cast me a sidelong look. "What'd we talk about before? You've got to let yourself off the hook a little. No one expects you to do it all yourself."

I expected me to do it all by myself.

Or at least be capable of it.

The truck stopped at a red light and Landon turned to face me. "You're the owner. The boss. It's natural to want to stay involved, but you also have to feel comfortable stepping back. Trusting your team. That's part of owning a business. Well, okay, you run a non-profit, but it's the same thing."

The light changed, and we continued on. I chewed my lip, mulling over his advice. I knew Landon meant well with his talk of self-care and breaks, but it wasn't something I was used to considering.

"I get what you're saying," I said after a moment. "I do trust everyone. And I know micromanaging isn't good for them or me. It's just hard breaking old habits, you know?"

"Oh, believe me. I know better than anyone." Landon chuckled, the sound low and rumbling. "When I first started my carpentry business, I wanted to keep my hands on every single project. Drove myself half-crazy trying to control everything."

"Did you really? That's hard to picture."

"Yep." He shook his head, recalling those early days. "I think I was working eighteen-hour days, never taking time off. But eventually I realized that wasn't sustainable. Or sensible. I had to empower my team to do their jobs while I focused on the big picture stuff."

I nodded. "That makes sense."

"Even now, after all these years, there are still days I want to chuck it all and just go build something with my own two hands," Landon admitted. "Some mornings I miss just firing up my tools in the workshop to take on a project from beginning to end, without all the stresses of running a company. Even when you've got capable help, it's hard to let go of doing the work yourself."

"Exactly!" I said. "Even with amazing staff, it's so tempting to just dive in. Fiona's money was such a blessing, but..." I didn't want to say it was a curse, because it wasn't—but it was challenging.

Landon smiled. "I get it. But Ellie, you've built something special. Something that's taken on a life of its own. You deserve to enjoy that success." He gave my hand another supportive squeeze. "Give yourself permission to loosen up the reins a little. Focus your energy on the bigger picture and trust your team to handle the day-to-day stuff."

I let out a long breath. "You think it's past time I start actually acting like the boss instead of trying to do everything myself?" I smiled over at him. "Maybe."

"No maybes. You know I'm right."

We pulled up outside the library, but before I could open the door, Landon placed a gentle hand on my arm.

"One more thing."

I smiled at him. "What's that?"

"I know you've always put taking care of Evie and your work first. Hell, Ellie, you're one of the most selfless people I know." His brown eyes softened. "But you sometimes forget to pencil in time and space for yourself. Even Wonder Woman needs a break sometimes."

After so many years focused solely on being a mom of a special needs kid and then building the shelter, carving out time for myself still felt foreign. A prickle of guilt would creep in whenever I considered taking a break or doing something just for me. My instinct was always to devote every minute to others.

But Landon was right—I needed to make self-care more of a priority. As much as I wanted to give, if I kept doing it endlessly, I was just going to stress myself out like a candle burning at both ends—and melting in the middle.

Actually, I wouldn't mind melting in the middle a bit. My pants have been feeling tighter lately thanks to one too many holiday cookies. Ah, well—a little extra winter insulation never hurt anyone. It's not just me scarfing down all the peppermint bark and eggnog.

Well.

Probably not.

"I'll do my best," I promised.

Landon grinned. "That's all you can do. Now, what

do you say we go see what secrets this library might hold?"

The library was hushed, a solemn stillness hanging heavy in the air. Our shoes squeaked against the glossy polished floors as we walked, our footsteps echoing through the cavernous lobby. It felt like trespassing in a museum after closing time, everything perfectly preserved in silence.

"Where is everyone?" I murmured. I swept my gaze across the vacant tables and aisles, confused. Hadn't there been advertisements for some major holiday event today? Where was the cheerful bustle of activity I'd expected?

"Good question," Landon said. "Place is deserted."

The room felt like it was watchful, waiting for... something.

I made my way over to the circulation desk, expecting to at least see Sarah busily working. But the swivel chair sat empty, not a soul in sight. Sets of books were stacked in piles on metal carts, untouched and awaiting shelving, while a half-filled mug of tea sat cold on the counter.

"Sarah?"

No answer.

I moved farther into the library, peeking down aisles

of bookshelves. Still no one. The whole place was oddly hushed, almost eerie. Like a ghost town.

"Hello?" I called out. "Sarah? Anyone here?"

No response.

Just then, the heavy thud of a book hitting the floor somewhere made us both jump. Landon and I exchanged startled looks as the noise faded, leaving a tense hush in its wake.

Then muffled voices drifted out from somewhere, the angry rise and fall of a man and woman locked in heated debate. I strained to make out the words, but only snippets punctuated by sharp tones carried over.

Landon held up a hand, signaling for quiet. His brow furrowed as he tilted his head, trying to pinpoint the source until, without a word, he moved swiftly toward the back of the library, his work boots scuffing softly over the carpet.

I followed close behind as he headed toward a door marked "Staff Only" in the back corner and stopped in front of it.

I could make out the angry voices more clearly now. Even slightly muffled, I instantly recognized one as Sarah's.

"...absolutely no idea what you're talking about!" she was yelling.

A deeper male voice snapped back. "Don't play dumb, Sarah. I know you have it!"

Jack.

I would swear that was Jack Jones.

"You're delusional! Why would I take something of Alice's? If you lost something and it's not here, I can't help you."

"You know exactly what this is about," Jack snarled back. "Now quit stalling. I want that ledger, and you know where it's hidden!"

"How many times do I have to say it? I don't know what you're talking about!" Sarah's voice rang out, quivering with fear. There was a sharp crack in her tone, like a thread pulled taut and about to snap.

A heavy scuffling sound followed, like... furniture scraping. A grunt of effort and a yelp of surprise—oh, my goodness. Were they actually getting into a physical fight back there?

"Landon?" I whispered.

"Get off me!" Sarah's words were followed by the sounds of a struggle, and a loud crash rang out, making us both jump.

"Stay here," Landon whispered, and then barreled through the door with a force that nearly tore it from the hinges.

Stay here?

Fat chance.

I followed close behind.

The storage room was chaos unleashed—shelves lay toppled like felled trees, contents spewed across the floor. Books were splayed open, pages crumpled and bent at unnatural angles. Cartons spilled files in drifting mounds, papers shuffled into disarray.

Sarah hunkered against the far wall and peered out fearfully through the tangled strands of her hair. Even at this distance, I could see angry red welts marking her forearm as if someone had grabbed her with force.

At our sudden entrance, Jack whirled to face us, momentarily startled. "I thought the door was locked! What are you doing in here?"

Sarah seized the distraction, scurrying out from behind him and rushing over to cower half-hidden behind me and Landon. She revealed her keys, which had a huge key fob marked front door lock, and then peered around us, eyes wide with fear. "Thank you," she whispered.

"What in blazes is going on here?" Landon demanded, his broad frame blocking Jack's path to Sarah.

"Just a... misunderstanding," Jack said tightly. It was as if he suddenly realized we'd witnessed something we shouldn't have. Recovering his composure, he said, "Sarah has something of mine. That's all. I simply asked for it back."

"That is such bull!" Sarah cried out, emboldened by our presence. "I don't have anything of yours except the stupid book you wrote, and right now I'm sorry I ever read it!"

"You're a liar." Jack glared at her over my shoulder. "This isn't over, Sarah," he told her. "It will be mine one way or another."

Sarah flinched at his approach, raising her hands as if in self-defense.

With that ominous threat, Jack walked toward the exit, and Sarah collapsed into a chair as the door swung shut behind him. "Oh, my gosh. I can't believe I had a crush on that absolute psycho." She looked up. "I'm so glad he spilled that he'd locked the door. I had my keys on me so I could unlock the place from back here, but I don't know what he would have done if you guys hadn't shown up when you did."

I hurried to her side. "Are you okay?" Up close, I could see the red marks circling her slender wrist, early signs of bruising. "Sarah, why didn't you call the police?"

"I had my keys, but I left my phone up at the front desk. But I'm fine." Sarah nodded shakily. "He just... he stormed in here ranting, demanding I give him some ledger, and I had no idea what he was talking about." She shuddered. "That made him furious. Then he tried to search my desk, and..."

She trailed off, wiping at her eyes beneath her glasses.

I gave her shoulder a gentle, comforting squeeze. "It's over now. We'll make sure he doesn't come near you again."

"I really thought he was so cool. What an idiot." Sarah dabbed at her eyes with a tissue Landon handed her. "What makes him think I'd even have something of Alice's?" she said in a small voice. "We never got along.

It's not like she would have trusted me with some secret ledger."

I hesitated.

Given what we'd witnessed, maybe we should share what we knew with Sarah. She certainly didn't seem like she had anything to do with the strange events that had been going on, and I felt she deserved an explanation for the violence she'd endured.

Glancing at Landon, I could tell they had the same hesitations and considerations running through his mind.

I raised my eyebrow.

He shrugged. "Can't make anything worse, can it?"

I sent up a silent prayer that we were doing the right thing. "We think we know what he was looking for," I began carefully. "Well, maybe."

Over the next several minutes, Landon and I explained everything—Alice's double life, Henry's inheritance, his stolen and then reappearing book, our confusion about Jack's behavior, and most importantly, our spotting what seemed to be Alice's ledger in Henry's possession.

We omitted the specifics of how we got some of that information—you know, anything to do with talking cats.

Sarah stared at us in stunned silence, processing everything we'd revealed. Finally, she dragged both hands down her face. "This is... insane. Alice, a book thief?" She shook her head in disbelief. "I mean, I knew she was involved in something shady here at the library, but nothing like that." She looked up. "I don't understand, though. What's in the ledger? Why does Jack want it?"

"We don't know."

Suddenly, her jaw dropped. "I wonder if that weird room has something to do with it." She looked up. "It has to, right?"

Landon and I exchanged baffled glances, then both said, "What weird room?"

Chapter Eighteen

SARAH'S HANDS SHOOK AS SHE CLUTCHED THE library key fob, her knuckles white.

"I don't want the front door open when Jack decides he's coming back. It's the Friday before Christmas, anyway. Everyone's probably on the road," Sarah said. She stood rigid, shoulders tense, eyes darting around like a frightened fawn ready to bolt at the slightest disturbance. I heard the shrill beep of the alarm system activating as the lights in the stacks dimmed to an eerie twilight. "Okay, let's go toward the back," she said, gesturing for us to follow.

The alarm's periodic beep was the only break in the heavy quiet that had descended.

We walked past haphazard rows of bookshelves and stacks of full carts, their contents jutting out at odd angles like crooked teeth. The low illumination cast an eerie pall over the previously well-lit room. Shadows draped the corners, and our footsteps seemed abnormally loud in the muffled stillness.

"You okay?" Landon asked.

I nodded and shivered. As I hugged myself even tighter, goosebumps pricked my arms beneath the soft fabric of my sweater.

The library felt like an entirely different place without the familiar murmured voices and shuffling sounds of patrons going about their business. An unsettling watchfulness permeated the space, as if the vacant building itself was peering at us through its tall windows and around its looming shelves.

Landon set his broad hand lightly on my back, steadying me as we walked, and I leaned into him. His solid presence was comforting amid the suddenly unnerving atmosphere.

"I know. It's weird, isn't it?" Sarah asked.

"What is?"

"This place," she said with a sweeping gesture, taking in the cobwebbed rafters. "I always told Alice we should turn it into a haunted house on Halloween. Most people don't realize how ancient this building is, with all these little rooms and winding corridors." She turned back to look at me, her eyes glinting in the dim light. "I guess now I know why she didn't want people running around in the back rooms."

"Why's that?" I asked.

"You'll see."

Sarah seemed to know things we didn't, and I

hurried to keep close as she led us through a web of storage rooms.

We passed through a doorway into another small, almost claustrophobic, cluttered storage area. More shelving units lined the walls, stuffed with more boxes and more bins in haphazard stacks.

Sarah moved through it all without a glance, weaving through the maze of shelves toward the back wall of the small room, until she stopped in front of a large shelving unit crammed tight with bulging boxes.

"There's a door here that blends right in," she said, gesturing toward the back panel. "You'd never notice it unless someone showed you. Or you spent a lot of time looking for it. Like I did."

The contents rattled noisily as Sarah shifted it several feet to the left, books and boxes threatening to topple off. Landon took a step forward, his forearm muscles flexing as he grabbed the middle rail and helped tug it the rest of the way.

"Oh, my gosh," I gasped.

"You see it, don't you?"

Just as Sarah said, a narrow wooden door set flush into the rear wall. It was painted the same dull beige as the surrounding panels, and it's outline was almost imperceptible. I could have wandered this room a hundred times and never noticed.

Sarah reached into her cardigan pocket and withdrew a ring of keys, sorting through them until she located a tarnished brass one. "I found this ring of keys hidden in Alice's desk after she was killed," she explained as she slid it into the lock. "Since I'd been poking around before I got fired, it didn't take me long to find out what some of the keys unlocked."

As she turned the key, the lock mechanism clicked, and the door creaked open a few inches. Sarah drew it wider, revealing a dimly lit stairwell that descended into shadows. From below, cold, stale air whispered up from steps that vanished into the darkness.

Landon and I looked at each other nervously.

"Well, this seems perfectly safe and not at all like the beginning of a horror movie," I deadpanned, raising an eyebrow at Landon.

"I know it seems sketchy, but it's safe," Sarah said. "I'll get another light on for you. Maybe that will help."

Sarah flipped an electrical switch, and a single dim, bare bulb flickered to life, casting a weak, sallow glow on the stairs. It didn't make the windowless passageway any less creepy, and the sickly light only added to the eerie atmosphere.

"That did not help," Landon told her.

"Oh, come on." Sarah stepped on to the stairway and descended out of view.

I hesitated.

Going into a hidden underground room with someone we barely knew didn't seem like a good idea. After all, Sarah was one of our first murder suspects, and we'd cleared her solely because of her upbeat personality. Considering she was leading us down into a darkened basement no one knew about, that didn't exactly inspire confidence in my judgment of character lately.

I looked over at Landon, meeting his eyes.

In them I could see a reflection of my own hesitance and mounting doubts. Should we continue being friendly and trust her for now? Or politely excuse ourselves from what was potentially a reckless adventure?

Landon cocked an eyebrow at me. "What do you say, Nancy Drew?"

"I say this could be a mistake."

"Anything could be a mistake. What does your gut tell you?"

"That there are answers down there," I admitted.

"Then after you, Nancy Drew."

"Stop calling me that." I elbowed him in the ribs as I moved past to follow Sarah down the shadowy steps.

The temperature plummeted with each cautious footfall, and I shivered in my thin sweater, the knit fabric no match for the cool air. It was like descending into a meat locker, the frigid draft seeping through my clothes and into my bones.

About halfway down the steep staircase, black splotches on the rough concrete wall caught my eye. I paused, squinting in the dim light. "Hold on, are those... scorch marks?"

Sarah reappeared below me on the stairs. "Oh, yeah. Cool, isn't it? You'll see in a minute, but this used to be part of the old county jail. This whole place is super old. That's from some pretty gruesome parts of its history."

I shivered again, but not just from the cold this time. The remnants of violence clung to this place like ghosts.

After about thirty crumbling steps, we reached the bottom.

Heavy iron bars blocked entry to four small cells lining the underground room's back wall of the rough-hewn cellar. Ancient manacles dangled from rusty chains anchored into the stone, swaying ever so slightly as if recently disturbed. The metal cuffs hung open and empty, but still sent a chill down my spine.

I averted my gaze from the eerie cells and began scanning the rest of the basement. I couldn't imagine this cold, dreary space as part of the bustling library upstairs. "So this used to be the county jail, but now it's just abandoned?" I asked, scuffing my shoe on the dirty floor.

"Pretty much." Sarah moved farther into the cellar. "From what I read, it was used to jail prisoners in the western frontier during the nineteenth century. Someone escaped, so they shut the place down and built a new jail."

"Why didn't they demolish it?" Landon asked.

"They did, at least the part that was above ground." Sarah shrugged. "I guess because a library went in upstairs over all this, they just sealed this part off and left it."

"This place is seriously creepy," I muttered under my breath. Some places absorbed the energies of their past, retaining echoes even long after falling silent. This empty pit in the earth seemed to exude some of that traumatic imprint left by those who had suffered and died here.

"I know this is wild, but it's not what I wanted to show you."

I tore my gaze away from the disturbing holding cells.

Sarah stood by a second door nestled to the right of the barred cells. She slid another antique key into the lock and turned it with some effort until the mechanism creaked and the door cracked open.

"It's in here."

I followed her through the door into a small, windowless room, and as I stepped inside, I gasped.

The room was pristine, as if the limestone walls had been scrubbed and bleached. Two entire walls were lined floor to ceiling with a few hundred books on shelves, their leather spines faded with age. The air held a distinctive vanilla, earthy scent of aging paper mixed with leather.

"Wow," I breathed, trailing my fingers gently over the antique tomes. It took effort not to pluck one off the shelf and caress its timeworn cover, leafing through pages that had appeared to have weathered generations.

I turned to Sarah. "Do you know what these are?"

"Well, they're not on the library's inventory. I can tell you that much," she said, coming to stand beside me. "And they're rare. First editions, single books from printings that got destroyed. I wasn't sure where they were from when I found them, but after what you two just told me, I think I understand. This must be where Alice was collecting and hiding the rare books she stole."

Landon let out a low whistle as he took in the extensive collection.

I moved slowly around the room, peering closely at the titles. Some I recognized—leather-bound first editions of Charles Dickens novels, an original Grimm's Fairy Tales. Many more were unfamiliar, their gold-embossed titles faded beyond recognition. All appeared incredibly old.

"Why wouldn't Alice have moved these to a safer place than this?" I mused aloud.

"This is actually a pretty good place to store books. That?" Sarah pointed. "It's a HEPA filter machine to keep dust to a minimum. That thing next to it? That's a dehumidifier. There are no windows down here, so no sun. It's not damp, so no water. I know cave temperatures in Wildebridge County are always stable—that one in Woodville claims to be seventy-two degrees year round. This room seems to always be comfortable. So, I have to disagree with you—this is a perfect place to keep books. Not to mention that everyone clearly forgot this room was even here."

I turned in a slow circle, considering possibilities. She had a point—this secreted underground vault seemed the perfect place to conceal illegal treasures away from prying eyes.

Sarah moved to an antique roll-top desk in the corner. "I need to show you something." She withdrew a leather-bound journal from the center drawer, identical to the one we had glimpsed in the video footage of Henry Davis's library. She held it up. "I think this is Alice's ledger."

But... that didn't make sense.

I took the ledger carefully, almost afraid it would disintegrate in my hands. The worn brown leather cover felt smooth and supple, the pages edged in gilt. This unassuming book might hold the key to unraveling Alice's secrets.

Of course, then again, it might not.

With a deep breath, I opened it to the first page.

Neat handwriting marched across the parchment in straight lines. Just as Ginger described to us, it was a meticulous ledger cataloging Alice's bibliophilic exploits.

Each entry began with a name, followed by notes on what I assumed were the person's attempts at censorship or book restriction. I recognized some of the names, which ranged from wealthy business owners to prestigious academics to high-ranking politicians. Others I didn't know, but their crimes against books were listed regardless of their celebrity.

I slowly turned the pages, reading random passages aloud.

"Senator Howard Mills. Attempted to slash library funding in his state by sixty percent. The Time Machine by H.G. Wells, First Edition, 10 August 2005."

I flipped ahead several pages.

"Reverend Theodore Barstow. Campaigned to ban The Golden Compass from school libraries for supposed 'heresy.' The Golden Compass first edition, 18 February 2010."

Entry after entry of the people she had secretly targeted, as well as the rare books she had stolen from their collections in retaliation. Her ledger was a thorough record of her illegal, but never-ending, crusade against censors.

I shook my head in disbelief, still struggling to reconcile this evidence of Alice's hidden depths with the polite, modest librarian I thought I'd known.

"This is incredible," I murmured. "She documented everything."

Sarah nodded. "I know. I could hardly believe it myself when I found this. And your story of what you found? Well, that explains what was going on." She moved to the shelves and trailed her fingers along the leather spines. "The books listed in the ledger are here on these shelves. Well, some." Sarah pointed toward the leather book. "The ones with lines through the titles? Those books are no longer here. Sold off, maybe."

Landon and I began comparing titles as we moved along the shelves. Sure enough, many of them were exact matches to books in the mysterious ledger.

"This is pretty amazing," Landon said, shaking his head. "An entire secret library of stolen volumes squirreled away down here."

I turned to Sarah. "Where did you say you found this ledger again?"

"I didn't, but in Alice's desk drawer upstairs. It was with the keyring."

I looked at the ledger. It looked exactly like the one Henry Davis was tapping his fingers on while talking to Matt. "Sarah, I..." I hesitated and looked at Landon, hating to doubt her story. "We saw a video of this exact ledger in Henry Davis's possession. Are you telling us the truth?"

Sarah's cheerful expression faded. "What do you mean?"

I quickly explained that I had noticed what appeared to be the same journal in the background of Matt's video interview with Henry on Wednesday morning. Matt and Mario, I explained, were going to visit Henry about it as we spoke.

Sarah stared at me. "But... that's impossible. I found this ledger right here on Wednesday morning."

I wanted to believe her.

If Henry had had this ledger in that footage, how did

it get back here into the drawer and into Sarah's hands? I turned the book over in my hands, carefully inspecting it. It looked exactly like I remembered from the video. "Sarah, please. Just tell me the truth. Where did you really get this?"

"What? No!" Sarah grabbed the book from me roughly, clutching it to her chest. She backed away, shaking her head. "You're trying to gaslight me. I told you the truth. I found this right here in Alice's desk in the library! I swear!"

Heavy scuffling sounds came from down the hall before we could react to Sarah, accompanied by the crash of objects clattering to the floor. Someone was tearing apart shelves, it sounded like.

"What's that?" Landon asked, his voice low.

"No one," the librarian said in confusion. "I locked the front door. You saw me. Why would I leave the door open?"

The foot stomps echoing toward us said otherwise.

"Did you kill Alice? Are you in on this with Henry Davis?" I asked as Landon raced toward the heavy door.

Her head snapped up, eyes flashing. "No! I didn't call anyone! And I found this exactly where I said I did!"

Before I could respond, a thunderous crash exploded from the front entrance, fracturing the rock wall and sending shards of stone raining down.

"Get behind me!" Landon yelled, rushing to protect Sarah and me.

He rushed to pull the metal door to Alice's hidden

room closed, hoping to lock us safely inside. But the heavy door creaked and groaned in protest, sticking halfway.

"It's jammed!" Landon cursed through gritted teeth as he strained to force it shut.

"How did he get in here?" Sarah cried, her voice shaky and panicked as she clung to my arm.

"He never left," Landon replied grimly, giving up on the door to face our attacker head on. "He must have hid upstairs and followed us down."

My heart dropped like a stone.

We were trapped.

I whipped my head around desperately, looking for another way out, but the only exit was blocked by a skinny silhouette, his eyes dangerously cold. In his hand glinted a wicked hunting knife.

Landon shifted to put himself between us, muscles coiled tightly as he prepared to fight for our lives. I clung to Sarah, terror rising in my throat. We were cornered prey with nowhere to run.

Jake's wild eyes focused on Sarah.

"You," he spat. "I warned you what would happen if you didn't give me that ledger." His gaze dropped to the ledger now laying open on the floor between us and the exit, and his eyes widened in recognition. In two quick strides, he snatched up the leather book, scanning the pages eagerly. "You found it. The ledger of all the bank accounts—" A slow, angry frown spread across his face. "Where are the bank accounts?"

"There's no bank accounts in that thing!" Sarah shrieked at him. "It's just a list of books!"

He looked up, pointing an accusing finger at Sarah as comprehension dawned across his features. "You must have torn out the pages with the bank accounts! You had this all along, so you must have them!" He took a threatening step toward her.

Sarah shrank back, whimpering.

Landon stepped forward, his feet shoulder-width apart, his fists clenched at his sides. His steely gaze fixed on the knife in Jack's hand as the muscles in his jaw flexed. "Son," he said, "if you think I can't take that thing away from you and gut you like a fish before you can cry out for your momma, you're sorely mistaken."

Jack just laughed, utterly unperturbed by Landon's hulking presence and obvious threat. He held up the book triumphantly. "This is proof that Sarah was Alice's partner, and she has all the money. I figured it out." His eyes gleamed, half-crazed. "The game is over. I've won."

A chill ran through me at the unhinged look on his face.

Chapter Nineteen

THE COOL BASEMENT AIR SEEPED THROUGH MY THIN
sweater, causing my skin to prickle once more with
goosebumps.

Well, it was either the temperature of the air or the
situation.

It was probably the situation.

My heartbeat was pounding in my ears. Jack Jones,
his knuckles white around the handle of the hunting
knife, blocked the only way out.

Landon had positioned himself between us and Jack,
acting as a human shield to protect Sarah and me from
the wild-eyed man. His broad shoulders were tense, and
his feet were planted wide.

Ready.

"If you knew how to disarm someone with a gun,
why didn't you just do it that time with Joel?" I asked
Landon once after seeing him demonstrate self-defense

techniques with Waldo at a hardware store opening. "Why wait?"

Landon made a shaky motion with his head. "Because, unless absolutely necessary to save someone, you should never escalate the level of aggression. When a fight becomes physical, the risk of serious injury skyrockets."

Waldo chimed in. "He's completely correct. Just because someone has a weapon does not mean they will use it," he explained. "In a situation like that, it's better to try to de-escalate rather than attack. Attacking only incites violence."

Well, here we were again.

At least it wasn't a gun this time.

Sarah's nails dug into my arm, her slender frame trembling against mine. I searched the shadowy basement for a way out, but the jail was better sealed than its history of escapes would have suggested.

We were trapped underground with a thief.

And... and probably a killer.

Jack's wild gaze fixed over my shoulder, his focus on Sarah with eyes blazing. "You," he spat angrily, taking a threatening step toward her. "I warned you what would happen if you didn't give me that ledger." He gestured sharply with the knife clenched in his fist. "Now hand over the pages you tore out! I know you have them!"

Sarah huddled against my back, her eyes wide with dread. "I already told you, I don't have anything!" she sobbed, her voice quivering. "That leather book only contains a list of rare books and people. There are no bank accounts!"

Sarah flinched violently as Jack let out a frustrated growl and slammed his knife against the bars. "Don't lie to me!" he roared. "You know where Alice hid her money, and you're going to tell me one way or another!"

He held the knife menacingly.

"You take a step toward either of them and it'll be the last thing you ever do, son," Landon warned Jack in a low, steady voice.

"Once I have those missing pages, you can all go! There's no reason for you to hold on to them!" he told us. "Where did you hide them? Down here? Stuffed in another book somewhere?"

Stuffed in a...

His statement slammed into me with the force of a freight train.

That was it.

There wasn't one ledger.

There were two.

Sarah held Alice's ledger, a record of the books stolen, the reasons for the theft, and where or from whom the books were stolen. The second, kept by Alice's partner, contained the financial records—donations, amounts, and bank accounts.

And Alice's partner was Henry Davis.

It *had* to be.

It explained almost everything, particularly Josephine's behavior. It wasn't the murderer she had been trying to shield; it was Henry and Alice's illegal dealings that she was obligated to keep concealed. Alice may be dead and buried, but her client, Henry, was still out there.

If Henry didn't kill Alice, and Sarah didn't kill Alice...

"Jack, listen to me," I said, carefully concocting a credible-sounding truth without elaborating on the additional information I now believed I knew. "Sarah is telling the truth—there are no hidden bank account pages. We've been working on this case since Alice's death, and we've found no money. I suspect Alice gave all of it away."

Jack froze and stared at me.

Landon tensed beside me, ready to react.

Instead of responding, the agitated author cast an accusatory glance at Sarah. "You may have the crazy cat lady fooled, but it's obvious you and Alice have been in cahoots all along. You lied to me this whole time about—"

"For goodness' sake, Jack, you're like a broken record!" Sarah's voice rang out sharply, cutting Jack off mid-accusation. "No! For the last time, I was not Alice's partner in any secret operation!" She threw her hands up in exasperation. "Come on, Jack. Think about it." She fixed him with a determined stare. "You know I got canned from the library for poking around back here in restricted areas. Why would I have been fired for that if Alice I were supposedly working together?"

"Getting fired was a calculated move to make yourself appear innocent." But both you and I know better." He pointed the knife accusingly at her. "From the beginning, you and Alice were partners in this. You purposefully had yourself dismissed so that no one would suspect your involvement."

"You're like a damn brick wall, refusing to listen. You've always been like that, so sure you're right and everyone else is wrong!" She jabbed an accusatory finger at him. "What you just said makes no sense. Why would I have torpedoed *my own job* if we were working together *in the library?*" Anger flashed in her eyes now, her cheeks flushed. "You know what? I'm not going to waste my time explaining this. I swear to you—I don't have what you want. Heck, I don't even know if what you want exists."

Sarah was annoyed, and she was done playing nice.

Which made the whole situation much, much more dangerous.

"I'm not always right." He insisted, his voice taking on a desperate, pleading edge. "But it doesn't matter now. Alice is gone, and you have what I need to find the money. So stop stringing me along and give me those ledger pages!"

"Did you hear a word I said?" Sarah whirled to face me, throwing her hands up in frustration. "I'm speaking plain English here, right?" Her words dripped sarcasm. "Spelling it out nice and clear?" She jerked her thumb over her shoulder at Jack, lip curled in a scowl. "Because no matter how I say it, Captain Paranoid back there just won't listen."

"Where's a fruitcake when you need it," Jack muttered.

Jack's erratic gaze darted between the three of us, his agitation growing with each passing second. despite the fact that he had a knife in his grip and was clearly unhinged, something told me he wasn't a hardened killer. Probably just a desperate, unstable man who'd turned to violence as an easy solution.

"Jack, let's all take a deep breath here," I said gently. "I think there's been a big misunderstanding about these ledgers that's caused everything to spiral out of control."

His eyes narrowed as he focused on me. "Oh, now you want to chat, huh?" He swung the knife in the air. "Well, it's too late now. All I want to know from any of you is where the money is."

I put up my hands. "I'm not sure about money, but maybe we can figure this out. Let's go over what happened between you and Alice."

Jack hesitated, skepticism etched across his features. But the knife lowered slightly.

He was listening.

"You and Alice must have been close once if she trusted you to get close enough that you discovered her secret." At this point, I was just guessing and saying things to boost his ego. Convince him I understood his point of view. I knew little about his connection with Alice—Ginger told me he'd been to Alice's apartment a few times and that the two had known each other through the library, but that was it.

"You must have cared about each other."

Jack shuffled his feet, looking down. "We were friends," he muttered.

"How did you find out about what she was doing?" I asked.

"It was an accident. I stopped by her apartment one night unannounced. It was a Saturday, and she wasn't home—I figured she was working late at the library. I, uh, let myself in—I had a key because I'd fed her cat when she went to a library conference once. While I waited, I found..." He trailed off, pained emotion flickering across his face.

"You found what?" I prodded.

"Disguises. A hidden panel in a closet full of wigs, theatrical makeup... everything someone would need to completely alter their appearance. She had identification, too. Different ones." Jack scrubbed a hand down his face. "I confronted her about it when she got home. She broke down and confessed everything. Her double life stealing books."

Just like that?

I found that hard to believe.

"That must have been difficult, discovering her secret like that," I said.

Jack's gaze flickered away from mine, just for a moment. He gave a slight, almost involuntary nod. It was fleeting, barely perceptible. But it was there.

Deception.

Something about his story wasn't true.

"I was shocked. Appalled. But I still cared about her. I wanted to protect her from getting caught. We fought over it, but finally she agreed to stop the thefts if I helped sell off the remaining books she had hidden. Split the money between us."

I didn't think he was shocked or appalled.

I thought he was greedy. And I thought that because he didn't know why she was doing what she was doing. Jack didn't realize Alice didn't keep the money.

Things were becoming clearer now.

I just had to keep him talking.

"I see. So you agreed to help her quit the business?"

"Yes. But she refused to hand over the books. It was hard for her to quit, you know? Like, she was an addict or something. She had to steal. Things between us got heated." Jack resumed pacing agitatedly. "I told her if she didn't cooperate, I'd go to the police. Turn her in myself to stop this insanity."

Did he now?

There it was again.

That inability to meet my eyes.

Some of his story was nothing more than a shined up turd.

I fixed my eyes on his. "I believe you," I said evenly,

the lie slipping smoothly off my tongue. "But *something* must have set you off that night at the library, to confront Alice so violently." I held his shifty gaze as I made my assumptive close. "What was it that sent you over the edge, Jack?"

Jack hesitated, warring emotions playing across his face. I could see it. He wanted to confess. He wanted to take the chance I was giving him to be the good guy, the guy that was trying to stop the book thieving villain of the story.

The hero of this tale—for half the proceeds.

"She thought I'd left to go to the tree lighting, and I overheard her on the phone telling someone to process a donation to a library I never heard of." He drew in a shaky breath. "She was screwing me over! She was getting rid of all the money so she couldn't be caught, and I confronted her. I agreed to keep quiet for half."

He thought she was getting rid of the money.

And he wanted it.

"So you fought?" I asked.

He nodded. "We... argued. Not fought."

"But eventually you fought."

"She attacked me."

"And then you grabbed the nearest thing to you. A fruitcake. I mean, no one would ever think a fruitcake would actually kill someone. It was just an accident. Right? You never meant to hurt her. Things just got out of hand."

Jack stared at me.

The knife lowered and slipped from his trembling fingers, clattering to the stone floor. "I didn't mean to kill her," he whispered. "But the books I write just don't sell enough pay the mortgage on my house, and it wasn't fair that she had *so much money* from stealing books when I was going bankrupt writing them..."

Landon stepped forward and snatched the hunting knife off the floor.

I shook my head. "No, Jack. Of course it wasn't fair."

The ledger dropped from his hands as he sank to his knees.

***

Landon seized Jack's arm and pulled him up and over to the barred cell's lone seat—a narrow ledge along the wall. "Here, have a rest," he said, settling the dazed man. "I need to go check on the ladies. You gave them quite a scare back there."

"Right. Sorry."

Jack sank with his head in his hands on the ledge. He didn't even look up when Landon exited the cell, the thick metal door slamming shut with an echoing clang that rang out through the subterranean space. The frenzied light had faded from his eyes, leaving him with a vacant stare.

Landon walked toward us, the sound of his footsteps echoing off the hard stone walls.

"Those still work?" I asked him, shocked the ancient iron-barred cells could contain anyone.

"I don't really want to ask myself why, but yes," Landon answered.

When Jack overheard this, he seemed to snap out of his regretful trance and dash for the door, shoving his hands through the bars toward Landon. "You duped me! I need to get out of here! I thought you believed me!" he yelled angrily.

"I don't have a key," Landon responded.

"And Jack, even if we do believe you," I told him, "and I'm not saying we do, you still need to explain it all to the police. You can't just hide what you did and avoid any accountability for your actions."

"Let me out, damn you!" he yelled, his face flushed with rage. Spittle flew from his mouth as he cursed words I won't repeat. His eyes were wild once more, his teeth bared, and every muscle strained as he fought against the unyielding bars that remained motionless, unfazed by his tirade.

Landon gently took my arm and steered us farther away from the jail cell. "I think you should go upstairs. I have no bars on my phone, so I suspect neither of you do, either. Go upstairs, call Mario, tell him what happened here," he suggested in a low voice. "Get him over here to take Jack into custody. I *think* those bars will hold, but I can't be sure."

I nodded, my gaze darting nervously toward the barred enclosure where Jack was still raging. "Okay," I said, returning my attention to Landon. "Will you be all right down here? Maybe you should come, too."

Landon gave me a reassuring smile. "I'll be just fine."

I despised the idea of leaving him alone with Jack, even for a short time. But he was correct—we needed the authorities to arrive as soon as possible.

The echoes of the basement jail faded behind Sarah and me as we dashed up the stairs, and the moment we burst into the storage room behind the circulation desk at the top of the stairs, I frantically punched Mario's name.

The line only rang once before Mario picked up.

"Mario, it's Ellie," I said without preamble. "You need to get over to the library right away. Jack Jones is here, and he confessed to killing Alice."

I gave Mario a quick rundown of what had happened, including the creepy details of the hidden subterranean jail. To his credit, he didn't press for information, instead stating flatly that he was on his way and would arrive in less than five minutes.

I thanked him profusely and hung up the phone, taking a deep breath.

Help was on its way.

Armed help.

The authorities would handle this mess.

The next few minutes passed at a painfully slow pace. However, the blessed sound of sirens soon cut through the night. We raced outside as Mario's police car approached, lights flashing and I'd never been happier to see those red and blue lights.

Well, maybe that time Joel held a gun on me.

Or that time...

Never mind.

"What's going to happen to me now?" Sarah wondered aloud as we approached the cruiser. "It's clear Jack only wanted me to work here because he mistook me for a book thief like Alice, and once the mayor hears that... Am I about to be fired? Again?"

Sarah had uncovered crucial evidence that had broken open this case, despite the fact that her methods were... dubious. While rehiring her so soon after Alice's death was based on the advice of a murderer, Sarah herself had done nothing wrong and had even helped us in the end.

"I bet once we explain all of this to Mayor Monroe, tell him how pivotal your situation was to revealing the truth, he'll understand," I said.

"You think so?" Sarah sighed. "I hope you're right. I would hate to lose my job a second time."

For a brief moment, we stood awkwardly at the end of the walkway as Mario and two other officers rushed to meet us. We quickly led them through the library, through the back, and over to the hidden basement stairs. As we descended, I noticed Mario looking around the underground corridor and cells with interest.

"I know. It's bizarre, right?" I said.

Sarah smiled cheerfully. "So, the story is—"

"Unnecessary backstory," one of the officers following Mario remarked. "Let's skip that and get straight to securing the suspect."

"Right. Right. Sorry."

Three police officers and two city employees descended the steps quickly, tools at the ready. Jack stood motionless inside the barred cell, his face devoid of color as he stared at them with white-knuckled hands clutching the metal bars.

Landon moved to the side as Mario motioned to one of the workers carrying a large power tool.

"Angle grinder?" Landon inquired, nodding appreciatively to the mini saw.

"Yup," Mario agreed. "Cut right through these old bars."

"Nice," said Landon.

With a piercing whine, the grinder blazed to life, spraying sparks as he dragged it across the cell's bars. The shriek of protesting metal caused Jack to flinch visibly. Within minutes, the door (minus a few bars) swung open.

Jack offered no resistance as they handcuffed him and read his rights to him. He shuffled along compliantly between them toward the stairs, defeated.

Mario paused before following. "I'll need full statements from all of you about what happened here today. Especially what he said when he confessed," he said. "But for now, go home and take care of yourselves. It's all over."

Chapter Twenty

"So, Jack killed Alice?" Evie asked as Landon and I came back to the cat rescue after the dramatic events at the library. She searched our faces, looking for any sign that what she had heard wasn't true. "That's just crazy. I mean, I know we thought he might have done it, but I read the guy's book. I liked it."

"How did you hear about it so fast?" I asked, surprised that the news had already spread. I took a deep breath, the earthy smell of litter mingled with a homey aroma of baked goods from the nearby kitchen. It was an odd scent, to be sure, but very much like home.

"Old Carl came in for lunch ranting to anyone who would listen that Jack Jones got arrested for murdering Alice," Evie explained, shaking her head. "Apparently, Mario took him into custody in front of the library, and Carl saw the whole thing go down as he drove by. He said he nearly jumped the curb, he was so busy gawking at the scene."

Right on cue, the crotchety voice of Old Carl rang out from his usual perch at the front counter, his raspy baritone carrying into the lobby.

"You're darn tootin' I saw it all!" he declared loudly, thumping his wooden cane on the floor for emphasis. "I watched Mario marched that scoundrel right outta there in cuffs! Near scared me right outta my britches watching all that chaos unfold again, but I kept calm, pulled over, got behind a tree, and watched it all." The old man was hunched over his mug of black coffee, one gnarled hand clutched around it while the other jabbed a crooked finger in the air.

The café was almost empty, just a few stray customers scattered at tables. I suspected much of the small town of Tablerock had already hit the road to visit friends and family, getting an early start on Christmas weekend.

Despite a smaller audience, Carl waved his wrinkled hands through the air as he painted the scene, his raspy voice rising and falling for effect. Eyes twinkling, he played up every gasp-worthy detail—the squad car's screaming arrival, Jack's scrawny frame being shoved against cold brick. "Cuffed him quick as you like and dragged him out while he was yelling and putting up a fuss!"

The few nearby customers glanced over in amusement at Carl's theatrics, exchanging knowing looks and stifled chuckles. The regulars were familiar with his habit of embellishing for impact, and they humored him just the same.

"Goodness, Carl, no need to shout," I said dryly. "I think they heard you clear over in the next county."

Old Carl paused his energetic retelling just long enough to shoot me a wry glance, bushy brows pinching together. "Well, pardon me, Miss Ellie, but seems to me this is big news in our little town." The old man sat back with a satisfied nod and took a triumphant swig of his coffee, clearly relishing his role as the eyewitness to such an exciting event. "Ain't every day we get a murder," he huffed.

"Oh, I don't know about all that," mumbled a lone trucker nursing a cup of coffee at the counter. "Feels a bit like we have a murder every day," he said, flipping through a newspaper.

Well..

He wasn't wrong.

We'd had our fair share of tragic events lately, much as I wished otherwise.

Carl saw an opening in the silence and started up again.

"Anyway, soon as I saw Mario slap those cuffs on that no-good murderer, I high-tailed it over here to spread the word that Alice's murder was solved. Wanted to make sure folks knew." He looked around the café with a satisfied nod, as if personally responsible for informing the few people in attendance. "It won't be long before everybody still in Tablerock knows Jack Jones killed poor Alice. Mark my words!"

"I'm sure you're right, Carl," I said, hoping to rein in his enthusiasm before he embellished a shootout at the library corral. "We appreciate you making sure we all heard the news."

"Well, someone's gotta spread the word 'round here," he replied with a sly wink, some of the earlier theatrics leaving his voice. "Shoot, nothing happens in Tablerock that Old Carl doesn't hear about first!"

I stifled a laugh at the smugly satisfied look on Carl's wrinkled face.

Let him have his moment.

"Say, Miss Ellie, you and Landon were right in the thick of things when it all went down, eh?" Carl prodded eagerly, his eyes glinting with curiosity. "I saw his truck. What happened in that dang library to rile folks up so? What did you see?"

Before I could respond, Evie jumped in diplomatically. "You know, Carl, it's really still an active investigation, so maybe we shouldn't discuss the details yet."

Carl muttered something unintelligible into his coffee mug but seemed to accept our reticence as Landon slipped a supportive arm around me, as if sensing my need for comfort and quiet.

"Let's go up. I can make us some hot cider," he suggested, steering me toward the stairs up to our private quarters. "We probably should tell Ginger about Jack, but then I think you and I should put our feet up for a few."

I nodded, suddenly feeling bone-weary. "That sounds perfect."

As soon as we stepped onto the second floor, Landon and I headed toward the isolation room where Ginger and Belladonna were sleeping. The hallway was dim and quiet, a welcome relief from the chaos (that centered on Old Carl when he got riled up) downstairs.

Landon carefully turned the handle and we slipped inside.

The room was bathed in shadows, the only light coming from a recessed overhead light in the center of the room. Ginger and Belladonna lay curled up on the talking plate like the cubby was their throne, their faces peaceful in the warm glow.

Well, their faces *were* peaceful.

Ginger lifted his head from where he was curled up, his ears twitching, but Belladonna moved more slowly, unfurling at a leisurely pace from her cozy ball in the cubby. Once both heads were raised, their alert stares followed us intently.

"Why are you here?" Belladonna asked bluntly.

Landon hung back near the door, keeping a respectful distance.

"We have some news," I said. "Jack was arrested

today for Alice's murder. The police took him into custody outside the library."

Ginger's eyes went wide. "He killed her?"

"Yes."

I didn't want to overwhelm the cat with more information than he needed to process, so I waited patiently for any questions—but none came. No questions about why he might have killed her, what he said. Ginger simply gazed up at me, his yellow eyes calm and inquisitive, and asked, "You are sure?"

"Yes."

He seemed to take it all in stride—though with cats it was sometimes very hard to tell how they were feeling unless they wanted you to know. Ginger remained still, his tail curled neatly around his paws as he stared at me. "I guess that's the end of that, then. What's going to happen to me now?" he asked, uncertainty entering his voice.

Belladonna's claws slid out, pricking the metal tray beneath her paws. Her eyes narrowed, pupils constricting to slits. "You're not going anywhere," she stated, an unmistakable edge to her tone. Her small body radiated authority and menace in equal measure.

This was not a friendly suggestion, but a command.

Luckily, she was right. Well, lucky for me, really.

I'd hate to think of what she would have done to me if I'd disagreed.

"Belladonna's correct." I crouched down to Ginger's eye level. "Nothing is going to happen to you. This is your home for as long as you want it. We'll make sure you're taken care of, no matter what. And if you meet someone you want to go home with—"

"They will move in here," Belladonna said with finality.

Arguing with her crazy idea would be futile, I sensed. Belladonna had decided, and woe to anyone who tried to defy her iron will. "We'll discuss it when the time comes," I said. "For now, this is your home."

Ginger nodded, seeming to relax a bit. "Well, uh, thanks," he mumbled.

Belladonna turned to Ginger and held his gaze, her amber eyes narrowed in scrutiny, before being satisfied with whatever she saw there. With a final warning look shot in my direction, she laid her sleek black head back down on her paws to resume her nap.

"You can go," she purred lazily, tail flicking once.

"Well, I guess we can go," I said wryly to Landon.

I sank gratefully onto the plush sofa in the sitting room in my bedroom suite, away from the Carl-flavored chatter of the café. The afternoon sun glowed high over the shelter's sprawling back lawn through the large windows, casting a warm amber light across the room.

"Fiona must have been lonely in this big house, but it's really beautiful," I said, gazing out the large bay window that overlooked the sprawling gardens. Beyond the glass, the grounds were dormant to prepare for winter, flowerbeds dotted with mulch and the bare earth exposed. A few brave blossoms still swayed on their stems, defying the chill breeze with vivid pops of color against the barren beds.

"It is."

"I love it here. I didn't think I would," I confessed, eyes trailing over the manicured hedges and empty marble fountains. In the spring, this landscape would burst into extravagant life, but the bare bones had a beauty too, stark and haunting.

As lovely as it all was, I could picture Fiona and Belladonna wandering these many rooms and paths alone, her heels echoing down the cavernous hallways as the sleek black cat's claws ticked beside her. She lived in such grandeur, but ended up its sole inhabitant for too long.

"Beau Blackwell was such a jerk."

Landon chuckled softly as he wrapped a cozy throw around my shoulders, leaving my observation unanswered for the moment. He disappeared into the kitchen, and soon the comforting scent of mulling apples and cinnamon wafted in, making my mouth water. After a few moments, he returned with two steaming mugs clasped in his hands.

"This should warm you up," he said with a smile, passing me one of the mugs.

As Landon settled beside me on the sofa, his eyes crinkling happily as I took the first sip, I cradled it close, breathing in the fragrant tendrils of steam wisping up from the rich amber liquid. The mulled cider was perfect—warming, sweet, and spiced with just a bite.

For a moment we just sat in silence, the only sounds the occasional faint clink of mugs on the coffee table.

"Quite a morning, huh?" Landon finally said quietly.

I nodded. "That's putting it mildly." I shook my head, still trying to process everything. "I can't believe it was Jack this whole time. He seemed so..."

"Normal?" Landon said.

"Yeah." I took a long sip of cider. "On the surface, at least. Well, Alice wasn't exactly normal, either. Or Henry, come to think of it." I frowned. "Is Henry going to be arrested now?"

Landon rubbed my shoulder. "Mario should swing by here once he's done with what he needs to do. I guess we'll find out then. I don't know how much Mario can prove, but to be honest, I think what matters is Jack can't hurt anyone else now."

"True." I nestled closer to Landon's steady warmth. "I just have so many questions. How did Jack really find out about Alice? I don't buy his story at all. And who stole Henry's book? Did anyone steal his book? You know, it occurred to me when we were down there that the whole Henry stolen book thing might have been a ruse to get us involved. Josephine could have just—"

"Stop," Landon said gently, turning to face me with solemn eyes. "It doesn't matter. We did the best we could with the information we had at the time. No one else got hurt, and Mario has the murderer in custody. Things are good." He tenderly brushed a loose strand of hair back from my face, his voice reassuring. "We don't need to expose every single secret."

I managed a small, unconvincing smile in response. "You're right," I agreed, trying to believe his words. I leaned my head on his sturdy shoulder. "I'm just so thankful you're safe."

And it was true. I was beyond grateful for that.

But... my mind still spun with unanswered questions, dark possibilities, nagging what-ifs. I wanted rational explanations to make sense of the senseless.

Landon pressed a kiss to my hair. "Me, too, love."

The tranquility was shattered by a brisk knock at the door cracking through the quiet like a gunshot. Before we could rise, the door burst open and Josephine came storming in with a whirlwind of noisy silks and perfume.

She didn't wait for pleasantries.

"There you two are! Thank heavens you're all right," she exclaimed, heels clicking sharply across the floor as she hurried over. "Another near-death encounter with a murderer, I'm told? Honestly, you two, I may have to start keeping a tally."

It was comforting, in its own way, to have her breezing in unfazed as always, returning a veneer of normalcy to our relationship—but I was still annoyed by her disappearance.

"We're okay, Josie. Just a bit shaken up still."

"Understandably so." Josephine smoothed her skirt and settled gracefully onto the sofa beside me. "Now, I should apologize for my necessary distance this past week. I'm sure it caused no end of frustration and confusion. You must have missed me terribly."

I bit my tongue, holding back a sharp retort.

I mean, she *did* apologize.

That was unlike her.

"It's all right, Josephine," I said evenly. "I take it you're allowed to talk to us again now that your client's been caught?"

Josephine blinked, clearly taken aback. "My client caught? What are you talking about? I didn't represent Jack Jones. And, by the way, my clients don't get caught. They're all as innocent as vestal virgins entering the temple."

"That's pretty innocent," Landon said.

"Henry Davis was Alice's partner in crime, so I assume that's why you had to drop us like a hot potato." I said. "He's your client, right?"

"I can neither confirm nor deny who my clients are."

"You already said he was."

"Oh. Right." Josephine smoothed her skirt demurely before replying, "I want to go on the record to say I never once stated Mr. Davis was innocent or guilty of anything."

Landon looked at her oddly. "No one's keeping a record of this, Josephine."

"Oh Landon," she tutted. "One can never be entirely certain. There's always the possibility of being recorded—and in this scenario, my obligation was clear: to offer counsel and steer the course rather than getting in the middle of everything. It's the legal tango I dance, my friend."

"Counsel to who, exactly?" Landon asked.

"Why, Landon, I do not know what you mean." Josephine blinked innocently. "My sincerest apologies, but I find myself utterly befuddled by your inquiry."

Landon looked at me.

I stifled an eye roll. Josephine was clearly being evasive about her involvement, cloaking it in verbal smokescreens. Her insistence on vague half-truths was giving me a pounding headache. "Look, I don't have the energy for this verbal gymnastics routine right now."

She sighed. "Okay, then let me be *generally* frank— who exactly did you envision an attorney representing, if not people accused of crimes?" Josephine arched an eyebrow. "I assure you, many colleagues represent far more unsavory characters than a harmless old book collector."

"Book thief," I corrected sharply.

"I have no idea what you're insinuating," she said, blinking innocently.

I frowned, out of patience with her act. "You're such a liar. And you're giving me a migraine."

"I know. The long and short of it is I made a calculated decision, the reasoning for which I cannot divulge," Josephine said firmly. "I told you, I cannot elaborate without breaching privilege. That was truthful."

I huffed in frustration—even though I knew she was bound by ethics.

"What I can tell you is I hoped you would connect certain dots, and since the murderer is locked away, you obviously connected enough of them." Josephine gave a delicate shrug. "The outcome was good enough."

Landon and I exchanged puzzled glances.

"What dots?" Landon asked. "You've lost me. What are you trying to say?"

Josephine simply smiled enigmatically.

"The missing book report," I said. "Henry called Matt's uncle and got Lodestar investigating so we'd have a reason to speak with him. I'd bet Josie told him to do that—I said I believed the book really was never misplaced, and that's why he—"

"I cannot confirm any client's motivations, as I've stated." But Josephine's eyes held a satisfied gleam.

"He wanted us to figure out he was Alice's partner all along," I said. "Why not just tell us?"

"Because no one knows and no one can prove he was Alice's partner," Landon guessed. "I mean, we can't prove he was Alice's partner. Ginger didn't tell us anything about it and if that cat didn't know, they must have been pretty careful to hide it. Or we're wrong."

"Are we wrong?" I asked Josephine.

She just smiled.

"We only suspect he is because we saw the matching ledger on the video and because of the will," Landon said. He turned toward Josie. "Wait, did you represent Alice, too?"

"I can neither confirm nor deny any of your off the wall theories."

Josephine's carefully crafted non-answer made me want to scream. I sank back against the cushions and asked another question I'd probably never get an answer to. "Do the police know Henry was involved with Alice's book thefts?"

"Oh goodness me, I haven't the faintest idea what the authorities do or don't know," Josephine replied airily. "I'm merely an attorney providing legal counsel to an innocent old man. Nothing more."

"Right, right," I muttered.

I had to hand it to her—it seemed to me Josephine had expertly maneuvered on the razor's edge of legal ethics. And thanks to her sly maneuvering, Henry's role was exposed to us without either of them uttering a word of direct confession.

Maybe we'd never know every detail.

And perhaps Henry didn't deserve harsh punishment. On the surface, his philanthropy likely seemed altruistic, an old man simply donating money to libraries. I mean... do we really know how much he knew about Alice's life as the Bibliophile Bandit?

I looked at Josephine.

Her eyes, filled with knowing, told me she understood the situation better than I did. "Whatever happened? It's all over now. And it's Christmas, Ellie," Josie said, her voice gentle but firm. "Let it go."

She was right.

It was Christmas.

So I tried to let it go.

Chapter Twenty-One

THE ENTICING AROMA OF ROASTED TURKEY FILLED the air as our motley crew gathered around a makeshift large dining table in the café's dining room, which we'd fashioned by cramming several square tables together. Candles flickered happily along the centerpiece garland of pine cones and red berries, casting a warm glow across our faces.

I smiled around at the familiar faces of my makeshift family—Evie and Matt chatting amiably, Josephine scolding her husband Charlie to use a napkin, Laurie's assistant Francis trying to sneak cat treats under the table to the meowing felines.

"So even if your client is guilty, you defend them?" Evie asked, her brow furrowing as she leaned forward, genuine curiosity in her voice.

"That's right, my dear," Josephine replied matter-of-factly. "It's an attorney's duty to provide the best defense possible, regardless of personal beliefs."

"Ah, but my Josie's clients are innocent until proven broke," Charlie chimed in with a playful twinkle in his eye. He winked at his wife. "Isn't that right, my love?"

Josephine chuckled and shook her head, unable to hide her amusement. She reached for Charlie's hand and gave it an affectionate squeeze. "Oh, don't go giving away all my secrets now!"

I couldn't help but smile as I watched Josephine and Charlie's easy banter. It was nice to see Josie relaxing a bit after the tension of the past few days—after all, I had missed my friend, despite our different approaches to the past week.

Simultaneously, I felt a flare of annoyance at the mention of secrets. She was clearly still keeping them, refusing to explain so much of her behavior and sudden disappearance, and her tight-lipped return to the group bothered me a bit. Not everything was privileged —was it?

There were moments I wanted to take her by the shoulders and shake the full story out of her, but this wasn't the time or place for that confrontation. Not on Christmas, with her loving husband sitting right there gazing at her adoringly.

"Sorry I'm late!" Laurie said breezily as she rushed into the café's cozy dining area, the beads of her holiday necklace clacking together. "I was just checking in on the chocolate-ingesting dachshunds in the other wing. They're doing much better, by the way."

"Oh, thank goodness," Francis mumbled.

"Whew, I'm starving! What did I miss?" she asked brightly, already helping herself to a scoop of mashed potatoes.

"Nothing, we're just getting settled," I assured her, rising to help set down the rest of the food. Roast veggies, green bean casserole, sweet potatoes—everything looked and smelled incredible.

"Save room for dessert later," Estella said with a wink as she joined us. "I made my famous Mexican wedding cookies, and this handsome boy helped." She smiled proudly at Matt. "He's such a good baker."

Matt ducked his head, cheeks flushing. "Abuelita, no need to brag on me."

"Nonsense! You're my only grandson. I get to brag if I want," Estella tutted, patting his shoulder as she settled into a chair. "Evie, darling, I heard Agnes and Myrtle were giving you trouble the other day?"

Evie smiled at Estella's question. "Oh, Agnes and Myrtle—those two are characters for sure! They both had their hearts set on adopting the same cat, Hondo. And neither one wanted to back down."

"Did they?"

She nodded, recalling the tiff that had erupted in the shelter lobby. "Those ladies might be in their seventies, but they can squabble like teenagers when they dig in their heels. But I managed to defuse the situation."

"How did you do that?" Estella asked curiously.

"Well, I took each one aside separately and really listened to why that cat appealed to them. For Agnes, she loved Hondo's sweet, laid back personality since it would be a nice match for her high-strung Pomeranian at home. And for Myrtle, it was Hondo's cute face she couldn't resist."

Evie smiled. "So I showed them some other cats with those same traits that might be an even better fit—and that might not mind living with a Pomeranian, which Hondo definitely did. Agnes fell for a super mellow tabby named Oliver, and Myrtle adopted the most adorable rag doll kitten named Marshmallow."

My daughter discreetly left out the part where she had to bribe Hondo with catnip in order for him to sit on the magic plate and finish the conversation with her once she mentioned the Pomeranian. The idea of sharing an apartment with a "mop-looking yappy ankle-biter" did not sit well with the young cat.

Apparently, Hondo wasn't laid back about everything.

"They both left happy, and Hondo didn't get adopted but, honestly, he didn't really want to go anywhere. Sometimes it just takes listening and finding a solution that works for everyone."

"Mija, you handled that beautifully," Estella praised, patting Evie's hand. "You have a genuine gift for working with people and animals."

Evie blushed at the compliment. "Thanks, Estella. I really love what I do."

Matt smiled affectionately at my daughter. "She's pretty amazing."

Evie gave him a little kick under the table, but she was clearly pleased.

We were all seated and passing dishes around the table in no time. Cats of all colors and patterns scurried around our feet as we filled our plates, their tails twitching and eyes pleading for food. An exuberant tuxedo kitten leaped onto the table, almost knocking over the gravy boat, before Charlie gently lifted her down.

"No jumping on the table, Simba," I gently scolded as a striped orange tabby tried to climb up my leg. He meowed in protest, but jumped down when I offered him a tidbit of plain turkey from my plate instead. "Now go."

"I feel like we should have eaten on the second floor instead of in the café," Laurie said, slipping a bite of ham to the black and white cat in her lap. "Or put the cats up on the third floor until we were done."

"Oh, I think it's kind of fun," Charlie said with a playful toss of turkey over his shoulder to the eagerly waiting cats. "How often do you get to turn Christmas dinner into a game? It adds a little friendly competition to liven things up."

I laughed as I watched the cats chase the turkey scraps around the café floor.

Despite the unusual mix of guests crammed around

the long table, a spirit of lighthearted community prevailed—exactly as I'd hoped. After the darkness and chaos of the previous week, I was grateful to be celebrating life with loved ones.

After dinner, laughter rang out more than once as we took turns opening the gifts, cats jumping curiously at the crinkling wrapping paper and colorful bows. I chuckled as I unwrapped a pair of fuzzy cat socks, while Charlie roared with delight at the cat-patterned tie Josephine had picked out for him.

Belladonna observed the odd human tradition with a bemused tolerance from her place of honor atop the counter next to Ginger.

Toward the end, Matt shyly presented Evie with a small wrapped box, and I held my breath, wondering if he was about to ask her to marry him—and how I was going to feel about that when it happened.

I was able to breathe again once I remembered Matt's parents were on a holiday cruise. He was unlikely to propose while they were out of the country. I didn't know Julio and Maria very well, but I knew they'd box poor Matt's ears if he tried to get engaged while they were in the Carribean.

I exhaled entirely when Evie took a tiny silver necklace from within—even though the two exchanged a private smile that suggested they would share more than just gifts tonight.

None of my business, I reminded myself.

Evie was an adult now. Her life had not always been easy, but she had arrived at this point with grace. She'd—

A sudden buzz of the front doorbell jolted me from my reverie.

"Now who could that be?" I muttered under my breath.

I got up from my chair and smoothed the wrinkles out of my sweater before heading to the shelter's front door. Maybe Mario decided to come after all. It could be carolers hoping for treats or a neighbor stopping by to wish a Merry Christmas. Maybe it was a delivery person with a last-minute package.

With one swift motion, I pulled the door open...

...and stared.

"Mr. Davis?"

I was sure I looked surprised as Henry Davis and Jessa Winthrop stood on the doorstep, Henry holding an elegantly wrapped present. His expression was friendly and calm, whereas Jessa was defensive, her lips pursed in a skeptical pout.

"Hello, my dear," Henry said warmly. "I understand my attorney is here celebrating with you all, and I wanted to stop by and bring her this small token of appreciation for her help lately."

"And I'm only here because he insisted on this detour," Jessa said acidly. "I told Henry we have six more parties to hit tonight, but he refused to skip paying his respects to Ms. Reynolds." Her arms crossed tightly over a fur coat probably made of puppies.

"Now Jessa, mind your manners," Henry chided gently. "I'm sure Ellie doesn't mind one bit if we impose for a quick holiday hello."

He smiled congenially at me, and I resisted the urge to slam the door in his suspiciously cheerful face.

"Oh... of course, please come in," I stammered, the words tumbling out automatically as I stepped back in a daze. My mind was still struggling to process the unexpected sight of the suspected book thief darkening my doorstep. I gestured numbly for him to enter.

It was Christmas, after all. Time for charity and goodwill toward men.

Even sketchy, book-pilfering men dragging the town's demon spawn with them.

"Finally," Jessa mumbled under her breath, breezing past me with a flick of her perfect blond hair, her critical gaze sweeping over the cozy cat café in thinly veiled distaste.

I plastered a smile on my face that probably looked more like a grimace. "Can I offer you some hot apple cider?" I asked through gritted teeth.

"From a drink tray?" Jessa responded coyly, her eyebrow raised.

I hoped my face was as unreadable as my silence.

In the dining area, multiple conversations died an abrupt death as all eyes turned to the new arrivals. The

warm din gave way to a sudden hushed shock, except for
the soft meows of various cats lounging around the café
—and one loud hiss from the black cat on the counter.

"Consider the feeling mutual," Jessa told
Belladonna.

Nothing like unexpected, uncomfortable silence to
really get the holiday cheer flowing.

Josephine rose smoothly from her seat, surprise
flashing across her features before her expression
smoothed over. "Henry, what an unexpected pleasure,"
she said, moving to give him a brisk hug. "To what do we
owe the honor?"

"Just wanted to deliver a small Christmas gift, my
dear." He extended the festively wrapped box
toward her.

"He's obviously still inocente, eh?" Estella said
under her breath in Spanish, clucking her tongue disap-
provingly. "*Deep* pockets of innocence."

"Abuelita," Matt whispered, throwing her a
cautionary look.

Josephine ignored their hushed exchange and
accepted the gift graciously, her manicured fingers
brushing over the elegant wrapping. "How very
thoughtful of you. Please, since you're here, won't you
join us for some holiday pie? Estella brought some fresh
from the bakery this morning."

"Oh, that's quite all right, we really must be going
more quickly than I would like," Henry demurred.
"Seven more gatherings on our schedule tonight. I think

I've gone out more this Christmas than I have for the last few years."

"You're welcome," Jessa muttered.

Henry reached into his suit jacket and withdrew a slender, aged book. I recognized it instantly—the rare Grimm's fairy tale book that had supposedly gone missing from his library. The one Matt had been hired to find.

"Before we take our leave, I hoped you might indulge an old man by allowing me to read a brief tale from this cherished tome," Henry said, a nostalgic fondness in his eyes as he cradled the antique volume. "It has been a family tradition of mine since childhood to read this story each Christmas night."

I watched with interest as Henry's frame carefully lowered into a café chair, looking oddly out of place among the cats and lively decor. He licked his finger as he slowly turned the delicate pages until he reached what appeared to be the end of the book.

"Now, this is an odd little tale entitled 'The Golden Key,'" he explained.

As he began reading the fairy tale aloud, his voice took on a rich storytelling cadence. Despite myself, I found myself drawn into the cryptic narrative.

> Once in the wintertime when the snow
>   was very deep, a poor boy had to go
>   out and fetch wood on a sled. After
>   he had gathered it together and

loaded it, he did not want to go
straight home, because he was so
frozen, but instead to make a fire and
warm himself a little first. So he
scraped the snow away, and while he
was thus clearing the ground, he
found a small golden key. Now he
believed that where there was a key,
there must also be a lock, so he dug
in the ground and found a little iron
chest. "If only the key fits!" he
thought. "Certainly there are valuable things in the chest." He looked,
but there was no keyhole. Finally, he
found one, but so small that it could
scarcely be seen. He tried the key,
and fortunately it fitted. Then he
turned it once, and now we must
wait until he has finished unlocking
it and has opened the lid. Then we
shall find out what kind of
wonderful things there were in the
little chest.

When he concluded, a thoughtful silence hung in
the air. Henry closed the book gently and looked around
with a smile.

"So, wait—that's it?" Evie finally asked.

"Indeed. That is it."

"But what was in the locked chest? What did the key open?"

"Questions are endless and some tales are without end, my dear." He traced a finger over the gilt lettering on the cover. "To tell you the truth, child, I've read this very tale every Christmas since I was small and I still puzzle over it's true meaning. Every year, I seem to understand a little more." He gazed thoughtfully around the table. "I suppose that's the beauty of a good story—it reveals itself to you little by little over time, and what it doesn't reveal makes you think."

With that, Henry pushed himself carefully up. "Well, we've taken up quite enough of your evening. Thank you for allowing an old man his holiday indulgence." He leaned down and pressed a kiss to Josephine's cheek and extended his hand to Charlie. "I do hope you'll both come for dinner again soon."

Charlie stood up and shook. "Of course, Henry."

Henry turned to Jessa, who looked bored and irritated. "Shall we, my dear?"

Jessa glanced at her diamond-studded watch. "About time. We're already late for the Councilman's party."

After quick but polite goodbyes, Henry allowed the sour Jessa to take his arm solicitously as they made their way out of the café.

"What a lovely way to tell someone they won't get answers to all their questions," Josephine said mildly, smoothing her napkin over her lap. A knowing gleam flashed in her eyes. "Wasn't it? Now, who wants more pie?"

"Aren't you going to open that?" Landon asked her.

"It's probably a chest, right?" Evie added. "Like part of the story he told?"

"No, I'll wait until Charlie and I get home."

Landon's eyebrows drew together as he met my gaze. Our wordless exchange spoke volumes.

"I don't want more pie. I want to know how Sarah knew where that underground jail was," Evie said, leaning forward. "How did she know to go there, and how did Jack know to hide in the library to follow you all?"

Laurie shot an incredulous look at Evie, one eyebrow raised. "That's your question?" she asked. "I want to know why Jack clobbered poor Alice over the head with a fruitcake. Okay, well, two things—why attack Alice in the first place, and why choose a fruitcake as the weapon?"

"Jack told us he didn't mean to," I said. "And as for my question—I want to know what's in the box." I pointed toward the present Henry brought Josephine. "Anyway, as far as I understand, Jack wanted money from Alice, and didn't get it."

"Maybe when Mario shows up, he'll explain," Matt said, and glanced at the door. "He is coming, right?"

"Not with Josephine here," Estella said. "He came by the shop earlier to pick up some pan dulce," she explained, "and said he was going to have to rethink hanging around lawyers since they're all so sketchy and dishonest."

Josephine let out an affronted huff, her lips pressing into a thin line. "Well, that's just plain rude," she declared, clearly miffed.

"He's upset that you kept so many secrets from him," Estella told her matter-of-factly as she absently twisted a silver ring around her slender finger. "Says trust is supposed to go both ways. You create an uneven playing field, he said."

Josephine's gaze flickered away evasively. "I don't know what secrets he's talking about, and I don't play games," she said, a defensive edge to her voice. "I did my job, Estella. It's what I'm paid to do, and I'm one of the best in the county."

Estella leveled an unimpressed look at the slick lawyer, her eyes narrowing. "You're a civil attorney, not a defense attorney, and I bet that's exactly the sketchy, dishonest comportamiento he was talking about," she said pointedly, and then leaned in to her grandson Matt and whispered, "Ella es tan mandona y arrogante, se cree la ultima Coca-Cola del desierto."

I knew that phrase. It was a saying: *She is so bossy and arrogant, she thinks she's the last Coca-Cola in the desert.* What's more, I was pretty sure Josephine knew it, too.

"Abuelita!" Matt whispered back sharply, throwing her a pleading look.

Josephine bristled, her shoulders tensing as her eyes flashed with irritation.

"What? You have something to say, Josefina? You make choices, abogada, you live with them, yeah?" Estella continued bluntly. "What did you expect him to do? You should have convinced your *client* to come forward like a man, not play games." She glanced at me and then back to Josie. "You put your friend in danger." Her eyes narrowed. "Be glad it wasn't my grandson."

Josie opened her mouth to fire back, but seemed to think better of launching into a tirade at Christmas dinner. Clamping her lips shut, she merely shook her head in denial, though her knuckles were white on the handle of her cup.

"Honey," Charlie said, reaching for her with a sympathetic look.

"Shut up, Charlie," Josie snapped.

His hand pulled back, and he sighed.

An awkward silence descended on the table. Nothing like some passive aggressive chosen family drama to really spice up the holiday spirit.

Even the cats looked concerned.

"How about a carol?" Evie asked—and without waiting for anyone to agree, she launched into a soothing version of *O Holy Night*. After *O Come All Ye Faithful*, *Silent Night*, and a rousing rendition of *Joy to the World*, the tension around the table was finally gone.

Well.

Maybe not *gone*.

Questions still nagged in the back of my mind about Alice's murder and the threads of mystery surrounding what happened here in Tablerock. I wasn't happy that Mario was—once again—annoyed with a member of our group.

But, let's be honest.

It was becoming routine at this point.

I tried to let it all go and live in the present moment, choosing to focus on gratitude for what I had.

"To friends," Josephine proclaimed, raising her wineglass.

"To family," Estella added, smiling around the table.

Glasses clinked together.

"To love," Matt slipped an arm around Evie's shoulder, and she nestled against him happily.

I met Landon's warm brown eyes, feeling blessed by the quirky extended family circumstances had brought together.

Today, no shadows could diminish the light.

For now, that was more than enough.

Thank you for reading! I hope you enjoyed the fourth book in the Silver Circle Cat Rescue Mysteries!

As the last page turns, things continue to unravel in the frosty fifth installment, "Snowballs, Fluff, and Murder."

Brace yourself for a chilly adventure as Ellie, Evie, and their quirky gang find themselves snowed in at the shelter. With nothing but steaming cups of coffee to warm them and icy tensions beginning to rise, they're in for more than just a snow day.

KEEP UP WITH LEANNE LEEDS

Thanks so much for reading! I hope you liked it! Want to keep up with me?

Visit leanneleeds.com to:

Find all my books...

Sign up for my newsletter...

Like me on Facebook...

Follow me on Twitter...

Follow me on Instagram...

Thanks again for reading!

Leanne Leeds

Find a typo? Let us know!

Typos happen. It's sad, but true.

Though we go over the manuscript multiple times, have editors, have beta readers, and advance readers it's inevitable that determined typos and mistakes sometimes find their way into a published book.

Did you find one? If you did, think about reporting it on leanneleeds.com so we can get it corrected.

Artificial Intelligence Statement

Portions of this book were created with the assistance of AI tools used for editing, proofreading, and refining the text. However, the ideas, storyline, characters, and overall creative vision remain my own original work.

While some aspects of the cover image were generated using AI tools, it was done so under my creative direction and curation.

I want to acknowledge the use of these technologies as part of my creative process, while affirming that the essence of this work comes from my own imagination and effort.

Leanne Leeds

Made in the USA
Monee, IL
01 December 2023

47875652R10194